By J. A. Jance

J. P. Beaumont Mysteries

UNTIL PROVEN GUILTY • INJUSTICE FOR ALL
TRIAL BY FURY • TAKING THE FIFTH
IMPROBABLE CAUSE • A MORE PERFECT UNION
DISMISSED WITH PREJUDICE • MINOR IN POSSESSION
PAYMENT IN KIND • WITHOUT DUE PROCESS
FAILURE TO APPEAR • LYING IN WAIT
NAME WITHHELD • BREACH OF DUTY
BIRDS OF PREY • PARTNER IN CRIME
LONG TIME GONE • JUSTICE DENIED
FIRE AND ICE • BETRAYAL OF TRUST

Joanna Brady Mysteries

DESERT HEAT • TOMBSTONE COURAGE
SHOOT/DON'T SHOOT • DEAD TO RIGHTS
SKELETON CANYON • RATTLESNAKE CROSSING
OUTLAW MOUNTAIN • DEVIL'S CLAW
PARADISE LOST • PARTNER IN CRIME
EXIT WOUNDS • DEAD WRONG
DAMAGE CONTROL • FIRE AND ICE

Walker Family Thrillers

HOUR OF THE HUNTER • KISS OF THE BEES
DAY OF THE DEAD • QUEEN OF THE NIGHT

Ali Reynolds Mysteries

EDGE OF EVIL • WEB OF EVIL
HAND OF EVIL • CRUEL INTENT
TRIAL BY FIRE • FATAL ERROR

J.A. JANCE

DISMISSED WITH PREJUDICE

A J.P. BEAUMONT NOVEL

HARPER

An Imprint of HarperCollins*Publishers*

Grateful acknowledgment is made for the excerpt from the poem "A Child," *The Selected Poems of Shuntaro Tanikawa*, copyright © 1983. Translated by Harold Wright. Published by North Point Press and reprinted by permission.

HARPER

An Imprint of HarperCollins*Publishers*
195 Broadway
New York, NY 10007

Copyright © 1989 by J. A. Jance
ISBN 978-0-06-199930-7

First Harper premium printing: October 2011
First Avon Books mass market printing: June 1989

HarperCollins ® and Harper ® are registered trademarks of Harper-Collins Publishers.

Printed in the United States of America

Visit Harper paperbacks on the World Wide Web at www.harpercollins.com

HB 10.31.2023

To Alice and Alan,
the happy campers
and
To Doc Thornton,
J.P. Beaumont's personal physician

CHAPTER 1

THE JANGLING TELEPHONE REVERBERATED THROUGH my head, ramming its way through champagne-stupefied senses, jarring awake both me and a pounding headache. Without opening my eyes, I grappled blindly for the phone, knowing the only way to stifle the awful racket was to answer the damn thing.

Except I couldn't pick it up. When I tried to close my fingers around the handset, they wouldn't. The receiver slipped out of my hand and clattered noisily across the bedside table.

Even hung over, I'm usually not quite that clumsy.

Puzzled, I opened my eyes and looked at my hand. The three middle fingers, bandaged securely to metal splints, stood stiffly at attention. No wonder my hand wouldn't close. With each heartbeat, a dull throbbing pain echoed from my fingertips up through my hand and wrist. I stared stupidly at the injured fingers as if maybe they belonged to somebody else. What was wrong with them? Were they broken or what? How had it happened?

"Hello? Hello?" A tiny angry voice buzzed up to me from the fallen receiver on the tabletop. "Beau? Are you there? Answer the phone, goddamnit!"

Reaching down, I again attempted to scoop up the phone, this time using my thumb and the palm of my hand rather than the useless fingers. That didn't work very well either. Once more the phone skittered away from me. This time it bounced off the table onto the carpet.

"Just a minute," I snarled at the phone and who-ever was on it. I sat up and swung my legs over the side of the bed. "Hold your horses."

I had to pause there for a moment to steady my-self while the room spun and the jackhammer in my head threatened to loosen teeth.

"Beau, what the hell's taking so long?" I recognized Big Al Lindstrom's muted voice.

Detective Allen Lindstrom is my partner on the Seattle Police Department Homicide Squad. Even from a distance and at much reduced volume I could tell he was pissed.

I snatched up the phone with my left hand. "So I'm up already. What's the big rush? My alarm didn't work, and Peters didn't call."

Peters, my former partner, had spoiled me. For months he had routinely given me an early morning wake-up call from his semipermanent residence on the rehabilitation floor at Harborview Hospital. Gradually, I had gotten out of the habit of setting an alarm, counting on him to wake me up in plenty of time to get to work. He was out of the hospital now, and back at work a few hours a week in the Media

Relations Department, but the pattern of early morning phone calls had continued.

"You jerk," Big Al snapped. "You expect him to call you while he's off on his honeymoon? Get real, Beau, and get dressed. I'll be there to pick you up in ten minutes. There's a case breaking right now. Sergeant Watkins wants us to handle it. By the way, how are your fingers?"

I held up my right hand and examined the bandaged fingers, turning them this way and that. "Fine," I mumbled.

"They don't hurt? The doc said they probably would, once you sobered up."

"No. They're okay," I lied, attempting to ignore the low-grade throbbing that got stronger as soon as the idea came up. I found it disturbing that Big Al seemed to know more about my injured fingers than I did. I couldn't remember anything at all about hurting them or about seeing a doctor, either. I guessed I'd really tied one on.

"Be there in a few minutes," Big Al said shortly when I said nothing more. He hung up. I sat on the bed for a few seconds longer, trying to piece together what might have happened. Finally, giving up, I stumbled into the bathroom and studied my face and body in the mirror. Other than the fingers, there was no visible sign of injury, so whatever had happened couldn't have been too serious—something less damaging than a multistory fall or a car wreck. And if it was a fight, the other guy never laid a glove on me, at least not on my face.

I closed my eyes in concentration and tried to

remember. The previous day had seen the arrival of the long-awaited wedding between Ron Peters and Amy Fitzgerald. The ceremony itself, in a small church on top of Queen Anne Hill, had been simple and quiet. The reception in the Chart Room of Belltown Terrace had started sedately enough, but it hadn't stayed sedate long. When cops feel free to let down their hair, they've got a lot of letting to do.

And Jonas Piedmont Beaumont was right in there swinging with the best of them. As someone whose usual drinking menu seldom varies far from Canadian in general, MacNaughton's in particular, I should never, never have allowed myself to be suckered into swilling champagne one glass after another. At my age, I ought to know better.

I remembered the part at the church clearly enough, but there was only a dim recollection of the cake cutting at the reception, with its hazy, happy laughter and flashing cameras. After that, the remainder of the evening was a total blank. That worried me.

Gulping down some aspirin, I staggered into the shower and turned it on full blast. The hot, rushing water helped clear my head some. Once out of the shower, I discovered it was a real struggle to get dressed. My underwear, zippers, and buttons are all built to be right-handed, and the splints got in the way of everything from brushing my teeth and putting on my socks and shoes to tying my tie.

It was nothing short of miraculous that I was down on the sidewalk outside Belltown Terrace when Detective Lindstrom swung off Broad onto Second Avenue in one of Seattle P.D.'s notoriously unreliable Reliants. I climbed in. The car coughed, sputtered, and choked as Big Al eased down on the gas and pulled away from the curb.

"You look like something the cat dragged in," Big Al commented as we started down Second toward Seattle's high-rise core. "And your tie's crooked."

"It's on, isn't it?" I replied curtly. "Give me a break." I wanted to get off the subject of J. P. Beaumont, his fingers and his foibles, as quickly as possible. "What's going on, Al? Bring me up to speed."

Al shrugged. "Suicide, most likely. Down in one of those new industrial complexes south of the King-dome. Landlord came in this morning and found one of his tenants dead."

"Not a good way to start the week," I said.

Big Al nodded in agreement. "Ya sure, you betcha," he responded in his best Norwegian parody. "You can say that again."

Al and his wife Molly live in Ballard, a Scandina-vian enclave in Seattle with such strong Old Coun-try connections that people sometimes joke about needing a passport to go there. In the months we've worked together I've learned that the best thing to do with Big Al when he gets cute is to ignore him entirely. Otherwise, he gets worse.

"What kind of suicide?"

"High tech," Al responded.

"What'd he do, electrocute himself with his com-puter?"

Big Al shook his head. "I mean the guy was into high tech. Nobody mentioned how he did it."

Al reached into the inside pocket of his jacket and drew out a tattered notebook, opened to an almost empty page. He tossed it over to me. The notebook clipped the top of the splinted fingers, fell to the floorboard, and slipped under the seat.

"Sorry," Al said, as I fumbled clumsily to pick it up. Once the notebook was held securely in my left hand I read the hurriedly penciled note scrawled across the top of the page: *Microbridge, 1841 Fourth Avenue South.*

"What the hell's a microbridge?" I asked.

"Beats me. Not big enough to walk on. Something to do with computers, I think," Big Al replied. "I don't know anything more about that stuff than you do."

Which is to say, not much. Big Al Lindstrom and J. P. Beaumont are two of a kind when it comes to that. We're both manual typewriter people trapped in a computer world.

The address on Fourth South turned out to be in a brand-new low-rise complex called Industry Square, a campus that occupied several full blocks. The building numbered 1841 was surrounded on three sides by a border of parking lots while the back with its waist-high loading dock butted up against a Burlington Northern railroad track. The main entryway was marked by two tall wrought-iron gates that opened onto a small interior courtyard and garden. A six-foot-high SPACE FOR LEASE sign had been tacked onto the wall next to the gate.

A small group of civilians, presumably workers from the building who had been displaced by the investigation, stood clustered on the far side of the first line of cars. Numerous Seattle P.D. patrol cars were scattered near the front entrance while a King County Medical Examiner's van, directed by a uniformed police officer, was just backing up to the opening.

"How come they're here before we are?" I asked, nodding toward the M.E.'s van.

"Their people must have been awake when the call came in." Big Al's response was liberally laced with sarcasm, but I knew he had covered for me with Sergeant Watkins, and I let the dig pass without comment. Struggling to open the car door with my gimpy hand, I got out and started toward the van. As I came around the side of it, I almost ran over a little round-faced bald-headed guy. Startled, we both zigged and zagged, trying unsuccessfully to stay out of each other's way.

The uniformed officer looked up, saw me, and nodded briefly in my direction, but he spoke to the man in front of me. "So you're going to have to stay back, Mr. Rennermann, at least until we finish getting people and equipment in and out."

"But this is my property!" Rennermann objected, backing away a step or two. His already florid face reddened to a slightly brighter shade. "You've got no right . . ."

"We have every right in the world," the officer replied calmly. "This is a police investigation."

He turned to me while the two technicians from the Medical Examiner's van hurried through the gate carrying a stretcher between them. "Hello there, Detective Beaumont. The body's upstairs. Doc Baker said to send you up as soon as you got here."

"Who's he?" I asked, nodding in Rennermann's direction. "The landlord?"

"That's right. He's the one who found the body."

I fumbled a notebook out of my pocket. One abortive attempt at writing was enough to convince me it was a lost cause. As long as the splints were on my fingers, holding a writing implement of any kind was out of the question. I stuffed the useless notebook back in my jacket, got out my ID, and flashed it in the landlord's direction.

Rennermann looked like the sales-crazed manager of a disreputable used car lot. He paced back and forth, his unbuttoned orange plaid sports coat jacket flapping wildly with every bouncing step. His tie was knotted slightly to the left of center, and he was perspiring heavily.

"Hello, Mr. Rennermann," I said, finally getting him to hold still. "I'm Detective J.P. Beaumont of the Seattle Police Department. My partner, Detective Lindstrom, and I will be handling this case."

Big Al reached my side just in time to nod a brief acknowledgment to my introduction. "This is the guy who found the body, Al. Do you mind taking down his information? My hand won't work."

Disgustedly, Al got out his own notebook. "Give me your name," he said.

"Rennermann. Bernard Rennermann. My friends call me Bernie."

"And where can we find you when we finish up here?"

"Over there. In the next building. That's where my office is."

Big Al jotted down Bernard Rennermann's name and phone number and snapped his notebook shut. "You'll be there all morning?"

"Yes, but—"

"We'll come see you just as soon as we finish up here," Big Al said. "We'll need to ask you some questions."

A panicked look washed over Bernard Rennermann's flushed face. "But the new tenant is coming to look the place over today. What am I going to tell him?"

"Tell him he's going to have to wait." Big Al, running low on patience, started moving away while he was still speaking. He pushed past Rennermann as a second uniformed cop appeared at the gate. "Which way?" Al asked.

"Upstairs," the officer replied. "The elevator is just inside, right around the corner."

Al disappeared through the gate, but I wasn't ready to follow. "Did you say new tenant?" I asked, as Rennermann stared after Big Al's retreating figure. "Does that mean this one was moving out?"

Rennermann nodded, a little uneasily, I thought, although it was only a fleeting impression with nothing to back it up.

"He was in Chapter Seven," Bernard Rennermann continued. "You know, involuntary bankruptcy. It's been in all the papers."

"I don't read papers."

"Oh," Rennermann said. "Well, there was a long court fight, something about patent infringement. I guess the lawyers cost him an arm and a leg and ate up all the cash flow. Lawyers are like that. He lost anyway. In court. Lost the whole ball of wax. Kurobashi was scheduled to be out of here by the end of the month. In this market I was lucky as hell to find someone in the same kind of business who was willing to come in and take over the space without my having to do a whole lot of tenant improvements."

Big Al poked his head back through the gate. "Are you coming or not?" he demanded impatiently.

"I'll be right there. You be sure to stay in your office so we'll be able to find you, Mr. Rennermann. We won't be that long."

"But what about all these people out here who work for my other tenants in the building? When are they going to be able to go inside and start work?"

I glanced across the parking lot where a mobile food vendor was making an unscheduled stop, unloading a batch of undrinkable coffee and stale Danish.

"The roach coach is here, so at least they won't starve," I said. "They're going to have to wait outside until we give the word. Nobody's allowed in the building until after the crime-scene investigators have finished up, understand?"

Rennermann sighed, nodded his head, and swiped at his damp forehead with a dingy, wrinkled hanky. "This is real bad for business, you know. Bad public relations."

I left him standing there, still mopping his face. As the cop had said, the entrance to the building's elevator was just around the corner from the wrought-iron gates. Al was holding the buzzing elevator door open for me while the second uniformed patrolman, Officer Camden, waited patiently inside.

"What took you so long?"

"I was talking to the landlord. He said the dead guy was losing his business."

"No wonder," Camden said.

"No wonder what?"

"That he killed himself then. It's ugly in there," he added. "He did a hell of a job of it."

"What did he use? A gun?"

"Knife. Some kind of dagger. Cut himself up pretty badly."

"The M.E.'s pretty sure it's suicide then?"

The officer nodded. "So far," he said.

Once off the elevator on the second floor, we made our way down a short corridor and into a small reception area.

"He's in there," Camden told us, pointing toward a half-open door and making no attempt to accompany us through it.

The black-and-gold nameplate on the door said TADEO KUROBASHI, PRESIDENT. Through the narrow opening I could see the periodic flash of a police photographer's camera. Big Al and I went inside.

The room seemed smaller than it actually was. There was a desk with a gray computer terminal on it and next to the computer, facing into the room, was a tall gold-plated trophy of a woman on horseback. I read the inscription: *Kimiko Kurobashi, Best All Around Cowgirl, U.S. Intercollegiate Rodeo Championship, 1982.* The only other items on the desk were two pieces of a slender rosewood container, slightly curved and less than two feet long, a swatch of shiny black silk, and a bill to MicroBridge in the amount of $1,712.19 from a company called DataDump.

"The body's over here, you two," Doc Baker said, motioning to us across the room. Dr. Howard Baker, King County's chief medical examiner, is spending less and less time at crime scenes these days, so I was more than a little surprised to see the man himself.

Big Al went ahead to have a look. He stopped short, grimaced, and swallowed hard. "Harry karry?" he asked.

"*Hara-kiri*," Doc Baker corrected firmly. "If you're going to say it, you'd better say it right or you'll have half the folks in the International District jumping down your throat. But yes, that's what it looks like to me. I've called George in from the crime lab just to be sure. He should be here in a few minutes."

George Yamamoto is the head of the Washington State Patrol Crime Laboratory. He is also one of Seattle's more visibly prominent Japanese-American citizens.

"We've got a tentative ID from the landlord," Doc Baker added.

Dreading the sight that had given Big Al Lindstrom pause, I moved to a point where I could see. The dead man was lying on the blood-soaked carpet, his body twisted half on its side as though he had simply slipped out of his chair, the back of which had been shoved against the wall. A rusty, gore-covered knife lay on the floor nearby, its ornate handle only inches from the lifeless bloodstained fingers, while a mound of internal organs spilled onto the floor beneath him.

Suicide is usually ugly, but this was worse than most. No matter how many years I do this job, no matter how much I think I've seen it all, it never gets any easier. Sickened, I looked away.

Five feet above the dead man, a framed but faded

color photo sat askew on the wall, revealing behind it the open door of a small concealed safe. I looked at the picture closely, grateful there was something in the room besides the dead man to occupy my attention.

It was an enlarged snapshot of a child on a horse and a middle-aged man. The man was standing near the horse's head and beaming proudly up at the child in something akin to adoration. The child seemed tiny, especially in relation to the fully grown animal, a gray Appaloosa. The girl couldn't have been much older than nine or ten. The dark hair and almond eyes said Japanese, but she was wearing an ornate, fringed cowgirl outfit and white pointed boots in the best cowboys-and-Indians tradition. Her hair was braided into two long Annie Oakley plaits, while a huge white cowboy hat framed her small oval face and dark hair. She was grinning for the camera, mugging in typical kid-gets-first-horse fashion.

Looking away from the picture, my attention strayed to the open door beside it. The concealed safe was empty, absolutely empty, without even a layer of dust to indicate what might have been kept inside.

"What was in there?" I asked.

"Nothing," Doc Baker answered glumly. "Not a damn thing. If we knew that we'd probably be a long way down the line toward understanding exactly what went on here."

Dodging bloody footprints, I stepped close enough to look down at the screen of the computer on Kurobashi's desk. In the bright light of the room, pale amber letters glowed faintly on the CRT. Close examination revealed that the entire work space was covered with what looked like alphabet soup. The words were composed of English letters. Other than that, they were totally unrecognizable. I discerned a pattern, though. It was the same two lines repeated over and over.

"What does that say?" I asked.

Doc Baker shrugged. "Nobody here can read it. That's the other reason I've called George in. Somebody said they thought it was Japanese."

As if on cue, George Yamamoto appeared at the door. He paused in the doorway for a moment, pulling on a pair of rubber gloves. Doc Baker saw him a moment after I did.

"There you are, George. We've been waiting for you. He's over here."

George Yamamoto didn't move forward immediately. He stood gazing at the nameplate on the door, seeming to draw into himself, as if marshaling his resources for some terrible ordeal. His face was pale, his mouth set in a narrow line, and he said nothing. There was none of the usual banter that Baker and he often volley back and forth when they encounter one another at crime scenes.

Big Al and I moved aside to make room for him. George Yamamoto squared his shoulders, stepped resolutely to the side of the desk, and looked down at the corpse. As he did so, a barely perceptible tremor passed through his body.

"It's Tadeo," he said quietly.

"Tadeo!" Doc Baker's head came up sharply. He

eyed George Yamamoto questioningly through his thick, bottle-bottom glasses. "You knew him?"

George nodded. "His name is Tadeo Kurobashi. He was my friend."

With those few words, what had started out as a routine investigation into an ordinary suicide wasn't routine anymore. Like an automatic camera whirring into focus, Tadeo Kurobashi's ugly death suddenly took on the sharply delineated lines and proportions of personal tragedy. A friend's personal tragedy.

And in that instant, everything that was routine about it went straight out the window.

CHAPTER 2

I HAVE WORKED WITH THESE TWO MEN FOR SO LONG, spent so much time in both the medical examiner's office and the crime lab, that I know Doc Baker and George Yamamoto far better than I know some of the Seattle P.D. brass upstairs in the Public Safety Building.

The two men are a study in contrasts. Baker is a big burly man, a human tank, who habitually goes over or through people rather than around them. His volume control is permanently stuck on loud, and when he speaks, he gesticulates wildly, flapping around like some overweight bird attempting to become airborne. Baker's suits look like they were pulled as-is off the rack at the nearest big-and-tall shop. They're often wrinkled and unkempt. He looks like the proverbial rumpled bed much of the time, and his socks seldom match whatever else he's wearing.

George Yamamoto, on the other hand, is absolutely precise, from the meticulously folded and creased cuffs of his Brooks Brothers trousers to his carefully articulated manner of speech. When he speaks, he punctuates his words with small, deft hand gestures. Where Baker orders his subordinates around, George's quietly efficient management style inspires both loyalty and dedication. Of the two, I'd have to say, George Yamamoto's crime lab is a much tighter run ship than Doc Baker's medical examiner's office.

Now, as George stood over the body of his dead friend, I was struck by his unflinching self-control. Tadeo Kurobashi may have been one of George Yamamoto's close friends, but you couldn't tell that by looking. The head of the Washington State Patrol Crime Lab is nothing if not a complete professional. His friend was dead, but it was George's job to help us find out how and why. That didn't mean he wasn't hurting; he was, but he didn't let it show, and he didn't let it get in the way.

"What do you have so far, Howard?" he asked.

For once even Doc Baker seemed subdued. "George, I had no idea he was a friend of yours, or I never would have called you in."

Yamamoto finished donning his protective clothing. "It's all right," George replied, waving aside the apology. "You had no way of knowing."

He made his way around to where Doc Baker was standing, and together the two of them knelt on the floor beside the body. Speaking in hushed, careful tones that were astonishingly low for someone as noisy as Doc Baker, they took their time examining Kurobashi's corpse with its gaping, horrifying wound. Finished at last, both men stood up simultaneously.

"Well?" Baker asked pointedly, almost but not quite reverting to his normally brusque, blunt style. "What do you think?"

"It's definitely not *hara-kiri*," George announced.

Baker frowned. "It isn't? But I thought . . ."

George shook his head. "Absolutely not, although someone may have wanted us to think it was."

"How can you tell?"

"It's just not right. *Seppuku* is a form of ritual suicide with a long and honored tradition. Originally it was done with sharpened bamboo. But this is wrong. Totally wrong."

"What's all wrong?" Baker asked.

"For one thing, he's in a chair, not on a *zabuton*. That's a floor cushion. For another, he's not wearing a kimono. Tadeo was a stickler for tradition with an eye for detail as well."

"What detail?" Doc Baker was frowning.

"The traditional dress for *seppuku* is a white kimono."

The frown became thunderous. "You mean to tell me it isn't *seppuku* because he's wearing the wrong goddamned clothes? What about the sword? That is a samurai sword, isn't it? And isn't this *hara-kiri* or whatever the hell you call it a samurai tradition?"

Baker was reluctant to give up his pet theory even in the face of expert information to the contrary.

"It is that," George Yamamoto agreed; "and it may still turn out to be suicide, but I doubt it."

Up until then, Doc Baker had been treating George Yamamoto with uncharacteristic deference and consideration, but anyone casting doubt on one of Baker's prize assumptions is going to get run over by a truck.

"You're saying it's *not* suicide then? You think it's murder?"

George nodded. "Of all people, Tadeo wouldn't have violated the ancient traditions."

Baker rolled his eyes in disgust. "You mean he'd commit suicide by following some ancient recipe? Come now." Some of Baker's customary truculence was leaking back into his manner, but George wasn't intimidated.

"Tadeo knew more about samurai traditions than almost anyone in the country," he replied quietly. "He spent a lifetime learning about it."

Big Al and I had lingered in the background. We didn't want to disturb their deliberations, but we didn't want to miss out on something important, either.

"What did you call it?" I asked.

"*Seppuku*," Yamamoto repeated. "You probably know it as *hara-kiri*. It's the ritual disembowelment of the samurai."

Big Al stirred uneasily. "What's all this crap about samurai? This is Seattle, for Chrissakes, not Japan. Besides, I thought all that samurai bullshit went away a hundred years ago."

"More like a hundred and twenty," Yamamoto corrected. "It's gone, but not forgotten."

"And that rusty old knife over there is supposedly a samurai sword?"

George Yamamoto regarded Big Al with an air of impatience bordering on irritation. He nodded slowly.

"A *tanto*," he said. "A hidden sword, sometimes called a woman's sword."

Al Lindstrom grunted. "That thing's so rusty it's hard to believe it could do that kind of damage."

George knelt down on one knee and examined the weapon. "Don't let appearances fool you. It can cut, all right. Those ancient swords were made from such high carbon content steel that they'll rust in minutes just from not having the blood wiped off, but they're still sharp as hell. From the looks of it, this one could possibly be very valuable."

"An antique, then?" I asked.

George nodded.

"Do you think it belonged to him?"

George glanced at me. A shadow of personal grief flickered across his carefully maintained professional facade. He stifled it as quickly as it had appeared. "I don't know. If it did, he never mentioned it, at least, not to me."

"You said he was an expert. Why? Was he descended from a samurai warrior?"

"Not that I know of, but from the time I first knew him, he was interested in samuari history and lore as well as the swords and all the accompanying sword furniture."

"What kind of furniture?" Big Al asked.

"The other equipment besides the blades themselves that were part of a warrior's equipment."

"How long did you know him, George?" I asked gently.

There was a slight pause before he answered. "We had met earlier, when we were little, but we became friends in Minidoka." George Yamamoto made the statement softly, evenly, looking me square in the eye as he did so. "During the war," he added with quiet dignity.

George turned away. Once more he stood looking down at his friend's body in a room that was suddenly oppressively quiet. The $20,000 reparation being paid to survivors of Japanese War Relocation Camps may have mystified the rest of the country, but not the people who live here in the Northwest. We had a larger concentration of Japanese-Americans before the war. As a consequence we're more aware of the irrevocable damage done to those 125,000 people who were stripped of their rights and packed off to detention camps during World War II. Around here the scars are still very close to the surface.

Most the the detainees were citizens, born in the U.S. or naturalized, but they were nevertheless suspected of complicity with the Japanese, summarily deprived of their livelihood and possessions, and shipped into the interior. Minidoka, a raw barracks camp in the wilds of the Idaho desert, was where many of Seattle's Japanese-American folk, suffering alternately from terrible heat and terrible cold, waited out the war.

I knew vaguely that as a young teenager George Yamamoto had been incarcerated in one of those camps, but this was the first time he had ever spoken of it, and although I was barely born at the time, I felt ashamed of what had happened to him and to his family. Ashamed and chastened—a variation on a theme of the white man's burden.

The silence in the room had lengthened uncomfortably. I'm not sure George even noticed. He stood, lost in thought, gazing down sadly at the mutilated body of his dead friend.

"What does Minidoka have to do with samurai history?" I asked.

George walked over to the window before he answered. "Tadeo was interested in it, that's all. Interested and curious. He spent hours every day talking to the old ones there, asking them questions, listening to their stories. He came out of the camp as an unofficial samurai expert. He was particularly interested in swords. The rest of the time he spent fiddling with radios. He single-handedly kept the few radios in the camp running on scavenged parts."

"Swords and radios?" I asked. "That's an unlikely combination."

George smiled and nodded. "Tadeo is . . . was a very unusual man, equally interested in both the very old and the very new. Once the war was over, he went on and got degrees in electrical engineering from the University of Washington. We were in school there at the same time."

I could tell from the set of his shoulders that grief was hammering at him, and George Yamamoto was doing his best not to give way to it. Listening to him, I had, for the first time, a sense of what their meager existence in Minidoka must have been like. Obviously, living there together had forged a long lasting comrade-in-arms bond between Tadeo Kurobashi and George Yamamoto, the same kind of bond that comes from surviving other varieties of wartime experiences.

"Is that where he met his wife?" I asked, once more

trying to break up the silence before it swallowed us whole. "In the camp?"

George swung away from the window. "Machiko?" he asked, spitting out the name as though the very sound of it was offensive to him. "No," he answered. "Not her. She came over as a war bride in 1946 during the occupation. Tadeo married Machiko after her first husband died. He was still working his way through school when they married."

From the way he said it, I could tell that George had disapproved of his friend's choice of wife, that he had despised her in the past and still did in the present, even after all the intervening years.

Moving away from the window, George stepped over to the desk, standing in front of it and studying the items that lay on the smooth, polished surface. Without touching anything, he focused briefly on each of them, stopping eventually on the two halves of the wooden box. "Come look at this," he said.

Big Al and I did as we were told. Both the top and bottom of the slightly curved rosewood box had been carefully crafted and polished to a high gloss. The outside surface had been worn thin by years of opening and closing, but I was certain from looking at them that the two pieces would still fit together perfectly. On the top surface, a delicate inlaid ivory squirrel gathered an equally tiny mound of mother-of-pearl acorns. The exquisite inlay work was some of the best I've ever seen.

"It's beautiful," I said.

George Yamamoto nodded. "It is that, and I'm convinced that under all the blood we'll find the same design repeated on the handle of the *tanto* itself. Once the blade is cleaned up, we'll be able to see who made it."

"How can you do that?" Big Al asked.

"A sword that fine would have been signed by the artisan who created it."

"You said a few minutes ago that it may be valuable. Just how valuable?"

George shrugged. "That's hard to tell. Several thousand maybe. Possibly more, depending on whether or not we're dealing with a name-brand sword maker. Why do you ask?"

"The landlord told us that Kurobashi was losing his business, that he was supposed to be completely moved out of the building by the end of the month."

"I didn't know that," George murmured. "I can't imagine how it could have happened. Tadeo was always careful with money." He shook his head. "Getting back to the sword, even if it is valuable, selling it probably wouldn't have helped him enough to make any difference." He paused and looked around the room. "If he was losing his business, I suppose that makes the idea of suicide a little more credible, but still . . ."

Impatiently, Howard Baker stripped off his surgical gloves with a series of sharp snaps. "And as of right now, that's my preliminary finding, pending the autopsy, of course. All this talk of traditions and rituals doesn't mean a damn thing. We're going to find his fingerprints and nobody else's on that knife handle. I'd bet money on it."

Baker moved quickly to the door to summon his peons, the two technicians from the van who, along with their stretcher, were still waiting patiently in the outside reception area. "You can move him out as soon as George and the detectives give the word."

George waved for them to come ahead, while Big Al and I stepped back far enough to allow them to bring the stretcher into the room. George Yamamoto watched in silence as they carefully wrapped the hands to preserve trace evidence, covered the body with a disposable sheet, and eased it into a body bag and onto a stretcher.

Although the rubber-gloved technicians worked in almost total silence, Doc Baker's voice, booming away in the next room, provided more than enough background noise.

When they finally carried the stretcher out the door, Doc Baker stuck his head back inside. "I'm leaving," he said.

"When will you be doing the autopsy, Howard?" George Yamamoto asked quietly.

"I don't know exactly. That'll depend on whatever else is scheduled. Why?"

"I'd like to be there."

Baker frowned. "How come?"

Doc Baker can be pretty overbearing at times, but George Yamamoto didn't back off an inch. "Tadeo was a friend of mine, Howard. I'm asking as a personal favor."

Finally Baker nodded reluctantly. "That doesn't sound like such a good idea, but all right," he agreed. "Except I don't know how much advance notice there'll be."

"Whenever it is," George replied, "I'll be there."

Baker looked from Yamamoto to me. "Crime-scene

team's up next, you guys. They've been waiting out-side." With that, Dr. Howard Baker marched out of the room. George started after him.

"Wait," I said, stopping him. In the flurry of ac-tivity, Baker had forgotten to ask George to look at the words on the CRT. "While you were over by the desk, did you happen to get a look at what was on the computer screen?"

"No. What was it?"

"Check it out, would you? Can you read Japanese?"

"Some," George replied noncommittally. He turned and made his way back to the desk, walking gingerly around behind it, avoiding the blood-soaked part of the carpet from which the body had been removed. With a forefinger resting thoughtfully on one cheek, Yamamoto stood peering down at the computer's screen for several long seconds.

"It's part of a poem," he said eventually, nodding, "written in Romaji—romanized letters. I recognize it. I'm sure I've seen it before, but I can't remember the name of it or who wrote it. It's the same two lines repeated over and over."

"What does it say?"

Again, George Yamamoto studied the screen for a long time. "It's something about a child," he said.

"What does it say exactly?"

"I'm a criminalist, Beau, not a poet, but it's some-thing to the effect that even in this fouled-up world, a child still gives hope."

I gave George Yamamoto full credit for keeping himself under very tight rein. Given the circum-stances, I think I would have utilized far stronger terminology than *fouled-up*, but George is too straitlaced, too dignified to let something as profane as the "F-word" escape his lips.

"Is that his child?" I asked, motioning toward the picture on the wall behind the desk.

George nodded. "That's her," he said. "Kimiko. Kimi, we used to call her."

"Where does she live? Here in Seattle someplace?"

"Not anymore. She's a graduate student over in Pullman, working on her Ph.D. at WSU." He pronounced it "WAZOO," the way generations of Cougars and non-Cougars alike have referred to Washington State University.

"Kimiko?" I repeated. "Al, did you get that?"

Big Al was taking notes for both of us, and he wasn't exactly being Cheerful Charlie about it. "Got it," Al answered grudgingly.

George Yamamoto looked closely at my injured hand. "What happened to you?" he asked.

His question caught me flat-footed. I had no idea what had happened to my hand, and no ready-made answers leaped to my lips. Fortunately, Big Al Lindstrom came blundering to my rescue.

"Grace Beaumont. That's what we're calling him down in homicide these days. Got his fingers stuck in a car door. Pretty stupid if you ask me. How do you spell that name again, Kimiko?"

What door? I wondered as Big Al continued taking notes. And how had it happened? And why didn't I remember it? But being a detective has its advantages. At least now I had more information than I'd had before.

Behind us the door to Tadeo Kurobashi's office opened and two crime-scene investigators entered the room. Quietly but firmly they shepherded us out of the office. In the reception area outside, Big Al determinedly kept gathering family information.

"So the wife's name is Machiko, and they live in Kirkland?"

"It's called Bridle Trail Downs now," George said. "And yes, it's part of Kirkland. Back when they bought it, though, it was still in the county. They moved there when Kimi got her first horse. She must have been around eleven at the time."

Big Al jotted some information in his notebook, then looked at Yamamoto appraisingly. "Since you're a friend of the family, do you want us to handle the notification, or would you like to do it?"

George shook his head. Throughout the painful ordeal, he had seemed totally self-possessed. Now, for the first time, he appeared to be unsure of himself.

"I don't know. I knew Tadeo very well, but I was never close to his wife. Kimi and my two boys were friendly back and forth during high school, but that was years ago. Kimi would still remember me, I'm sure. I don't think her mother would like having me around at a time like this."

"So the two families socialized some?" I asked.

"A little. At least Tadeo and Kimi did. Machiko lived like a recluse in that house of theirs. She never did anything or went anywhere."

There it was again, in his tone of voice, in what he said about Machiko Kurobashi, the same anger and resentment I had noticed earlier. If other people in their social milieu had felt the same level of antipathy toward Machiko Kurobashi that George

Yamamoto did, then living as a recluse was probably a fairly good choice.

Looking for more breathing space in the small reception area, I backed around behind the receptionist's desk. Like Tadeo Kurobashi's, the desktop computer was still turned on, amber words glowing dimly on a dark screen in the office's bright fluorescent lighting.

I'm no linguist, but it looked to me as though that screen was showing the same thing as Tadeo Kurobashi's. To the left of the receptionist's desk was another small office, little more than a cubicle, with still another computer, this one sitting on a rolling stand. I hurried over to that one and discovered the same thing, a screen entirely filled with two brief lines, written in Japanese, repeated over and over.

George Yamamoto had watched me in silence while I moved from one computer to the other. When I stopped in front of the second one, something in my attitude must have tipped him off. He cocked his head to one side. "What is it?" he asked.

"Same as the first one," I said.

"What do you mean?" Yamamoto came around the desk and paused beside me. "You're right," he said, looking down. "It is the same thing."

"What do you think it means?"

"I don't know. If Howard is correct in his assumption and if Tadeo did commit suicide, then this is probably nothing more or less than an electronic suicide note." He paused. "For Kimi," he added.

"For Kimi?" I asked quickly. "For his daughter and not for his wife? Doesn't that seem odd?"

"What's odd is that he left it on all the computers like that. It seems to me as though Tadeo would have wanted it to be more private."

Whatever was on that screen was a clue, a direction finder. I needed to know what it said as well as what it meant. Somehow I needed to capture the words for later, preserve them in order to discover whatever evidence might be contained in those untranslated, repetitive lines.

I turned back to Big Al. "Is Nancy still out there?"

Nancy was Nancy Gresham, a Seattle P.D. police photographer. Lindstrom shrugged. "Probably. Want to talk to her?" I nodded and he hurried out into the outside hallway to find her. He was back with her a moment later, but when I told her what I needed, she shook her head doubtfully.

"I can try, but the resolution is pretty iffy."

"You don't think we'll be able to read it?"

"Probably not. If I were you, I'd have someone copy it by hand verbatim, just in case."

Because of my fingers, that onerous task fell to Big Al Lindstrom.

"Who, me?" Big Al protested. "I'm a Norwegian. You expect me to be able to write in Japanese?"

"You can copy the letters," I said. With only minimal grumbling, Big Al Lindstrom hunched his massive frame over the computer. There was no question of touching either the computer or the stenographer's chair in front of it for fear of disturbing evidence. Laboriously, one and two letters at a time, he began copying the unfamiliar words into his dog-eared notebook.

"Tell me more about the daughter, George," I

said quietly. "About Kimi. Why would he leave the note for her?"

"They've been at war for years."

"Who has, Kurobashi and his daughter?"

George Yamamoto nodded. "They were always very close when she was younger, but they had a falling out shortly after Kimi went away to school in Ellensburg. That's where she got her undergraduate degree, at Central. As far as I know, they never got over whatever it was. They never made up."

"Do you have any idea what the feud was all about?"

"No. Tadeo didn't say, and I didn't ask. I didn't want to pry."

"And how old is she now?"

"Kimi? Twenty-eight or twenty-nine."

"Ten years is a long time to carry a grudge," I observed.

George nodded. "I'm sure it ate at Tadeo, although he never talked about it. Kimi's an interesting girl, Beau, bright and stubborn both. She's right between my two boys in age. She never was the stereotypical lotus blossom. *Tomboy* is the only word for it. She was always out roughhousing with the boys, and she could hold her own with them, too.

"She was smart in school—good in science and a whiz at math. She took after her father in the brains department. I remember Tadeo telling me she was getting her Ph.D. in electrical engineering. He was proud of her, but I think he was a little baffled when he found out she was following in his footsteps. He was a double E too."

"A what?"

"A double E, an electrical engineer."

"So even though they were what you call 'at war,' Kurobashi kept in touch with her?"

"I could be wrong, but I think the bad feelings were pretty much one-sided on Kimi's part. After all, he did have her picture on the wall in there."

"And the trophy," I added.

"Okay," Big Al said, standing up and closing the notebook. "I've got it as good as it's gonna be got. I don't know if anyone else will be able to read the damn thing, but it's the best I can do. So what now, notify the next-of-kin?"

I nodded. George Yamamoto flinched at my answer, but he didn't offer to go along, and I didn't press him. "We'd better," I said, "before the Noon News does it for us."

We rode the elevator down in silence. Just beyond the gate a maroon Nissan Pulsar NX with a black plastic condom over its face was parked in a no-parking zone with its Jesus Christ lights flashing. A man in a gray three-piece suit and a dark red power tie was arguing loudly and heatedly with the uniformed officer at the gate as though using his blinkers gave him carte blanche to block the fire lane.

"I'll go in a minute but first I've got to find him, and no he isn't over there with all those other people. I've already checked. If we don't leave right now, we'll never get to the courthouse in time."

"What seems to be the problem here?" I asked, stepping through the gate.

The officer saw me and nodded gratefully. "This man says his client is inside and he needs to pick him up to go downtown. They're due at an appointment in twenty minutes."

"Who's your client?" I asked.

The gray-suited man glared at me. "Who are you?" he demanded in return.

"Detective J.P. Beaumont." I struggled my badge out of my pocket, marveling at how difficult even the most mundane tasks become when your fingers no longer work the way you need them to. The man in the gray suit sneered at my difficulty, which didn't make me like him any better. I've seen enough young, overly ambitious attorneys in my time to recognize the type. I made it a point not to genuflect. "Who's your client?"

This guy was medium young, thirty-four or so, with a long thin frame and narrow sloping shoulders. His car and clothing both screamed cool macho dude. He was someone who needed all the macho help an image-maker could give him. His cheeks were puffed up like a chipmunk's and his protruding eyes were set too closely together. When he started to speak, a mouth full of silver braces flashed like a chrome grill in the midmorning sun.

"Mr. Kurobashi," he answered.

I took a wild stab in the dark. "This appointment wouldn't have anything to do with bankruptcy proceedings, would it?"

"That's none of your business," he snapped. "That's privileged information." The braces caught the sun again and glinted wickedly. They were so at odds with his speech and mannerisms and cool macho dude getup that they somehow struck my funny bone. In my book, braces are for kids. I'm of the opinion that if your attorney is wearing braces, he's probably too young for the job.

"Mr. Kurobashi is dead," I said bluntly. "The medical examiner's already taken him to the morgue."

Stunned, the attorney reeled backward as though he'd been struck. He caught his balance on the shiny hood of the Pulsar and leaned on it heavily.

"Kurobashi, dead?" he croaked. "You can't be serious!"

"Yes, I'm serious. Now give my partner here your name and address so we can get back in touch with you later."

His name was Christopher H. Davenport, and his address was 1201 Third, the newest pricey address in town.

Davenport still looked shocked. "What happened?" he managed.

"It's privileged information," I shot back. "Right now we're on our way to notify the next-of-kin. Please don't make any attempt to contact the Kurobashi home until we've had a chance to make a personal visit."

He nodded. "Of course not. I wouldn't think of it."

I left Davenport still dazed and sitting on the fender of his Nissan as I turned back to the cop. "Get word to Mr. Rennermann. Tell him that we'll have to stop by to see him sometime later today or tomorrow."

"Right," the officer said, "will do."

Once out of the building, George Yamamoto headed for his car and we went toward ours. Big Al was grumbling about having to play both chauffeur and secretary while my fingers were screwed up, but I wasn't paying much attention. My headache was back and I was hours and miles away from any possibility of aspirin.

We were waiting at the stop sign for traffic to clear on Fourth South when George Yamamoto pulled up beside us and honked his horn. I rolled down the window.

He had changed his mind. "I guess I'll go with you after all," he said. "You'll probably need someone to interpret. Machiko doesn't speak English very well or at least she didn't the last time I saw her."

"You know how to get to their place?"

He nodded.

"We'll follow you, then. Lead the way."

Al waited long enough for George to pull out in front of us. "I could have found it all right, you know," he said.

I think he resented George going along, regarded his presence in somewhat the same light as Howard Baker did, as a hindrance rather than a help.

"Yes," I said, "but unless I miss my guess, your Japanese isn't all that hot. Mine sure isn't."

We drove to Kirkland in relative silence. At mid-morning, traffic on the Evergreen Point Floating Bridge was fairly light. The entire trip only took about half an hour.

As we drove, I couldn't get the picture of Kimi Kurobashi out of my mind. What monster had reared its ugly head between that happy-go-lucky, horsy kid and her adoring father? What had set them at each other's throats? Whatever it was, now it was permanent. There would be no more chances for reconciliation. Those were gone. Used up.

Whatever hidden meaning might be locked in the cryptic message Tadeo Kurobashi had left for his wife or daughter in those final words on his computer screen, the feud between him and his daughter was never going to get any better. Their quarrel would never be over, never be resolved, not as long as Kimiko Kurobashi still lived.

People die. Quarrels don't. That inalterable realization made me sad as hell.

For everyone concerned.

CHAPTER 3

THERE ARE A LOT OF THINGS ABOUT THIS JOB THAT aren't wonderful; doing mountains of paperwork and dealing with the media are two items that come immediately to mind. But by far the worst part, bar none, is notifying next-of-kin. Delivering bad news, fatal bad news concerning a loved one, costs everybody—the people receiving it as well as those dishing it out.

Anyone who knocks on the door and walks into the home of survivors of a homicide victim is walking into an emotional mine field. There's no way to prepare in advance for what may happen because everyone reacts differently. Some survivors accept the news calmly and quietly, while others burst into hysterics, either crying or laughing. I've seen both. On some occasions I've been made to feel welcome and even been invited to stay to dinner, while at other times I've been bodily thrown out of the house. Once I was assaulted by a grief-crazed widow who held me personally responsible for her husband's death.

She came after me tooth and nail, ready to flay the skin right off my face.

But all of those are overt reactions—things cops can see for themselves and either accept or avoid by taking some kind of evasive action. For homicide detectives, though, there's often another dimension, a hidden element of risk.

Law enforcement statistics show that murder victims are usually killed by someone they know. One way or the other, survivors hold the keys to what went on before the crime. As a consequence, answers to mysteries surrounding murders and often even the killers themselves lurk just below the surface of those initial, painful next-of-kin visits. A detective has to go into those interviews with all his instincts fine-tuned and with his attention to detail honed to a razor-sharp edge.

And since at that stage of the investigation we didn't know for sure whether Tadeo Kurobashi had been murdered or if he had died by his own hand, we had to go to his home with our eyes open as well as our minds.

We followed George Yamamoto off 520 and up the I-405 corridor to the N.E. 70th exit. We headed east for a mile or so and then south on 135th toward Bridle Trails State Park. As the name would imply, it's a horse-acres neck-of-the-woods, with plots divided into five-acre parcels containing sprawling houses attached to two- or three-car garages. Stables with paddocks and thoroughbred horses take the place of conventional backyards.

Tadeo Kurobashi's house, set in a shady stand of towering alders, was at the end of a long cul-de-sac that bordered on the back of the state park. A FOR SALE sign had been pounded into the ground next to the mailbox, and the word SOLD was fastened underneath.

It could have been any standard American tri-level set in a well-kept but natural setting. The shingles on the roof and the siding of the house had weathered to a matching shade of slate gray. A closer examination of the roof, however, revealed that the ends of the roof peaks had been curved slightly upward, and a length of timber protruded underneath, giving the house's whole appearance a distinctly Japanese flavor.

We followed George Yamamoto into the circular front driveway and parked behind his car. Before anyone had a chance to get out, a woman came striding around the side of the house toward us. Her glossy black hair was pulled back and held in a long ponytail. The way she walked made her seem taller than she was, and her clothing—western shirt, faded Levi's, and worn cowboy boots—gave her an old-time wrangler appearance. At first glance I thought she was much younger than she was, a teenager maybe. Close up, however, I recognized her as a twenty-year-older version of the grinning child from the picture in Tadeo Kurobashi's office.

Kimiko Kurobashi wasn't grinning now. A deep frown furrowed her forehead, her mouth was set in a thin, grim line, and her chin jutted stubbornly. She stopped a few feet from the cars and stood waiting for us, feet spread, hands on her hips.

Since I was the first one out of the cars, I was the target of her initial blast. "If you're the new owners, we were told we didn't have to be out until three P.M. We're not ready."

George Yamamoto exited his car and started toward her. "Kimi—" he called, then stopped, as words stuck in his throat.

She turned when he spoke to her. Recognition registered on her face, but she made no move toward him. Instead, she stood like a granite statue, waiting for him to come to her. "What are you doing here?"

George's professional demeanor had fractured during his long solo ride across the lake. Criminal justice professionals of all kinds learn to detach themselves from death. They have to. They build a wall around their emotions and stay safely inside that protective circle, but if something breaches that wall— the death of one of their own, a family member or another cop, for instance—then they're in big trouble, just as George Yamamoto was now.

He stumbled blindly toward Kimiko Kurobashi, his arms outstretched, groping for words. Nothing came out of his mouth but an unintelligible croak. Once he reached her, George gathered Kimiko in his arms and crushed her against him.

"Kimi, Kimi, Kimi," he murmured over and over.

She placed both hands against his chest and pried herself away. "What's wrong? What's the matter?"

Shaking his head, George Yamamoto didn't answer directly. "Where's your mother?" he asked.

"She's out back, but tell me. What's wrong?"

"It's your father, Kimi."

"My father! What about him? Is he dead?"

Her question registered in my consciousness like

an arrow zinging straight into the bull's-eye. Not "Is he hurt?" Not "Has there been an accident?" or "Is he in the hospital?" But right to the heart of the matter: "Is he dead?"

"Yes."

Her wide-set eyes, so brown they were almost black, filled quickly with tears. She stiffened and backed away, brushing the tears away quickly, fiercely. Several feet away from all of us, she stood with her arms crossed, face averted, holding herself aloof from George's murmured expressions of sympathy. Her reaction appeared to be nine-parts anger and one-part grief.

"When?" she asked.

"Last night sometime," George answered slowly, fighting to control the timbre of his voice, trying to keep it from cracking. "We don't know exactly."

"How?" Single-word questions seemed to be all she could manage.

"Kimi, I—" Unable to go on, George stopped and shook his head helplessly.

"Tell me!" Kimiko demanded. She stepped toward him, her voice dropping to a strangled whisper. "Did he do it himself?"

George shrugged his shoulders. "We don't know yet."

"Yes you do. You must. Tell me the truth! Did he?"

George was not a tall man, and Kimi Kurobashi was smaller still, but she seemed to grow taller as she stood there staring at him while her whole body vibrated with barely controlled fury. George faltered under the weight of her withering gaze. I would have, too.

"Maybe," he answered reluctantly. "Dr. Baker seems to think so, but I don't."

Kimi turned away from him again. She stood hunched over and trembling, her white-knuckled fingers biting deep into the plaid material of the shirt that covered her upper arm.

"That son of a bitch!" I heard her mutter. "That no good son of a bitch!"

Shocked, George Yamamoto reacted instantly. "Kimi! He was your father. You mustn't talk about him that way."

"I'll talk about him any damned way I please," she blazed back at him. "Don't tell me what I can and can't say."

"But Kimi—"

"I asked him straight out," she continued, "and he lied to me. He lied!"

While listening to this heated exchange, I was still busily processing her initial reaction. "What did you ask him?" I interjected. "And when?"

She shuddered and let out a jagged breath. "Last night. I asked him last night, at his office."

"You went there?"

"Yes."

"Why?"

"To find out what was going on."

"I don't understand."

"I didn't either. He called me yesterday morning at home. They had to call me in from the barn. He told me to come home right away and get my mother. He said it was urgent."

"Did he say why?"

"No. I tried to ask him while we were still on the

phone, but he said there wasn't time, that he wanted her away from here when it happened. He wanted her to go home with me to eastern Washington. He said she was pretty much packed and that she should stay with me until all this blew over."

"Until what blew over?"

"I don't know, not for sure. They were having difficulties evidently. Money difficulties of some kind. He told me that the house had been sold but that he owed more on it than they would get."

"Did he tell you he was filing for bankruptcy?"

Although Kimiko Kurobashi had been answering my questions for several minutes, now she looked at me as if my presence had finally registered. "Who are you?" she asked.

I fumbled out my ID and showed it to her. "Detective J.P. Beaumont of the Seattle Police Department. This is my partner, Detective Allen Lindstrom. We're investigating your father's death."

She glanced at George Yamamoto, who nodded a verification.

"No," she answered finally. "He didn't tell me that, but I knew anyway. I figured it out."

"How?"

"He told me my mother had packed up all the things she wanted to keep. That I should take them home with me along with my mother. Everything else is scheduled to be auctioned off next week. A moving van is due here any minute to pick it up."

She bent down suddenly, picked up a round river rock from the border of the driveway, and heaved it with surprising strength through the stand of alders until it disappeared into a blackberry thicket in the park behind the house. She made a muted noise, a derisive, angry sound that was neither sob nor laughter.

"After all those years of lecturing me on my duty, how could he leave her to face this . . ." She stopped suddenly as if she had just thought of something. She looked from me to George and back to me again. "How?"

"How what?"

"How did he do it? With the short sword?"

There was no sense trying to skirt the issue, especially since she already seemed to know about it. "Yes," I said.

She wavered at first when she heard it, but then she straightened up as though hearing it said aloud had somehow refueled her anger and given her new-found resolve. Turning on her heel, she started back around the house the way she had come.

"Let's go find my mother," she said. "She's out back saying good-bye to the fish."

When we walked around the side of the house, we passed a stable with a tall fenced enclosure built around it. No horse was visible at the moment, and from the look of the compound, there had been no four-footed occupant in the place for some time.

Behind the house, a car and trailer had been backed up to an open door. The faded green-and-white Suburban looked as though it had been picked up at a surplus vehicle auction from either the U.S. Forest Service or Immigration. It was a huge old rig, much the worse for wear. A decaying bumper sticker asked, HAVE YOU HUGGED YOUR HORSE TODAY? Hitched to that hulking wreck, however, was one of the classiest horse trailers I've ever seen. Impeccable black lettering on the cream-colored metal side announced HONEYDALE APPALOOSA FARM. And on one of the open back doors, in smaller but equally black lettering was the trailer's own pedigree: PHILLIPS TRAILERS, CHICKASHA, OKLAHOMA.

The contrast between the battle-worn Suburban and the pristine trailer was so striking that it almost made me laugh. Clearly, the horses' riding comfort was of more importance than the comfort of any human passengers.

I sidled around to the opened end of the trailer and glanced inside, half expecting to see the rump of a horse. Instead, the interior of the trailer was stacked high with furniture and boxes. I understood as soon as I looked inside. Considering their financial difficulties, it would be far less expensive for the Kurobashis to move their household goods in a borrowed horse trailer instead of a rented van or U-Haul. Once the trailer had been cleaned out, of course.

Kimiko stopped in front of me so abruptly that I almost ran her down. George and Big Al blundered to a stop behind me.

"Wait here," she ordered. "I'll go get her."

Kimi Kurobashi hurried through a wooden arch into a small, peaceful Japanese garden. She crossed a fountain-fed pond on a miniature arched concrete bridge and paused beside a carved stone bench where a woman sat tossing something to several enormous orange-and-white carp that circled lazily in the sun-dappled water.

The woman looked up startled and began to rise as Kimi came forward, speaking in rapid-fire Japanese.

I couldn't understand a word that was spoken, but I was sure from Kimi's tone that she wasn't pulling any punches. A look of shocked dismay passed over the older woman's face as she heard the news. Dismay gave way first to denial and then to total anguish as the full meaning of the words finally struck home. Her face crumpled. She faltered backward while Kimi reached out to steady her. Together they sank down onto the bench.

Even from where we were standing, it was apparent that the daughter was very much a younger, fresher version of her mother. There was the same determined set to the chin, the same delicate molding of eye and cheekbone, although the lines on Machiko Kurobashi's face were beginning to blur a little with age. Her hair was steel gray and cut short, but I could imagine that it had been long and black, full and lustrous once. In her day, she must have been a striking beauty, just as her daughter was now.

They sat on the bench for several minutes, while Machiko Kurobashi wept silently. At last the older woman took off her glasses and wiped her eyes. Despite Kimi's objections, the mother rose and started toward us.

She was wearing an old-fashioned blue cotton dress with a zipper down the front that reminded me of the everyday dresses my mother used to wear, housedresses she called them, that were good enough for working inside the house but not for going to the grocery store or for entertaining even unexpected guests. Machiko seemed to share my mother's housedress philosophy. She self-consciously brushed crumbs from her lap and checked the zipper as she walked toward us.

She was older than I had thought at first, older and frailer. Coming closer, she leaned heavily on her daughter's arm with one hand and on a twisted wooden cane with the other. When she reached the wooden archway, she stopped and looked questioningly at each of us in turn, her eyes enormous behind the beveled lenses of her gold-framed glasses. When her glance reached George Yamamoto, it stopped, freezing into a hard glitter.

Machiko Kurobashi's transformation was sudden and complete. She seemed to grow younger, stiffer, and inches taller all at the same time. Letting go of her daughter's arm, she raised one trembling hand and pointed an accusing finger at the head of the Washington State Patrol Crime Lab.

"You," she hissed. "Out!"

A dark flush swept out from under George Yamamoto's collar and up his neck, leaving his ears a vivid shade of crimson. "I'm so sorry, Machiko . . ." he began.

She shook her head stubbornly, cutting him off. "Out," she repeated, glaring at him. "Go!"

He started to object and then thought better of it. He went, retreating dispiritedly past the trailer and Suburban until he disappeared around the corner of the house while Machiko Kurobashi stared after him as if concerned that he might change his mind and come back.

Surprised, I looked down at the bird-boned old woman who had ordered George Yamamoto away, who had managed to treat a more than sixty-year-old bureaucrat the same way a hard-nosed teacher might treat a misbehaving kindergartener. Obviously, the rancor between George Yamamoto and Machiko Kurobashi was deep-rooted and inarguably mutual.

Once George was out of sight, Machiko turned toward me. "I sorry to be rude. That man not welcome here." Her English was broken and heavily accented, but quite understandable. Once again I fumbled my identification out of my pocket and handed it to her. She didn't bother to look at it.

"You are police?"

I nodded. "I'm Detective Beaumont, and that's my partner, Detective Lindstrom. We came to tell you about your husband."

"Kimi told me," she said. "Come."

Instead of going toward the house, she turned and headed back into the garden. The rest of us followed. She resumed her place on the bench, patting it to indicate that I should sit beside her. Big Al and Kimi sat on another bench a few feet away.

"Sorry," she said. "Furniture all gone. Nowhere to sit inside."

"That's fine," I said. "This is very beautiful."

"Tadeo make it for me. Like home, so I not be homesick." The aching hurt in her simple words put a lump in my throat. My heart went out to this fragile old woman who seemed to be losing everything at once—husband, home, security. Somehow she didn't seem defeated.

"Homesick for Japan?" I asked, wanting to be clear about what she was saying.

She nodded.

"Didn't you ever go back?"

She shook her head.

"Not even for a visit?"

"No."

From the look of the surroundings, the kind of home they lived in, the kind of business her husband had run, they surely could have afforded the price of an airplane ticket.

"My home in Nagasaki," she said simply.

Nagasaki. Hiroshima's sister in devastation, the one you seldom heard about. For the second time that day the specter of World War II rose up before me, its horror and destruction made personal in a way it had never touched me before. Looking at Machiko Kurobashi, I wondered what tricks of fate had placed her home and family in the path of exploding atomic bombs.

"There's nothing left?" I asked.

She shook her head. "No one. Nothing. Only this, that Tadeo made for me. Now it gone too."

Tears sprang once more to her eyes. For several long seconds no one spoke. The brilliantly colored fish alternately lazed in and darted through the shallow water.

"Tell me about my husband," she said.

And so, as gently as I could, I told her everything, including how George Yamamoto had been called in to help determine whether or not Tadeo's death had involved the ancient practice of *hara-kiri* or *seppuku*. I noted what seemed to be a sharp intake of breath when I mentioned the sword, but she said nothing and I continued. Finished finally, I waited to hear what she would say.

"No."

She spoke the word so softly that I almost missed it. "No what?" I asked.

When her eyes met mine, they were blazing with a new intensity, a desperate defiance. "My Tadeo not kill himself. This I know."

And that was all she said, her only response. They may have disagreed on everything else, but on that score, George Yamamoto and Machiko Kurobashi were in full and total agreement. Neither one of them believed for one moment that Tadeo Kurobashi had committed suicide.

Their insistent belief led me to agree with them.

CHAPTER 4

THE DEEP-THROATED HONK OF A SEMI'S HORN SOUNDED three short bursts out in front of the house. Kimi glanced at her watch then jumped up and started out of the garden. "The movers," she explained. "I'll go tell them what's happened, that they'll have to come back later."

"No," Machiko said. She didn't say much, but what she did say was definitive.

Frowning, Kimi stopped and turned to her mother. "What do you mean, no?"

"Your father say today. He give his word. We go today."

"But—"

Machiko held out her hand, a gesture which both stifled protest and asked for help. Kimi pulled Machiko to her feet. "You stay," the older woman ordered. "I go."

It was more a command than a request, and Kimiko unwillingly assented to it. She stood watching with furrowed brows as her mother, leaning on the gnarled cane, hobbled slowly across the bridge and out of sight around the house while the truck's horn honked impatiently once more.

This time when Kimiko turned back to us, tears were streaming down her face. She made no effort to wipe them away. "How could he do this to her?"

"Do what?"

"Bail out. Leave her like this with next to nothing. Worse than nothing. The house is gone, along with everything else."

"But your mother seems to think he was murd—"

Kimi interrupted with an angry snort. "She'd defend him no matter what, right or wrong. It's always been that way."

She paused long enough to blow her nose. Kimiko Kurobashi's bitterly hostile words didn't sound like those of someone grieving for a dead father, at least not yet. It was still too soon. She was still too angry with him for dying. It's a common enough reaction, and I didn't fault her for it.

The time had come to begin the inevitable questioning process. Big Al picked up the ball and ran with it, speaking directly to Kimiko for the first time. "You said you talked to your father last night at his office?"

Kimi nodded.

"What time was that?"

"About eight-thirty, I guess. He called around eleven yesterday morning while I was working. It took me several hours to get squared away at work, to make arrangements to have someone fill in for me both at school and on the farm."

"The farm?" I asked, suddenly remembering the words printed on the side of the horse trailer. "Would that be Honeydale Farm?"

People don't expect you to pay attention to the little telltale clues they leave scattered around them. If you ask someone wearing a Yellowstone T-shirt how they liked Old Faithful, they'll be mystified as to how you knew. They react as though you have some secret, black magic way of knowing things about them when it's actually nothing more than using basic powers of observation. Kimi Kurobashi was no exception. She had long since stopped seeing the Honeydale Farm lettering on the horse trailer.

"I live there," she said, giving me an uncertain look. "I help out around the place for board and room both for me and Sadie."

"Who's Sadie?"

"My horse. Teaching assistants don't earn enough to support horses."

"Your parents haven't been helping you then?"

"Are you kidding? My father threw me out when I was nineteen years old. I've earned my own way ever since, every penny of it. When he called me yesterday, it was the first time I had spoken to him in almost nine years."

"That's a long time," I said.

"He was a stubborn man," she said, adding thoughtfully after a moment, "I must take after him."

"Getting back to yesterday," I prompted.

"As I said, it took me a while to get things lined up. It was after one before I was able to get away. It takes a full five hours to get across the mountain pass, a little longer pulling the trailer, especially in weekend traffic, and it was windy coming across the Columbia. I didn't get here until almost six-thirty.

"Mother must have spent weeks packing. She had been here working by herself all day long and was so tired she could barely stand. There wasn't a crumb of food left in the house—everything was packed. I took her into Kirkland to have something to eat. She doesn't drive. I dropped her off after dinner, and then I went to see my father."

"At his office?"

"Yes."

"Was there anybody else there?"

"One person that I saw. A young guy who was moving files."

"Moving them where?"

"I don't know. I met him coming out of my father's office carrying a full file drawer. He brought the empty drawer back later and got another full one. I assumed he must be packing them into boxes somewhere."

"Doesn't that strike you as an odd way to move files?"

"Odd? Maybe, especially on a Sunday night, but I didn't question it, if that's what you mean. I still don't think you understand about my father, Detective . . ."

"Beaumont," I supplied.

"Detective Beaumont. His word was law both at work and at home. Questioning wasn't allowed. Period."

"So what happened when you got to his office?"

"As I said, in the doorway I met this young man

in overalls who was carrying the file drawer. I waited
long enough for him to come out and then I went in."

"And your father was there?"

She nodded. "Sitting at his desk, polishing that
damn sword."

"Had you ever seen it before?"

"No. Never."

"Do you have any idea where it came from?"

"No."

"And what did he say to you?"

For the first time in her narration, Kimiko faltered,
pausing to swallow before she answered. "Thank
you," she said.

"Thank you for what?"

"He said thank you for coming home to take care
of Mother."

"And you took that to mean?"

"That he was going to kill himself," she replied
matter-of-factly.

"Why?"

"I'm a Japanese-American, Detective Beaumont.
I grew up on samurai stories, cut my teeth on them
while my friends at school were reading the Hardy
Boys and Nancy Drew. It looked like a samurai short
sword to me. I know all about *seppuku*, about choos-
ing death over disgrace. It's a time-honored Japanese
custom."

"But he didn't *say* outright that he was going to do
it, did he?"

"No. In fact, when I asked him, he denied it. I told
him he had no right to leave my mother. She's always
been totally dependent on him. Far too dependent.
He kept her here in this house, waiting on him hand

and foot, but she never said a word against him, never objected to the way he treated her."

"And how was that?"

"Like he was lord and master and she was his servant. His slave. Around the house things were done his way and that was it."

"What about you?" I asked quietly. "Did you always do things his way?"

"Up to a point." She gave me a shrewd, appraising glance. "You're a smart man, aren't you?"

"I try."

"Things were fine when I was younger. Kids think that whatever they're used to at home, that however they live, is the way life is supposed to be. They don't question it. He treated me like the son he never had, took me places, taught me things."

"Is that why you're studying engineering?"

She shrugged. "Probably," she said. "I'm good at it, but he made sure I was exposed to engineering at a very early age."

Lost in thought, she stopped and seemed to drift away. "Go on," I said.

"Back then I didn't worry about my mother, didn't even think about her very much. She was always there but almost invisible, always hovering in the background, always doing things, never complaining. But eventually I grew up and went away to school. I got my consciousness raised in a Women's Studies program over at Central. When I came home from Ellensburg, I tried to talk to my father about it, tried to get him to see that what he was doing to her was wrong, how he'd made her too helpless, too dependent on him, kept her isolated and cut off from everyone but us. We had a major battle over it, and he threw me out."

"What did your mother say?"

"What do you think? She sided with him, as always. She said that I was wrong, that I was too young to understand. That's the last time I spoke to my father until he called me on the phone yesterday morning."

"But you stayed in touch with your mother."

"Yes. Other than him, I was all she had. My father had his work, his company. Without me, she had nothing."

"So what happened last night in your father's office?"

"We quarreled again. Except for that pitiful little stack of household goods out in the trailer, all my mother's things were packed up, ready to go to the auction to satisfy his debts, and there he sat holding that damn sword. I don't know where he got it or how long he's had it, but I told him that if she had to give up all her things, so did he. He told me about it then, bragged that it was made by a student of Masamune. He claimed that it had been in the family for hundreds of years, that it was priceless."

"But you had never seen it before?" That seemed strange to me. Priceless family heirlooms aren't usually hidden under bushels. People talk about them, brag about them, show them off.

"No. I had no idea he owned such a thing."

"Can you spell that?" Big Al was still glumly taking notes.

"What?"

"The name. It started with an *M*."

"M-A-S-A-M-U-N-E." Kimi spelled it out slowly

before she continued. "He's the Leonardo of Japanese sword makers. Swords done by him or by one of his students are considered national treasures in Japan. I'm sure it can't be genuine. How could it? How would he have gotten it?"

If Kimiko Kurobashi didn't have an answer to that question, I certainly didn't.

"Did he say anything else about the sword?"

"Only that he had finally thought of a way of putting it to use, that it would fix everything but that it would take time. In the meantime he wanted my mother out of harm's way."

"That's what he said?"

"Not exactly. He implied that all the disruption of selling the house and everything in it was upsetting to her and that he wouldn't be able to do whatever it was with the sword in time to stop the foreclosure or the auction, but he insisted that there would be plenty of money later."

Big Al's scratching pencil was suddenly quiet. Raising one eyebrow, he glanced meaningfully in my direction. "Insurance?" he asked.

I nodded. "Maybe. If the policy has been in effect long enough, suicide is usually covered."

"I thought about insurance, too," Kimiko said. "And when he told me about the money, I asked him again."

"And what did he say?"

"He laughed." She stopped abruptly. I could tell from her expression that Kimiko was reliving that painful scene, that she was still hurt and puzzled by his reaction. Considering subsequent events, her question didn't seem the least bit out of order. Laughter did.

"What about the office when you got there?" Big Al put in. "Was there anything unusual that you noticed? Anything out of place? For instance, what did you see on his desk?"

"Not much. His computer, the ashtray, a wooden box. I guess it's the box he kept the sword in. There was a piece of cloth, black silk maybe, that he was using for polishing. And then . . ." She stopped, unable to continue.

"And what else?"

"My trophy," she whispered.

"The rodeo trophy?"

"Yes. And a picture of me, too. An old one, hanging on the wall behind his desk. He was so angry with me that I was surprised to see those things there, surprised that he bothered to keep reminders of me anywhere in his life."

"Did you see any kind of a bill?"

"A bill?"

"An invoice."

"No. There were no papers of any kind."

I had to doff my hat to Al Lindstrom. He was asking good questions. If Kimiko Kurobashi was telling the truth, and we had no reason to think otherwise, then she may not have been the last person to see her father alive. The fellow in the overalls, presumably the guy from DataDump, had been.

"What about the door to the safe? Was it opened or closed?"

"What safe? I don't remember seeing a safe anywhere in the room."

"And where was the picture?"

"On the wall, right behind his desk."

That struck me as an important piece of information and another bingo for Detective Allen Lindstrom. The door to the safe had been closed and concealed behind the picture when Kimiko was in her father's office, when she last saw him alive, but it had been found open that morning, open and empty both, when our investigators had arrived at the crime scene.

"Do you have any idea what might have been important enough for him to keep in the safe?"

"I didn't even know he had a safe. How would I possibly know what he kept in it?"

"What about the computer?"

"What about it?"

"Was it on or off?"

"Off," she answered decisively, without the slightest hesitation. "Most definitely off. I already told you, he wasn't working. He was sitting there rubbing the sword with that piece of silk like he didn't have a care in the world while my mother was home working like a dog to get packed and out of there."

"What did you know about your father's business?" I asked.

"Not much. Only what everyone else knows, what I read in the papers. Until it was settled, the patent infringement lawsuit between MicroBridge and RFLink, Ltd., was hot news in newspaper business sections for months."

"What was it all about?"

"My father used to work for a man named Blakeslee. His job, as engineering manager, was to develop a system of local area networks. There were evidently hard feelings when he left, and Blakeslee claimed that when my father started MicroBridge a few months later, that he did it using technology and patents that rightfully belonged to Blakeslee's company. Blakeslee took him to court and won. Blakeslee was in the process of putting my father out of business."

"So you knew that your father was in some financial difficulty?"

She shrugged. "Vaguely, but I didn't have any idea how bad it was. And even if I had known, I wouldn't have been able to help. From what I've gleaned from my mother, he must have personally guaranteed a line of credit and put second and third mortgages on the house in order to meet payroll and keep the company afloat during the lawsuit. When he lost the case in court, the bank pulled the note."

She paused and shook her head. "My father and I didn't get along, but I always thought he was brilliant. I *believed* he was brilliant. I still don't understand how he could do such a stupid thing."

"What did he do that was so stupid?"

"He bet everything on winning that case—this house, their personal possessions, their chance of a comfortable retirement—everything. And he lost it all."

"He must have thought he was betting on a sure thing," I suggested.

"He was a fool!" Kimiko Kurobashi's dark eyes flashed with anger as she spoke. Her contempt for her father was absolutely unforgiving. Despite the years of hostility, the child in her was now being stripped of all lingering illusions. She was getting an adult look at her father's feet of clay, and she didn't like what she was seeing. Kimiko regarded her father's failure as a personal betrayal of her mother's simple trust, and seeing it for what it was tore her to pieces.

"Nobody but a fool bets on a sure thing!"

Machiko appeared at the corner of the house, limping slowly around the Suburban and the horse trailer.

"You know, she packed the entire house by herself," Kimi said, watching her mother's slow progress toward us. "Every bit of it. The boxes are there in all the rooms, carefully labeled in her own handwriting, waiting for the movers. It's like he forced her to dismantle her own life, piece by piece."

"Are they labeled in English or Japanese?" I asked.

"Japanese. I've spent all morning relabeling them. That's another thing. How is she going to get along? She never learned to speak English very well, and she doesn't write it at all."

Kimi didn't add, "My father wouldn't let her." She didn't have to. From the way she said it and from the look of disgust on her face, I knew this was yet another unpardonable sin laid at her father's door without Tadeo Kurobashi having a chance to defend himself.

Just as I suspected, the warfare between them was continuing unabated. If the message on Tadeo's computer screen was truly intended for his daughter, if Kimi was supposed to be the child that still offered hope, then Tadeo had screwed up again. Royally. He had bet big on yet another losing horse.

Falling silent as her mother approached within earshot, Kimi hurried forward to help Machiko cross over the bridge, where she sank gratefully onto a bench.

"Two hours," she said. "Done in two hours."

Kimi shook her head. "Two hours to move a life-time."

Machiko looked at her daughter. "Things are nothing. When they finish, we go."

"Go?" Kimi echoed in surprise. "Go where?"

"Home with you. Like your father say."

Kimiko Kurobashi looked shocked, dumbfounded. "But we can't," she objected. "There'll be all kinds of arrangements to make—the funeral, the auction."

Machiko was adamant. "No. We go today. Soon. In two hours."

While she had been off supervising the movers, Machiko Kurobashi had uncovered a daunting reserve of inner strength.

Kimi turned to me, pleading for help. "We can't leave, can we, Detective Beaumont? Shouldn't we stay here or in Seattle in a motel for a day or two until things get settled?"

"It would probably be better . . ." I began.

Machiko didn't give me a chance to finish my answer. Ignoring me, she slipped out of English and into Japanese, speaking quickly, urgently. Words flew back and forth between the two women in short, rapid bursts. The argument lasted for several minutes. I couldn't translate a word of it into English, but the outcome was obvious. Kimiko made zero progress. Machiko's mind was made up and she wasn't changing it.

Defeated, Kimi turned to me, shaking her head. "Mother insists that there'll be no service of any kind, no funeral. She wants the body cremated and the remains sent over to us later. She says that I should go with you now while the movers are here and sign whatever papers are necessary so we can leave as soon as they finish loading the truck."

I could think of no good reason why they shouldn't leave Kirkland as planned. There was no reason to think they were in any danger. From an investigative standpoint, neither was currently under any suspicion. Besides, they were only going east of the mountains, not out of state. They would be returning to Kimi's home and horse and job. It's not easy to go on the lam and take a thoroughbred Appaloosa with you. In other words, having them leave town would be a little inconvenient, but under the circumstances, it wasn't out of the question.

"Let's go now, then," I said. "Dr. Baker, the medical examiner, won't be able to release the body until after the autopsy, but you can sign the paperwork and designate where you want it sent."

Kimi nodded. "All right. Wait here while I go change."

She got up and strode off to the Suburban, where she took a small suitcase out of the back and disappeared into the house with it. Machiko watched her daughter go, her head bobbing up and down in approval.

"Kimiko good girl. Smart, too," Machiko said.

"You're lucky to have her," I said.

Machiko nodded again.

"May we ask you some questions?"

"I try to answer. Do my best."

"When was the last time you saw your husband?"

"Yesterday morning. He leave home early to catch ferry."

"Where was he going?"

She shrugged. "Do not know."

"Which ferry, did he say? Winslow? Bremerton?"

She shook her head.

"Did he call you?" I asked.

Machiko nodded gravely. "Yes. On phone."

"What time?"

"Noon."

"And what did he say?"

"He say, wait one more while. Things be better."

"When he didn't come home last night, did you think to try calling him at the office?"

Machiko shook her head.

"Did you send someone back down to MicroBridge to check on him?"

"My husband grown man. Come and go as he please."

Big Al Lindstrom had been watching this entire exchange with his head swiveling back and forth like an observer at a tennis match.

"If you don't believe that your husband committed suicide," he said, "then you must think he was murdered. Do you know of anyone who would want to see him dead?"

Machiko Kurobashi's eyes, enormous behind the beveled glass, turned full on Detective Lindstrom. "No," she answered.

"Did he have any enemies?"

"Yes. I think so."

"Do you know who those enemies might be?"

"No."

"Did it have anything to do with this lawsuit your daughter was telling us about?"

She frowned. "My English not too good. I do not understand."

"Was it about the lawsuit, the patent infringement?"

Machiko shrugged helplessly and shook her head.

Big Al tried again, louder, as though turning up the volume would somehow batter down the language barrier between them. It didn't. Machiko simply looked at him sadly and shrugged her shoulders once more.

I suspected that Machiko understood far more English than she was willing to let on, but we had reached a point in the questioning process where, for some reason, it was important for her to pretend otherwise.

I'll admit that I found Machiko amazing and puzzling both. For a woman who had just learned that her husband was dead, she was showing remarkable resilience, fortitude, and restraint. To say nothing of stubbornness.

Kimiko Kurobashi had hinted to us earlier that she thought she had inherited her stubborn streak from her father's side of the family, but I had news for her. Based on what I had observed, I suspected she had been given a hefty double dose of it. On both sides of her genetic heritage.

CHAPTER 5

I WAS SHOCKED WHEN KIMI KUROBASHI OPENED THE door and stepped back outside the house ten minutes later. I hardly recognized her. The threadbare Levi's, Western shirt, and down-at-the-heel boots had disappeared. She was wearing a well-tailored gray suit with a high-necked, pleated white blouse, and a pair of black, high-heeled pumps. The ponytail had been replaced by a complicated knot of hair, held in place on the back of her head by an oversized pearl-handled comb. She looked like a model fresh from the pages of Nordstrom's latest dress-for-success catalog.

I'm always dazzled when women pull off wizard changes like that, and I'm equally sure that dazzled is just what women want men to be. It's like they all have Fairy Godmothers stashed away that they can pull out at a moment's notice. Men are pretty much stuck with being the way we are, warts and all. Big Al Lindstrom, caught pushing the lawnmower in his yard on a Saturday afternoon, is still the same guy I work with every day.

Kimiko, emerging from her mother's house, was so transformed as to be almost unrecognizable. She bore little resemblance to the grungy ranch hand who had gone inside a few minutes earlier. I found myself gazing at her appreciatively. A sophisticated butterfly had been concealed in the faded work shirt and the grubby Tony Lama boots.

"Should I take the Suburban?" she asked as she came up to where Al and I were waiting with her mother. "It'll only take a few minutes to unhitch it."

I did my best to camouflage the lecherous stare. You can't hang a man for looking.

"No," I answered quickly. "We'll take you over and bring you back when we finish. It'll go a lot faster and give us a chance to talk to you on the way."

She nodded, spoke briefly to her mother in Japanese, and then started toward the car. Out front we found that George Yamamoto's car was gone and in its place sat a huge North American Van Lines truck with a crew of three loading boxes into it as fast as they could. Kimi walked past them with her eyes downcast, not acknowledging their existence.

Wincing at the pain in my fingers, I helped her into the backseat of the Reliant. It might have been more gentlemanly to put her in front, but I needed the extra legroom a whole lot more than she did.

It was silent in the car as we started back toward the freeway. I was hung over and half sick. It felt as though my pores were sweating pure champagne, and I reminded myself never to drink the stuff again.

Trying to take my mind off both my headache and my throbbing fingers, I began a mental review of what we had learned since arriving at Tadeo Kurobashi's office early that morning. Reflexively I reached for my notebook, wanting to consult my notes, but of course I hadn't taken any.

"Let me look at your notebook, Al."

He did, handing it to me carefully enough that it didn't fly out of my hand. Big Al's handwriting, a haphazard combination of printing and cursive, was difficult to make out. Remembering what Kimi had said about relabeling her mother's boxes, I thumbed through the pages until I reached the place where Al had laboriously copied down the Japanese words from the computer screen.

"Can you read Japanese?" I asked. When she didn't answer, I turned around and looked at her. Lost in thought, she was staring blankly at the back of Big Al's muscular neck. She jumped when she realized I had spoken to her.

"Excuse me?"

"Can you read Japanese?" I repeated.

"Yes."

"What about this?" I passed her the notebook.

Looking at the words, she held it in front of her for a long moment, long enough that I began to wonder if she had been mistaken and wouldn't be able to translate it after all. Closing her eyes, she leaned back against the seat, letting the notebook drop into her lap.

"Well?" I asked.

"Yes," she whispered. "I can read it."

"What does it say?"

She recited the verse in a leaden voice without opening her eyes, without once having to glance at the text:

> "*'A child is still one more hope*
> *Even in this careworn world.'*"

"You recognize it then?"

"Yes. It's a verse from my father's favorite poem, "A Child," written by a man named Shuntaro Tanikawa. How do you know about it? Where did you get it?"

"It was on his computer screen this morning when they found him. Detective Lindstrom here copied it down. We thought it might be important."

She seemed more visibly shaken by this than by anything else that had happened. "On his computer screen? He had typed it there?"

"Over and over," I replied. "Why, does it mean something to you?"

She still didn't open her eyes. "I was that child," she answered softly. "I was *supposed* to be that child. I heard that poem a million times while I was growing up."

Ten points for George Yamamoto. He had called that shot. Tadeo Kurobashi's message had indeed been meant for his daughter, not for his wife.

"Have you ever heard of the too precious child?" Kimi asked finally, her voice heavy, devoid of all animation.

Big Al shook his head. So did I. "Not that I know of," I said.

"It's the latest psychological buzzword," Kimi said, "but I think I am one. Or was."

"Too precious? What does that mean?" I asked.

The events of the morning and of the last two days had taken their toll. Her voice was barely audible above the road noise of the freeway.

"I was a change-of-life baby," she said. "My mother was forty-four when I was born, and she had long before given up on the idea of ever having children. When I was born, both she and my father thought it was a miracle. They gave me everything, pampered me, wanted me to be smart, have fun, do it all."

"That sounds like a lot of pressure."

She nodded. "It was. For everyone. Since my mother didn't drive, my father was the one who had to make arrangements for rides and car pools to get me to music lessons and riding lessons and soccer. He did too much, invested too much."

Kimi fell silent. I wanted to reach around, grab her by the shoulders, and shake her until her teeth rattled. What did she mean, her father did too much! He sounded like a helluva guy to me. Aren't parents ever right? They either do too goddamned much or too goddamned little, but they're never right, at least not as far as their kids are concerned. Count on it.

Not trusting myself to be civil on that particular subject, I took the notebook from her and went back to reviewing it, eventually reaching the part where we had been questioning Machiko outside her daughter's presence.

"Did you know that your father talked to your mother by phone yesterday morning?"

Kimiko shook her head.

"It must have been close to the same time he talked to you," I continued. "He didn't happen to mention to you where he was calling from, did he?"

There was no immediate response. I glanced back to see if Kimi was listening and found her frowning in concentration. "He said something, but I can't recall exactly what. I remember asking him if I could check with the people at work and call him back. He said no, that he was out of his office and wherever he was, he wouldn't be there long. Port something. Port Townsend, maybe. Port Angeles. Something like that."

"And he didn't give you any idea what he was doing there?"

"None whatsoever."

We made good time crossing Lake Washington. Big Al wheeled the car into a police vehicle parking place outside the medical examiner's office at the south end of Harborview Hospital. I got out, held the door open for Kimiko, and reached inside to help her out of the car. Once upright, she still clung to my hand. Her whole body was shaking.

"Am I going to have to identify him?" she asked, her voice small and tremulous.

"No," I said. "George Yamamoto already gave us a positive ID. That won't be necessary. All you'll need to do is sign the papers."

She sighed with obvious relief. I thanked George Yamamoto for sparing her that. After nine years of not speaking, it would have been a tough way to see her father again.

Doc Baker's receptionist ushered us straight into

the medical examiner's messy private office. His chipped blue vase, half filled with paper clips, sat by the window, but for once he didn't spend the entire interview trying to make baskets. He was solicitous and concerned as he shoved one piece of paper after another across his desk for Kimiko Kurobashi to sign.

"Have you scheduled the autopsy?" I asked when she finished.

He nodded, taking the last of the sheaf of papers and straightening the edge by bouncing it sharply several times on the hard surface of the desk. "This afternoon. Four o'clock."

"You've told George?"

"I've left word for him."

"Is an autopsy really necessary?" Kimiko asked.

Doc Baker peered at her, dropping his chin so he could see her through the part of his glasses where the bifocals weren't. "Yes, it's necessary, miss. In cases like this, the law demands it."

She flushed. "Will we have to pay for it?"

"No."

She nodded, relieved again. "And my mother wanted me to ask you about the sword. What will happen to that?"

"It's in the crime lab right now, being examined. It will be kept in the property room pending a determination of whether or not it needs to be held as evidence.

"But it will be returned to her?" Kimi insisted.

"Yes," Baker replied. "Eventually. Assuming she's the rightful owner, of course. And you'll have to handle that through the police department. They're the ones who are in charge of physical evidence. I understand you know Mr. Yamamoto over at the Crime Lab."

"Yes," she replied. "He was a friend of my father's."

"I see. Talk to him about it then. He can help you work your way through the bureaucracy, but you can plan on it taking quite a while. The wheels grind wondrous slow around here at times." He paused long enough to check through the papers before placing them in a manila file folder.

"This is all in order, then," he continued. "We'll release the body directly to the mortuary when the time comes. You should stop by and see them too, as long as you're over here. They may require full payment in advance, but I suppose you already knew that."

Kimi shook her head. "I didn't know, but I'll take care of it," she said, rising. The muscle in her cheek tightened over her narrow jawline. "Is that all?"

"Yes, Miss Kurobashi."

"And will we hear from you about what you find—in the autopsy, I mean?"

"The detectives here will keep in touch. You can ask them."

"All right," she said. Kimi walked out of the room with Big Al following her. I waited long enough for the door to close behind them.

"Would you mind giving George a message when he shows up here this afternoon? He is still coming, isn't he?"

Doc Baker nodded. "What kind of message?"

"Tell him that I think the sword was made by a student of Masamune."

"By who?"

I repeated the name Kimiko had given us and spelled it out for him while Baker wrote it down on a notepad.

"What's that supposed to mean?" Baker asked impatiently.

"According to the daughter, it's probably very valuable."

"That pretty much clinches it, then, doesn't it?" the medical examiner said.

"Clinches what?"

"That it was suicide instead of murder."

"Why?"

"Because if you had just offed somebody and had a clear shot at stealing a very valuable sword which also happened to be the murder weapon, would you be so stupid as to walk off and leave the damn thing lying there on the floor?"

"No," I answered. "I suppose not. Unless you wanted it to look like suicide."

Baker pushed his reading glasses up on his nose and glowered at me. "Get the hell out of here, Beaumont, and let me go back to work."

When I came out of Baker's office, Kimiko was using the phone at the receptionist's desk. She was speaking in low tones, but two bright red flush marks showed prominently on the otherwise pale skin of her slender cheeks.

Putting the phone down, she turned to me. "I'll need to go to a bank," she said.

"A bank?"

"I just talked to the mortuary. Since there isn't going to be a service of any kind, I'll have to pay with a cashier's check before they'll agree to do anything, and I'll have to pay for it myself. As far as I know, my mother doesn't have any money or even access to a checkbook. Besides, they told me they won't take an out of town check anyway."

Big Al drove her to a Seafirst branch on First Hill, and we waited in the car while she went inside.

"That's pretty shitty of the mortuary, if you ask me," he said as the glass door of the bank closed behind her. "Making her pay in advance like that. You think there is some insurance?"

"Beats me. That's anybody's guess. If there isn't, those two women are going to be in a world of hurt."

Grim-faced, Kimiko came back out of the bank a few minutes later, clutching a cashier's check, and we drove her to the mortuary, an old dilapidated one off Jackson. I offered to accompany her inside, thinking she might need an ally in fending off what I figured was the inevitable round of up-selling.

In theaters they try to get patrons to take a larger-sized drink or butter on their popcorn. In mortuaries, the high-priced spread is a snazzy, upscale, satin-lined coffin, and they sell them to grieving relatives when they are at their lowest ebb and most susceptible to high-pressure tactics.

Kimi ignored my offer and went inside by herself. While she was gone, Big Al and I bet lunch that they'd do a job on her even though no service was planned or wanted. Believe me, I've seen it happen often enough.

"How'd it go?" I asked cautiously when, still tight-lipped and grim-faced, she returned to the car.

"They asked about insurance," she answered. I caught Big Al's slight knowing nod.

"I told them he didn't have any," she added. "Naturally, Mother wants the very best, but I gave them the check and told them that was it. It'll have to do. There's no more where that came from. It's money I was saving for a stud fee."

With his worst mortician suspicions confirmed, Big Al shoved the car into gear and backed out of the parking place.

"Do you think maybe he did carry insurance?" she asked hopefully after a silence. Kimi Kurobashi was grasping at financial straws.

"Maybe," I said.

"And do policies pay off in case of suicide?"

"That depends," I said. "You'd have to have the policy itself in hand and talk to one of their claims people in order to find out. Have you seen any policies?"

"No, but everything at the house was packed. I'll have to ask Mother if she remembers packing any papers. Of course, there's always the possibility that he left them at the office." Her voice drifted away.

I turned and looked closely at Kimiko Kurobashi. She was wound tight as a coiled spring. For her mother's sake, she was doing what had to be done, tying up the loose ends, and keeping herself under control while she did it.

"Would you like to go there and look?" I asked gently.

"Please," she said, her eyes filling with tears. "If it wouldn't be too much trouble."

I knew how much it cost her to ask us for help. No way in hell could we have turned her down. At least I couldn't have.

"No trouble at all," I replied.

As he turned the car in the direction of Fourth Avenue South and Industry Square, Big Al Lindstrom made only the slightest grimace, one that was invisible to Kimiko Kurobashi riding in the backseat. He didn't approve, but he kept his mouth shut about it.

The crime scene team had completed their work and gone away. I figured we'd have to go find Bernard Rennermann to let us in. When we got to the complex, Big Al dropped us off and took the car to the next building to find Rennermann while Kimiko and I went inside to wait. We were standing talking in the hall outside the MicroBridge office when the door was opened by a tall scarecrow of a woman with a beaked nose and heavily hooded eyes that were red with weeping.

"I'm sorry but we're not—" the woman started, breaking off at once as soon as she recognized Kimiko Kurobashi.

"Oh, Kimi, you did come. I'm so glad. It's so good to see you after all these years."

"Hello, Mrs. Oliver," Kimi said.

"How is your mother? I wanted to call and talk to her and tell her how sorry I was, but the police wouldn't let me. They told me I shouldn't until we knew for sure that she had been properly notified."

"Mother's fine," Kimi responded. She stepped into the reception area and looked around. No one else was in evidence. "What are you doing here? I understood the place was shut down, out of business."

Mrs. Oliver shook her head and pressed a damp hanky to her nose. "I told your father that I'd stay until the end of the month, and I will, no matter what. Someone should be here to answer the phones if nothing else, to let people know what's going on. I don't know what to tell people though. The records are all gone."

"What records?" I asked quickly.

Mrs. Oliver gave me a quick, hostile look.

"It's all right, Mrs. Oliver," Kimi said. "He's a police officer, one of the detectives."

"The records. The customer lists, the sales records, the specifications and parts lists, his most recent design work. They're gone, all gone. Everything."

"Are you sure?" I asked.

"Of course I'm sure. When I came in this morning, I opened my file cabinet, and the drawers were empty. So were his. So was every file drawer in the place, here and down in engineering, and in the comptroller's office as well. Oh, there are still a few things left, your father's personal papers, some pension and tax records, that kind of thing, but the bulk of the company records, the important ones, are gone. I thought maybe the police had taken them, but they said no, that nothing had been removed except the . . ."

I could see Mrs. Oliver cringed at using the word *body* in Kimi's presence. She chose instead to leave the sentence hanging unfinished.

Mrs. Oliver was a woman in her mid to late sixties who walked with a stately, unbowed step. Leaving us standing, Mrs. Oliver went back over to her desk and eased her angular frame primly onto the rolling chair behind it.

"I was here on time this morning," she said, "but the officers wouldn't let me in. They finally allowed me inside my own office on the condition that I stay out of Mr. Kurobashi's."

"Did you?"

"Did I what, stay out? Of course, but I did go as far as the doorway and look around."

"Did you notice anything out of place?"

"His ashtray is gone. Maybe it just got knocked down behind the desk. I couldn't see that far."

"What kind of ashtray?"

"A marble one. I gave it to him at Christmas, but then he quit smoking in June."

I remembered that Kimiko had mentioned an ashtray, but I had no recollection of its being in the room, much less on the desk.

"Anyway, to go back to the files," Mrs. Oliver continued. "I didn't worry about them that much. After all, we were moving by the end of the month, but now I'm not so sure."

"Why not? What do you mean?"

"And look at this." She gestured toward her computer, and Kimi hurried around to where she could see the screen.

"That's the index," Mrs. Oliver continued. "That's all that's there, in every file and in every backup file on every computer in the place. I can't even read it, to say nothing of make it work. Your father had his fill of paperwork when he worked for Boeing. He preferred computer files to hard copy wherever possible, and we made archive files of every hard drive in the place, but all those floppies are gone, and this is all there is in the computer itself."

Kimi straightened up and met my questioning gaze.

"What is it?" I asked.

"A virus," she answered, her face hard beneath a sudden pallor.

"A virus? What are you talking about?"

"A computer virus."

I hurried around the desk to see for myself. The index showed a long list of files with the amount of disk space each occupied, but there was only one file name, written in Japanese and repeated over and over.

Kimi stepped away from the desk and leaned heavily against the wall.

"The poem again?" I asked.

She nodded. "The first few letters."

"What poem?" Mrs. Oliver asked, looking back and forth between us. "What are you two talking about?"

"Someone fed a virus into the computer system," Kimi explained. "When the virus program is activated, it works like a cancer, destroying all the files, filling it up with junk, in this case the first two lines of my father's favorite poem. Why would he do that?"

"Your father?" Mrs. Oliver was outraged. "He

wouldn't do such a thing, Kimi. Never in a million years. Your father wasn't like that. He had worked too hard. We all had. For years. How can you even suggest such a thing!"

She broke off, again lifting the hanky to her face, sobbing inconsolably.

"It's all right," Kimi said, reaching out and laying a comforting hand on Mrs. Oliver's shoulder. "I'm sure you're right. There must be records somewhere. There was a guy here from a moving company last night when I came to talk to my father. I saw him carrying files in and out. All we have to do is find out which company he works for and where he took them. They're probably all stacked in a warehouse somewhere."

And that's when I remembered the bill, the invoice on Tadeo Kurobashi's desk. In my mind's eye, I could see the yellow sheet of paper from DataDump as plain as day. What I saw most clearly, though, was the cute little company logo that ran across the top of the page: *Have shredder. Will travel.*

Shit, I thought. It took real effort not to say it aloud.

Kimi was looking at me. The unspoken reaction must have registered on my face. Maybe I choked. That's easy enough to do when you're busy biting your tongue.

"What's the matter?" she asked. "What's wrong?"

"We may have a problem with that," I said. "I don't think that guy you saw was from a moving company."

"He wasn't? What was he doing here then?"

"I'm not sure," I said.

Big Al appeared at the open doorway with little Bernard Rennermann nipping at his heels.

"I guess we don't need you to let us in after all," Al said over his shoulder. "Looks like everything's under control here."

Which was, in fact, something of a misstatement.

CHAPTER 6

LOCKED OUT OF HER FATHER'S INNER OFFICE, KIMI WAS able to get some of the information she needed from Mrs. Oliver. Yes, there was a modest amount of life insurance—a $50,000 policy as far as she could remember, and a will that had been drawn up fairly recently. She was sure Mr. Yoshiro, Mr. Kurobashi's personal attorney, would have a copy of it.

"What about this Davenport guy?"

"You know him?" Mrs. Oliver asked, sniffing with distaste.

"He was here this morning," I told her.

"His specialty is bankruptcy," Mrs. Oliver said. "He's not good for much else."

Taking what information we had, we headed back to Kirkland. It was three-thirty by the time we returned to the house in Bridle Trail Downs. The moving van was gone. In its stead we found a maroon Caprice Classic station wagon. At first I thought maybe the car belonged to some friend of the family come to offer condolences. That impression was short-lived.

We found Machiko Kurobashi huddled on one of the stone benches near the fishpond while a group of four screaming hellions streamed around her, clambering over fences, scrambling up and down trees, yelling at the tops of their lungs. The new owners had apparently arrived right on schedule to take possession of the property. The parents were nowhere in evidence.

Machiko waved gratefully when she saw us and started up from the bench, hobbling in our direction as fast as she could. Two of the children trailed along behind her, with one of them, a girl, doing an exaggerated pantomime of the old woman's gait.

"Did you used to live here?" the boy demanded rudely. "Was this your house?"

Machiko reached the safety of her daughter's arms and fell into them. "We go now?" she pleaded.

The children must have seen the look of unreasoning rage on Kimi's face. They stopped short a few feet away from her and backed off warily.

"Oh, come on, Jared," the girl said, grabbing her brother's arm and pulling him backward, away from Kimi and her mother. "Don't bother with her. She's old. She can't even speak English." The girl stuck out her tongue at Kimi, and the two children raced away toward the barn, splashing wildly through the fishpond as they ran, leaving the formerly placid water roiled and muddy, while frantic carp darted in every direction.

With that, Machiko lost all control. Clutching her

daughter, she burst into tears. Except for the distant squeals of those bratty kids, the only sound in the universe was that of her pitiful sobs, and there wasn't a damn thing anybody could do about it.

With a lump in my throat I watched Kimi turn her mother around and gently guide her frail footsteps toward the Suburban. She escorted Machiko to the passenger's side of the vehicle, then left her standing there for a moment, leaning on the cane, while Kimi opened the back door and pulled out a small varnished footstool. Putting that at her mother's feet, she helped Machiko climb up into the van.

Once her mother was settled, Kimi closed the car door and returned the footstool to its place in the backseat. Slamming the second door with a ferocious shove, she came around to the other side of the van. Dry-eyed and tight-lipped, she looked up at me.

"Thank you for your help," she said stiffly.

"You're going?"

She nodded.

"We'll need your phone number in Pullman."

"I don't live *in* Pullman," she said, "but the number's in the Pullman book. You can get it from information."

Awkwardly, I extracted one of my business cards and illegibly scrawled my home number across the back of it. I pressed the card into her hand. "My home number's on there, too, in case you need it."

Nodding, she swung herself up into the driver's side and drove away without so much as a backward glance toward the home of her youth. Machiko too, her daughter's older mirror image, stared resolutely ahead. The only good thing about that whole terrible can of worms was that at least they had each other.

Big Al was looking at his watch. "We'd better get the hell out of here too, Beau. It's already rush hour. We don't want to get stuck on the bridge."

Despite his dire prediction, we got back downtown without being stalled in traffic. Up on the fifth floor of the Public Safety Building we wrote our reports. Al finished up in a hurry and left. Hunting and pecking with my left hand, it took me a whole lot longer. When I finished at last, I took the extra few minutes to look up the number for DataDump in the phone book. Their answering machine said they were closed until 9:00 A.M.

I finally left the department around 5:15. Threatening clouds hung low over the Olympics, promising a storm for later that night while a chill breeze blew in off Puget Sound. Fall was coming. And winter would be coming after that. And I wasn't looking forward to either one of them.

I couldn't shake the disgust I felt about the way those damn brats had acted and at the hurt expression on Machiko's face as she watched those unruly little shits go crashing through her beloved fishpond. Life was not fair, I decided. Life was a crock.

It was nighttime. I wanted to go home and shower. I still reeked from sweating champagne, but I had also gone through the whole day without eating. Although I didn't feel particularly hungry, I knew my body needed fuel. I went to the Doghouse and ducked into the bar, ordering a MacNaughton's first and a chili-burger second.

I was well into the MacNaughton's when Winnie, the hostess, came looking for me. "You have a phone call, Beau," she said.

Being a creature of habit has its disadvantages—most important of which is that everybody knows where you go and what you do. As I walked to the phone, I did a quick mental rundown of where everybody was. I wondered if something terrible had happened to Peters and Amy on their honeymoon or to the girls or Mrs. Edwards. Or maybe Big Al had crashed and burned on his way home to Ballard.

Having sorted through all the possibilities of who the call *might* have been from, I was stunned when the person on the phone actually turned out to be George Yamamoto. I had never been in the Doghouse with him, and I had no idea how he knew it was one of my hangouts. Word evidently gets around.

"Thank God I found you," George murmured. "Wait for me right there. I'm on my way over."

"All right. I'll be in the bar."

I had finished the chili-burger and was having a dessert MacNaughton's when George showed up at the door. For the first time in all the years I've known him he looked agitated, upset. If I had any lingering visions of Japanese-Americans daintily sipping warmed sake from tiny porcelain cups, George Yamamoto dispelled that stereotype in a hurry. He ordered a double Scotch on the rocks and swilled it down like it was water.

"Have you heard from Doc Baker?"

"No, not yet. Why? What's going on?"

"The autopsy. We finished, just about half an hour ago."

"And?"

"I was right. It's murder, not suicide. We couldn't see it until after we moved the body. He died as a result of a blow to the head. A blunt object of some kind."

"The handle of the sword maybe?" I asked.

"No. If he tried that, the killer would have cut himself badly."

"You're saying 'he'?"

"Generic," Yamamoto replied. "He/she."

"But why the rest of it? Why the mutilation?"

George shook his head. "I don't know, unless they thought we'd miss the head injury and fall for the phony suicide bit."

I thought of the bloody carnage in Tadeo Kurobashi's office.

"A real sicko," I said.

George nodded. "Yes, but that's not all of it."

"What else?"

"Remember the message you left with Doc Baker?"

"About the sword being done by a student of someone, that Masamune guy?"

"It wasn't," he said. He turned and signaled the waitress for more drinks, ordering one for each of us.

"If it wasn't, then what's all the fuss about?" I asked, puzzled.

"I said it wasn't done by one of his students. It was done by him, by the master himself. It's an original."

Silence opened up in a deep pool between us as the waitress brought our drinks. I waited until she left.

"Are you sure?" I asked.

"It's signed by him, but no, of course I'm not sure. It'll take an expert to ascertain whether or not it's genuine."

"And what does it mean if it is?" I asked guardedly.

"It's priceless," he said. "Absolutely priceless. It shouldn't be in the property room. It should be locked in a vault in a bank or a museum somewhere. We're not equipped to be responsible for something that valuable. I'm worried sick about it, but what can I do? Even if it isn't the actual murder weapon, it's still part of the investigation, no getting around it."

"Fingerprints?" I asked.

"Several sets. They'll be running them through the AFIS as soon as they can get the computer time, but that'll only work if the killer is on file."

AFIS is the Automated Fingerprint Identification System, a recently purchased computerized program that had taken local law enforcement jurisdictions out of the Dark Ages and into the high-tech era of fingerprint identification.

"We should have results on that by tomorrow," George added.

I tried to assimilate all the information George Yamamoto had given me. Every way I looked at it, none of it made any sense. "This doesn't add up," I said. "If the sword was that valuable, why the hell would the murderer go off and leave it lying there on the floor?"

"He may not have *known* it was valuable. Maybe he was looking for something else, but what could be more important than a Masamune sword?" George asked.

"And how exactly did Tadeo Kurobashi come to be in possession of it?"

George took a long drink and shook his head. "I don't know. I just flat don't know. He couldn't have afforded to buy it, I'm sure of that, not even when he was making good money. It's a museum piece, Beau. We're talking about lots of money, a million, maybe more."

"That much?"

George nodded.

"But he was going through bankruptcy. If he had an asset that valuable up his sleeve, why was he losing his house, his business? Why didn't he use it?" I waited for a moment, giving George a minute to collect himself before I asked the obvious question. "Could he possibly have stolen it?"

"No. Absolutely not."

"Why else wouldn't he have unloaded it, then?"

"I don't know," George answered.

We were quiet for a moment, both of us thinking. "Well," I said at last, "going back to the killer or killers, if they weren't interested in the sword, they must have been after something else. Tadeo was an engineer. What exactly did he do?"

"He designed things, ways of putting microwave and computers together, and other things as well."

"Do you have any idea what specific projects he might have been working on in the months before he died?"

"No. In the last few years, we haven't been that close, but maybe a new project is what they wanted."

"More likely, they wanted to destroy it," I said. "Do you know anything about computer viruses?"

"Who, me? I know they exist," George answered, "but I don't know anything at all about how they work. Why?"

"Remember that poem we saw on Tadeo's computer screen?"

He nodded. "Sure. What about it?"

"It's a virus. We took Kimi by MicroBridge this afternoon. She wanted to go see if there was any sign of checkbooks or insurance papers there."

"Did you find any?"

"No. We got the name and address of Kurobashi's personal attorney, but what we discovered from the receptionist is that those lines we saw on his screen are actually part of a computer virus that's invaded every file in every computer in the entire company. Most of the MicroBridge records are gone."

"Gone?" George echoed. "Surely they kept backup copies of everything in the computer."

"We asked Mrs. Oliver about that. She said that all backup copies of disks were missing this morning along with the other hard-copy documents that were removed from the files. She seemed to think they had merely been moved somewhere else in preparation for moving. My guess is that they've all been systematically destroyed."

"What makes you say that? Files don't just get up and walk away over night."

"I didn't say anything about walking away. Remember the bill on Tadeo's desk this morning? It's from a place called DataDump. Remember what it said at the top of the bill? If I remember right, their motto is *Have shredder. Will travel.*"

"Damn," George said.

"Kimi told us that there was a guy there moving files when she was talking to her father."

"She must have told you that after I left," George said thoughtfully, "but that means Tadeo not only knew about the shredding, but probably even hired it done. If he had most of those documents in his computer, though, it wouldn't have mattered."

"Until someone infected the computer with a virus."

"And now it's gone completely," George added. There was a long pause while he fingered his drink. "Might they be in danger, too?"

"Kimi and her mother?" I asked.

He nodded. "Maybe they should stay in a motel for a while. Or should we ask the Kirkland police to keep an eye on them?"

I remembered how Machiko had summarily rejected that idea when, for another reason, Kimiko had suggested it. Still, now that George mentioned it, the idea that they too might be at risk bothered me more than I let on. "They're not in Kirkland," I said. "They left this afternoon to drive to Pullman."

"Pullman!" George exclaimed. "Why there?"

"Beats me. As soon as the movers finished getting the auction stuff out of the house, they took off."

"But what about the funeral? Who's going to handle that?"

"There isn't going to be one."

"No funeral? How come? Everybody has funerals."

"Machiko said no funeral, no memorial service. She was adamant. Big Al and I took Kimi downtown and had her sign all the necessary papers. Tadeo is to be cremated and the remains sent to them in eastern Washington."

"That witch!" George murmured under his breath. "She's got no right to do that."

"She has every right in the world, George," I reminded him. "She's his widow, remember?"

"As if I could ever forget." His voice was taut with emotion. There was something important lurking beneath the surface of his words, but I couldn't put my finger on it.

"What do you mean?"

"She always acted as though she had married beneath her, instead of the other way around, as though his friends weren't good enough for her. And now she thinks she can lock us out by not having a memorial service for him? No way, not if I have to do it myself."

I had never seen George Yamamoto so uncharacteristically emotional. Machiko Kurobashi definitely pushed all his hot buttons.

"Tell me about her," I urged.

"Tell you what about her?" he snapped back. "What do you want to know?"

"Tadeo wasn't her first husband?"

"No. She got hooked up with some sleazebag during the occupation."

"Sleazebag?" I asked.

"I kid you not. This guy was a real creep, a small-time hood. When he got discharged from the army, he went back to his previous lines of work. He was into horses and Indian reservation cigarettes and whatever else he could lay hands on. And he wasn't very good at any of it. They were living in a run-down apartment down in the International District when someone took care of him. My guess is, he owed money to somebody who decided to collect the hard way."

"When was that?"

"Forty-seven, forty-eight. Somewhere around there. It's a long time ago. I don't remember exactly."

"And how did Tadeo meet her?"

"He was working his way through school delivering groceries for a little Mom-and-Pop store down in that same neighborhood. With her rat of a husband dead, she went looking for somebody to take care of her, somebody nice who'd pay the bills and look out for her. Tadeo was it. As soon as she found him, she latched on to him for dear life."

"And when did they get married?"

"I remember that. Nineteen forty-eight for sure. Tadeo was only twenty years old, a junior at the university. I often marveled at what he managed to accomplish, dragging her around behind him like so much dead weight. He got both his B.S. and his Masters from the university here, and then he went down to Stanford and picked up a Ph.D."

"Smart guy."

"He worked down in California for a number of years, for Hughes or one of those other big defense contractor types, then he came back up here and went to work for Boeing. I figured he'd play it safe and stay there. They don't call it the Lazy B for nothing, but Tadeo couldn't handle the pace. He wanted to make things happen, wanted to be a mover and shaker. He quit Boeing to work for RFLink in the late seventies and has been off on his own for the last three or four years."

"Kimi said something about there being hard feelings when he left his previous employer, RFLink. Do you know anything about that or the people who work there?"

"No. He was pretty closed-mouthed about it when it happened. I got the feeling that his leaving wasn't entirely voluntary."

"You mean he was fired."

George Yamamoto nodded reluctantly.

"When's the last time you saw him?"

"Two months ago, down at the courthouse. I ran into him in the lobby. He had just lost the case, his patent infringement case."

"And did you know what losing that case meant to him?"

"No, and he never let on. He acted as though it was no problem, said not to worry, that he'd be back on his feet in no time."

"Would his secretary, Mrs. Oliver, know what kinds of things he might have been working on?"

"Mrs. Oliver? If she's still with him, she'd know everything there is to know."

"You say that as though she's been part of the picture for a long time."

"She has. She was his secretary when he worked for Boeing. When he left there, so did she. As far as I know, she's been with him ever since."

"And you think she'd be privy to all his business dealings?"

"You've got it."

"Anything between them?" I asked, knowing how the question would hurt, regardless of the answer.

"You mean romantically?" George shook his head. "No," he replied. "I don't think so."

But it wasn't the same kind of absolute answer he had given about whether or not the sword had been stolen. It made me wonder.

Our drinks had been empty for a long time. I ordered another round. George Yamamoto had told me a whole lot I didn't know about Tadeo Kurobashi, information I needed to get to the bottom of who had killed him and why. But there was still something missing, something about Tadeo and Machiko and George Yamamoto that I didn't understand, something that would unlock their history together and help it make sense to me. For all our talking, nothing in what George had said had given me a clue about the long-standing antipathy he felt toward his friend's widow.

I looked at George. Disconsolate, he sat holding his drink but gazing without seeing at the black-and-white picture of a German shepherd which, along with twenty or so other doggie portraits, lined the walls of the Doghouse's bar.

It would have been easy to let it go. There was little reason to think that the years of enmity between George and Machiko could have anything to do with Tadeo's death in the here and now. But detectives don't let things go. It's not part of our mental makeup.

"What do you have against her?" I asked.

George's head came up. He looked at me, saying

nothing, but he didn't ask me who I was talking about. He knew I meant Machiko.

"Why do you want to know?" he asked.

"It could be important."

"I doubt it."

"I'd still like to know, George."

"He and my sister met in Minidoka," he said evenly. "They weren't engaged, but they had an understanding. Tomi was prepared to wait until Tadeo got out of school. Then Machiko came along. Once she got her claws in him, that was the end of it."

"And what happened to your sister?"

"Tomi married someone else eventually. She died in childbirth when she was twenty-eight."

"That tells me what you have against Machiko," I said, remembering the woman's unleashed fury as she shook her finger at George and drove him out of her yard. "But it doesn't tell me what she has against you."

George Yamamoto met my gaze and held it as he answered. "It was all a very long time ago," he said. "I'm willing to let bygones be bygones. Machiko's not. I've thought for years that Tadeo could have done better. I still do."

I thought back to the devastated look on Machiko's face as she heard the news of her husband's death and at her gritty determination to follow through with whatever he had wanted, no matter what the personal cost to her.

For the first time I began to wonder exactly what kind of man Tadeo Kurobashi had been, what had made him tick. I looked at George, sitting there grieving over the loss of his friend. The dead man obviously had made a deep impression on the people closest to him, had engendered powerful and conflicting loyalties in his wife, his friends, and also his secretary. Only Kimiko, his embattled daughter, seemed immune to her father's charm.

Not only Kimiko, I thought grimly. Somebody else was immune as well, so immune that they had killed him. I felt a renewed sense of urgency to find out who that person was.

CHAPTER 7

WHEN I GOT BACK HOME TO BELLTOWN TERRACE IT
was after eight. The first thing I saw after I came in
the door was the repeated flashing of the red light on
my answering machine. Machines that count messages can be damned imperious.

I punched the playback button. One of the calls
was from a telephone solicitor for the Seattle Reper-
tory Theater, trying to sell me season tickets for
their fabulous upcoming season. One was from a guy
who wanted to be my stockbroker. All the rest were
from Ralph Ames, my attorney.

Each message from Ames was time-dated, and they
were scattered from early afternoon on, beginning
in a two o'clock, breezy see-you-at-the-meeting-at-
six tone and ending on a downright surly note at
7:59. Needless to say, I had not gone to the meeting,
didn't remember I was supposed to, and didn't know
where it was or what it was about. It was probably
something concerning the real estate syndicate that

owns Belltown Terrace, but that was only an edu-
cated guess.

Ames' final message said, "We've given up on
you. I've canceled the meeting. I'll probably be back
at the apartment before you are."

Who was "we"? I wondered. And how pissed was
Ralph Ames really? Knowing I had screwed up royally, I poured myself another MacNaughton's just
for the hell of it. With the drink in hand, and with
my injured fingers still throbbing painfully inside
their metal splints, I settled down to wait for the
other shoe to drop. It didn't take long. In less than
ten minutes, I heard the unmistakable scrape of Ralph
Ames' key in the lock.

I was sitting in the shadowy darkness of the living
room when he walked in and saw me there. I have to
give him credit for letting me have the slightest
benefit of the doubt. He graciously allowed me to
plead innocent until proven guilty.

"What happened?" he asked. "Get stuck working
late on a case?"

"I forgot," I said, not willing to play games or make
excuses.

"Forgot?" he echoed.

"Yes," I said. "I'm sorry."

Unfortunately, apologies were not the order of
the day. Ralph Ames blew his stack.

"Goddamnit, Beau, we set both the time and place
specifically so you could be there. Six other people,
not counting myself, built their day around that
schedule, and you can sit there and say you *forgot?*"

You get used to those kinds of recriminations

from a wife, and gradually, over a period of time, you develop a certain immunity. Coming from Ralph Ames, though, from a man who is both my attorney and my friend, they had a slightly different impact.

Still, feigning indifference, I took a sip of my drink while ice cubes clinked noisily against the side of the glass. Except for that, the room was silent. Ames reached back to the wall switch and turned on the light. He looked hard at the glass, but he said nothing more. Comment or no, the dumbest kid in the class would have gotten the message that Ralph Ames disapproved. Even a slightly smashed J. P. Beaumont read him loud and clear.

"How come you forgot?" he asked.

Time to go on the offensive. "Jesus H. Christ, Ralph! If I knew that, I would have remembered. I've had a tough day."

"You left the department at five-fifteen."

"You've been checking on me?"

"Damned right. I went by to give you a lift, but you were already gone, and since your latest reprimand, I didn't want to risk leaving a business message with Margie."

At the instigation of one of the newer detectives, a jerk named Kramer, Watty had climbed my frame about my receiving nonofficial phone calls while on duty. Of course, I wasn't alone, but nobody else in the homicide squad drives a Porsche 928, and the last thing I needed was any more trouble with the brass.

Saying nothing more, Ames went into the kitchen, poured himself a glass of orange juice, and came back to the living room, seating himself on the window seat across from me.

"How are the fingers?" he asked.

"Fine," I answered warily, not willing to admit that they hurt like hell and not sure if he was really off the subject or merely coming at it from a different direction. I've seen Ames in action often enough to know he makes a formidable opponent. I didn't like this feeling of the two of us being on opposite sides of the fence.

"You're lucky you didn't lose them."

"Yeah," I answered. "I guess I am."

There was a pause while we sat in not-so-companionable silence. Depth-charged silence was more like it. Naturally, I was the first one to break. After all, I was the guilty party.

"So what happened at the meeting?" I asked, keeping my tone light and casual.

"Nothing. Without you, there wasn't much point. I told them I'd try to reset it for later."

"Good," I said, not knowing what else to say.

Again the room became still. Ames was looking at me, studying me, building up to say something. Meanwhile, I paged through my mental catalog of smart-assed answers, preparing to pull one out and use it. I had a wisecrack all loaded up and ready to light when he surprised me by dropping the issue entirely.

"I saw in the afternoon paper that you're assigned to that case on Fourth South."

I breathed a small sigh of relief that he was willing to let it go. "Sure am," I said. "It started out looking like suicide, but it's not."

"Murder then?"

I nodded. As the tension between us eased, I went

on to tell him what I could about the circumstances surrounding Tadeo Kurobashi's death. He listened, seemingly attentive and interested, but beneath the smooth surface of conversation, I sensed we were playing a game, a set piece where two old friends make inconsequential small talk in order to avoid wandering into treacherous conversational territory.

When I reached the part about the Masamune sword, though, Ralph Ames was no longer merely listening for form's sake. He sat up straight, his eyes snapping to full alert.

"So you recognize the name?" I asked.

"Masamune? You bet I do. And George Yamamoto seems to think it's genuine?" he demanded.

"As far as he could tell, but then George isn't exactly a fully qualified samurai expert."

"No, I suppose not." Ralph seemed to mull the situation for a moment or two. "Are you of the opinion that the dead man may have come into possession of the sword through some illegal means?"

"That's how I read it. Otherwise, wouldn't he have used it to buy his way out of the financial trouble he was in?"

"Seems like," Ames conceded.

With a sudden loud splatter, wind-driven raindrops banged on the double-paned glass behind him. The storm that had been threatening all afternoon and evening burst through the night on the wings of a fierce squall. Ames gave no indication that he saw, heard, or noticed the pelting rain at his back. Chin resting on his hand, he appeared to be totally lost in thought.

"Except," he added quietly, "if—as this friend of

his says—if Kurobashi was always interested in the ways of the samurai, what may seem reasonable to you and me and what might seem reasonable to him could be two entirely different things."

"What are you getting at?"

"I have a friend," Ames said, "someone by the name of Winter, a fellow I went through law school with. He never practiced, though. Instead, he went back to school and picked up a Ph.D. in Oriental Studies. He lived in Japan for a number of years. Now he's living in New York and working as the Oriental antiquities guru for Sotheby's."

"Would you mind asking him about the sword?"

"No problem," Ames said, glancing at his watch, "but it's too late tonight. I'll check with him first thing in the morning."

Again we were quiet for a time, but now it wasn't nearly as uncomfortable. The heavily charged atmosphere had been defused. When Ames looked at his watch, I checked mine. It was after ten. Realizing plenty of time had passed for Kimiko Kurobashi to drive across Snoqualmie Pass and make it back home to Pullman, I picked up the phone.

"I should call the wife and daughter and let them know about the autopsy," I explained to Ames. "When they left, we were all still under the impression it was suicide."

"Except for the wife," Ames added.

I nodded, dialing Eastern Washington information as I did so. In answer to my question, a tinny recorded voice recited Kimi Kurobashi's phone number. I dialed, but it was busy. I tried dialing it several more times in the next half hour, and each time the result was the same. At first I wasn't particularly worried. After a death there are often distant relatives and friends who must be notified. Finally, though, shortly after eleven, instead of getting a busy, I was told that the number was currently out of service.

Alarm began to nudge its way into my consciousness. What would cause a phone to suddenly go out of service in the middle of the night? I remembered George Yamamoto's concern that Tadeo's killer was still on the loose and that his wife and daughter were also potential targets.

Without bothering to put the phone back in its cradle, I dialed information again and was connected to the Pullman Police Department. The dispatcher there passed me along to the Whitman County Sheriff's Department, where I found myself talking with a young man named Mac Larkin.

Speaking calmly but firmly, I attempted to express the urgency of my concern that Machiko and Kimi Kurobashi might be in jeopardy out at the Honeydale Farm. With the bland indifference of youth, Larkin assured me that I shouldn't panic about someone's telephone being out of order since there were scattered reports of telephone outages coming in from all over Whitman County that night.

I tried to let what he said allay my fears, but it didn't work. An insistent alarm continued to hammer in my head. The picture of Tadeo Kurobashi's mutilated body was fresh in my memory. His killer was free to kill again.

When I voiced my concern to Ralph Ames, he immediately began playing devil's advocate. "From what you told me about the hurried way they left town, how would anyone know exactly where they were going?"

"They wouldn't," I replied, "unless they followed them out of town." With that I was back on the phone to Mac Larkin.

"You again?" he demanded.

"When are they going to restore service to the Honeydale Farm area?" I asked.

"The phone company fixes phones," he replied curtly. "They don't tell us how to do our job, and we don't interfere in theirs. All I know is, they're doing the best they can."

Another line buzzed, and Larkin left me sitting on hold for the better part of five minutes. "Have you been helped?" he asked, when he came back on the phone.

"As a matter of fact, I haven't," I replied. "I'm still worried about those women. I'm telling you, the woman's husband was murdered last night. It's possible the killer will come after them next."

"And it's also possible that California is going to fall into the Pacific. Possible, but not very likely. This line is for emergency calls, Detective Beaumont."

"Couldn't you at least send a deputy by?" I asked.

"I've entered your call into the log, and I'll see what I can do, but I'm not making any promises." With that he hung up.

"Do any good?" Ames asked.

"Not much," I answered. "No way could I build a fire under that little jackass on the phone."

"You've done as much as you could," Ames said. "It'll probably be all right."

But his words offered small comfort. While I had

been on the phone, Ralph had turned around in the love seat and was sitting facing out the window, watching the pattern of splashing raindrops on the glass.

"Who all knew about the poem?" Ames asked thoughtfully a moment later.

"The one on the computer? Well, there was Doc Baker, George Yamamoto, Big Al—"

"No, no," Ames interrupted. "I don't mean who saw it on the computer this morning. How many people around him were aware that it was Tadeo Kurobashi's favorite poem?"

"Probably several. Yamamoto said it was familiar as soon as he saw it, but he couldn't remember where he'd heard it. Kimi knew it well, and I would imagine so would her mother. Why are you asking about the poem?"

"Because it sounds to me as though whoever fed the virus into the MicroBridge computers must have known Tadeo Kurobashi very well in order to pick that particular verse, to know unerringly that it was part of his favorite poem."

"So?" I asked. "What are you getting at?"

Ames cocked his head to one side. "Think about it. If you were a young woman struggling to get along on whatever crumbs the university dishes out to instructors and on what you could make shoveling horse manure in someone else's barn, and if you knew your father was busy squandering your entire inheritance, wouldn't you be tempted to do something about it?"

"I might," I said, "but not in this case. Kimiko Kurobashi isn't the type."

Ralph Ames looked at me sadly and shook his head. "Beau, you of all people should know better than that. It seems to me that we were both suckered very badly once by a lady who didn't look the part at all, remember?"

Remember? Of course I remembered, and the memory of Anne Corley caused a burning pain in my chest that didn't seem to lessen with the passage of time. I got up and poured myself another drink. That was easier than talking.

"I'll look into it," I said at last.

Ralph Ames nodded. "All right. In that case, I'm going to bed," he said.

I followed suit, but once in bed, I didn't go to sleep. For a long time, I lay there, doing all kinds of mental gymnastics in an effort to keep my mind off Anne Corley. By focusing completely on the hows and whys of Tadeo Kurobashi's murder and other more immediate matters I managed to keep her at bay somewhere outside my conscious memory. Eventually my mind wandered away from Tadeo Kurobashi's mystery to one of my own, one much closer to home and very much in need of a solution.

Where was my missing chunk of time? I worried the question like an old dog gnawing a bone. What had happened to the part of my life that contained my agreement to go to the mystery meeting with Ralph Ames and where I had somehow, inexplicably, smashed my fingers badly enough to require the attention of a doctor? How could I possibly have forgotten those things so completely? As if on cue, the constant throbbing reasserted itself, a pulsing reminder.

Try as I might to remember, though, there was nothing there, not a trace. It was as if a heavy black curtain had been pulled over the window of my memory. A blackout curtain.

As soon as the word came into my head, so did a sickening inkling of where that piece of my life had gone. I had forgotten things before on occasion. Everybody does that, but it had never been anything terribly important. I could recall misplacing my car once, finding it late the next day in the parking lot outside the Doghouse. But this time it was blatantly clear to me that, despite my desperately wanting to remember, I was missing pieces of my life that nobody else was. And there was a distinct cause-and-effect relationship that was hard to deny.

I thrashed around in bed and fought with the covers in a vain effort to deny the word's reality, to make the ugly possibility rebury itself somewhere far away, but it didn't. The word *blackout* was an evil genie let out of its bottle. It was out, and it wouldn't disappear.

And so I waited for sleep and mostly didn't find it until close to daylight. The rain had stopped. The last thing I heard before I fell asleep was the raucous squawk of a marauding sea gull. And that's when the dream came. I know it by heart. I see it over and over, and it's always the same.

Anne Corley, vibrant and alive and wearing the same red dress she wore when I first saw her, stands in a windswept park with the breeze rippling her hair. I call to her and she turns to look at me. She is holding a rose, a single, long-stemmed red rose. I go to her, running at that desperate nightmarish pace that robs you of strength and breath but covers no distance. At last I stop a few feet away from her, and she starts toward me. I reach out to clasp her in my arms, but as I do, the rose in her hands changes to a gun, and I step back screaming, "No! No! No!"

I awoke in a room awash in daylight with streams of sweat pouring off my body. Lying there alone in bed, waiting for the shaking to stop and my heartbeat to steady, I cursed Fate and any other gods who might be listening for making me be one of the few men I know who dreams in living color.

In black and white, it might not hurt as much.

An hour or so later, Ames and I were drinking coffee at the kitchen counter when the phone rang. I more than half expected the call to be from Peters— it was about time for him to check in—but the voice on the other end of the line was that of a total stranger.

"Is this the Seattle Police Department?" the gruff male voice asked.

"No it isn't," I answered. "This is a private residence."

"I'm looking for somebody named Beaumont. Anybody there by that name?"

"I'm Detective Beaumont. Who's calling, please?"

"Jesus Christ. Did that yo-yo give me your home number?" he demanded.

"Evidently."

"Sorry. I waited until I figured you'd be at work before I called."

"It's all right. Who is this, please?" I asked again.

"Oh, sorry. The name's Halvorsen. Detective Andrew Halvorsen with the Whitman County Sheriff's

Department. I've got a note here saying that you called in last night concerning a couple of women out at Honeydale Farm?"

My stomach tightened. So did my grip on the telephone receiver. "That's correct," I said carefully. "Is anything wrong?"

"Are these women related to you in any way, Detective Beaumont?"

"No, they're not. One is the wife and the other the daughter of a man who was murdered here in Seattle day before yesterday. I'm the homicide detective assigned to that case. Why? What's going on?"

"The old woman will probably be all right. She's not as badly hurt, although the doctors tell me that at her age any injury can have serious side effects. As for the other one, I understand they're calling for a Medevac helicopter. As soon as they can get her stabilized enough, they'll be flying her either to Spokane or Seattle for surgery."

My throat constricted around the last swallow of coffee. A terrible impotent rage rose through my body.

"That's what I was afraid of, for God's sake. Didn't that worthless son of a bitch do *anything?*"

"Now, now, Detective Beaumont," Halvorsen said soothingly. "Don't be too hard on Larkin. He did the best he could under the circumstances. This place was a zoo last night, and we were spread way too thin with the kind of problems we were having all over the county. He did enter the call in the log, however, and when I put the two together a few minutes ago, I thought I'd better get in touch with you."

With supreme effort I managed to keep my voice steady enough to speak. "Tell me what happened."

"We're still not sure. Rita Brice, the owner of Honeydale Farm, evidently got up about six and noticed that the horses still weren't out in the pasture. She went to Kimi's house, thinking she had overslept, and discovered the mother, bound and gagged. Rita untied the mother, left her there in the house, and went to the barn. That's where she found the daughter. Rita did what she could, then ran back to summon help. Luckily, by that time the phones were all working again."

"Is Kimi going to make it?" I asked.

"Too soon to tell. Larkin's notation said that you thought the women might be in some kind of danger. Do you think these two assaults are related to the murder in Seattle?"

"Absolutely."

"We'd better put our heads together, then. Do you want to come over here or should I go there?" Halvorsen asked.

"I'll come there," I said without hesitation. "As soon as I check in with my office."

"All right. Horizon flies directly into the Pullman-Moscow Airport. If you can let me know what time you'll be in, I'll come pick you up."

"Meet the next flight that leaves from Sea-Tac," I said. "If I can't make that one, I'll call and let you know."

I dropped off his call and immediately dialed Sergeant Watkins at home. Shaking his head, Ralph Ames listened as I explained the situation to Watty. As I expected, the sergeant told me to get my ass to

the airport, that he'd handle whatever official paperwork had to be handled, including notifying airport
security that I was on my way.

Ralph Ames handed me out the door and told me
he'd get me a reservation on the next available flight
while I made a dash for the airport.

It turned out that airport security wasn't that much
of a problem since Horizon's gate is so small that
they don't have a security check. I don't know what
strings Ames pulled, but I'm sure he yanked at least
one because the Pullman-bound Swearingen Metro-
Liner was still waiting on the ground when I got
there, even though it had been scheduled to leave
some ten minutes earlier.

And that's how, thirty-five minutes after Andy
Halvorsen's call, I was in the air on my way to Pullman, Washington, sitting scrunched into one of the
midget-sized seats, with my neck bent to one side
and my knees jammed into the backrest of the seat
in front of me.

Six foot three is too damned tall for Metro-Liners.

CHAPTER 8

THE PULLMAN-MOSCOW AIRPORT IS SET IN A NATURAL swale among rolling high hills. As the plane landed and the golden-grained landscape loomed up on either side of the runway, I gripped the handles of the seat and cursed myself for flying, although I suppose the safety statistics on red Porsches are a good deal worse than those for commuter airlines.

Not knowing how long I'd be away, I had stuck a briefcase with a change of underwear and a clean shirt in the nose of the plane, and since Metro-Liner passengers carry their own bags, I didn't have to wait for luggage to be delivered to a carousel inside the pint-sized lobby. There *were* no luggage carousels inside the lobby and not much of anything else, either. Two tiny but highly competitive branches of name-brand rent-a-car companies were busy. Both had lines—two customers at one and three at the other—which probably accounted for a major portion of that day's business.

Glancing around the lobby, I searched in vain for

someone who might be the detective who was supposed to pick me up. Seeing no one, I walked over to the plate glass doors that opened on a gravel parking lot. That's where I found Detective Andrew Halvorsen.

There was a good reason for his not being inside the terminal to meet me. They wouldn't let him. He was smoking a cigar, a well-chewed Churchill-sized Royal Jamaican.

Aside from that, Halvorsen seemed like a regular enough kind of guy—tall, well built, about my size, late forties, square-jawed good looks, neatly trimmed brush mustache, curly dark brown hair showing just a sprinkling of gray.

"Detective Beaumont?" he asked, catching sight of me.

I nodded.

"This way. The car's right here."

He led me to a white, four-door K-car. Lee Iacocca and his pals at Chrysler must have sold a handful of those hummers to every law enforcement jurisdiction in the country. Detective divisions always get stuck with them. Halvorsen popped open the trunk, and I tossed my gear inside.

"Any word?" I asked.

"None so far. They've airlifted the daughter to Sacred Heart in Spokane. They've scheduled emergency surgery for as soon as she gets there. The mother is still in Colfax Community Hospital, but I thought we'd drive by their place on the way so you could take a look around."

"Good idea," I said.

If I had any hopes that Halvorsen's car would have a no-smoking section, I was out of luck. The car was clouded by a haze of dense smoke that fogged the windows and made my eyes water. I'll never get used to that foul smell.

He closed the door to the car and exhaled a billowing plume before he ever turned the key in the ignition. I stifled the urge to ask him to put out the cigar. After all, if I wanted my own vices to be off limits to criticism from casual friends and acquaintances, then I'd best keep my mouth shut about somebody else's. What goes around comes around.

Talking as we went, Halvorsen drove us into and then through the hilly, winding streets of Pullman, a sleepy Midwestern-looking farming community with a stable population of about 8,000. Washington State University has been grafted into the middle of town, bringing with it a transient population of 20,000 or so students. God save me from ever living anyplace where minors outnumber regular people by a margin of three to one!

Within minutes we were out in the open again, heading northwest on Highway 195 driving through miles of ripened corn and wheatfields beside an unending line of stocky telephone poles.

"What about the phones?" I asked, eying the drooping lines. "Were the wires deliberately cut?"

It was the question that had been chewing on me all during the hour-long flight from Seattle. I had forgotten to ask Halvorsen about it earlier on the phone.

"You bet," Halvorsen replied.

"And related to this?"

"No question. Whoever did it wanted to create as big a disruption in communications as possible. They knew that if the wires were cut in just one place, the phone company would probably have been able to reroute calls from the central office and restore service in minutes. Instead, they cut wires in several places. That way, until repair crews fixed one break, they couldn't pinpoint the next."

Halvorsen took a long pull on his cigar. "It was deliberate all right. Deliberate, methodical, and smart, and it created enough of a smoke screen that we had no idea that the problem centered at Honeydale Farm."

"And what time did they start?"

"The outages? Right around ten, as far as we can tell."

"Time enough," I said.

"Time enough for what?"

"For whoever it was to follow Kimi here from Seattle, learn where she lived, and figure out how to cut off all lines of communication."

"Any ideas why someone would want to go to all that trouble?" Halvorsen asked.

"That one has me stumped so far. Whoever killed her father tried to cover it up by making it look as though he had committed suicide with an extremely valuable samurai sword. The killer took off and left the sword on the floor beside the body."

"So we can be relatively sure they weren't after the sword."

"That's how it looks at the moment. Not only that, at approximately the same time, someone messed with Kurobashi's company computer system. They fed a virus into it, destroying all the records. Because of that, there's no way to tell what they were after."

"What did he do?"

"Kurobashi? He was an engineer doing some kind of computer stuff. I'm still not sure exactly what."

"You think maybe they wanted to lay hands on some project he was doing?"

I nodded. "Either to steal it or wipe it out of existence."

"But that doesn't explain why they'd come after the women," Halvorsen mused. "What could they possibly know, or is the wife an engineer too?"

"Domestic engineer," I replied. "An ordinary housewife as far as I can tell." If Halvorsen noticed my quip, he didn't crack a smile.

"And the daughter?"

"She is an engineer, still a student. Same field as her father, but the two of them have been estranged for years. I don't see how she could know much of anything about his current business operation."

There was a lull in the conversation. When Halvorsen spoke, his face was grim. "The things they did to her weren't calculated to make her talk. These bastards got their rocks off doing ugly stuff, torture worthy of calling in Amnesty International. It must have gone on for hours."

"What do you mean?" I asked.

"First they dragged her out to the barn and killed her horse in front of her. Made her watch, I'd guess." Halvorsen paused, chewing angrily on the stub of his cigar. "And finally they raped her, with a bottle, a broken bottle. The medics said it was a miracle she didn't bleed to death before they got to her. She'll be lucky if she lives, to say nothing of ever being able to have children."

Outrage, like bile, roiled up in my gut. "Machiko too?"

"No. She was beaten up some, but nothing like what they did to the daughter. They must have thought Kimiko was the key to whatever it was they were looking for."

"You keep saying 'they.'"

Halvorsen nodded. "From what I understand there were two—one with a stocking over his face and the other wearing gloves."

"One they'd recognize and one they wouldn't?"

"The thought had crossed my mind," Halvorsen said.

Silence as thick as the heavy cigar smoke settled over the car. I didn't ask for more details. I didn't need them right then. Moral outrage over the atrocities committed on Kimiko Kurobashi would only get in the way of nailing the creeps who had done them. Instead, I settled for a kind of seething, controlled anger. There would be time enough later to know the other ugly details. Right now we had to concentrate on catching the sons of bitches.

The sense of urgency to do just that was almost overpowering. "When do you think it happened?"

"Looks like they left early this morning. They were gone before Rita Brice got up at six. I've got roadblocks up all over the county, but I don't know what the hell we're looking for—a car, a truck, who knows?" Halvorsen paused and glanced at me. "Any idea who might be behind all this?"

"Nothing solid so far. I've heard that Kurobashi had a big falling out with a former employer, and that the two of them have been involved in a dog-eat-dog lawsuit, one that essentially put Kurobashi out of business, but that's all I know so far. I would have interviewed the ex-employer today, but I'm over here instead."

"So Kurobashi's business had something to do with computers," Halvorsen said thoughtfully.

"Right."

"I wonder if that's what she was talking about."

"Who?"

"The mother. One of the paramedics claimed that on the way to the hospital, she kept mumbling something about a computer. He and his partner were busy with the daughter and didn't pay that much attention, but they both agreed she was trying to tell them something about a computer. Incidentally, do you speak Japanese?"

"No."

Halvorsen pounded the steering wheel. "How the hell are we going to interview her then?" he asked. "The medics said she barely speaks English."

"Don't worry," I said. "We'll get by. I'm pretty sure she understands more than she lets on."

We had swung off Highway 195 onto a narrow gravel road. "It's only about three miles from here."

Each turn of the K-car's wheels was taking us farther and farther into the vast rolling emptiness of the Palouse, fertile and full of shimmering oceans of golden wheat and ripened corn, but with only isolated farmhouses dotting the countryside. An intense wave of guilt washed over me as I thought of

Kimi and Machiko, alone and vulnerable, left to the wolves.

"Damn Mac Larkin!" I exclaimed.

"It wasn't his fault," Halvorsen returned. "He was doing the best he could."

The road we were on stopped abruptly at a wire gate. On either side of the gate, a white wooden fence stretched into the distance. Set in a stand of aging cottonwoods and huge drooping willows, Honeydale Farm looked far more like a Kentucky showplace than a horse farm far off the beaten path in the wilds of eastern Washington.

As I stood holding the gate open for Halvorsen to drive through, I more than half expected a guard dog to come snarling up and take a hunk out of the back of my leg. None did. The place lay still and quiet in early autumn's midmorning sunshine.

"People around here think she puts on airs," Halvorsen said as I got back in the car and we started down a rutted track.

"Who?"

"Rita Brice, the lady who owns this place. She's not a native, you know. She was married to a big-time Appaloosa breeder who had places both here and across the state line in Moscow, Idaho. When they split up, she got this place and he got the one over there. Now she's gone and set herself up in direct competition with her ex."

"Sounds fair enough to me," I said.

Andy Halvorsen gave me an odd look and then went on with his story. "She rents out most of the fields, but she runs the breeding operation herself."

"Alone?"

"Except for that young woman, the one who's in the hospital. That's the main house up there," he said, pointing toward a gaunt, weathered two-story frame house. "The help lives over there behind the barn and stables."

We drove through a motley collection of tin and wooden outbuildings which included a slightly tilted, but totally authentic, old red barn.

We stopped in front of a much smaller house, little more than a cottage really. The Suburban was nowhere in sight, but the horse trailer still was parked near the front door. Fifty feet away sat a white Whitman County patrol car. The uniformed deputy inside waved to us, and Detective Halvorsen waved back.

"Where's the car?" I asked.

"The Suburban? It's over there, in the garage. About the trailer—were those all the mother's things in there?" Halvorsen asked, motioning toward the trailer.

I nodded before I really comprehended the underlying message in his question. "Were?" I asked.

"It's all smashed to bits. Want to take a look?"

"I don't but I'd better," I said.

Halvorsen walked toward the horse trailer and reached for the latch. Worried about preserving evidence, I tried to stop him.

"It's all right," he said, cutting through the orange evidence tape that had been placed across the door. "We're not exactly hicks around here. We've already dusted for prints. We'll have the trailer towed into the crime lab in Spokane as soon as the wrecker is free."

With that, he swung the door wide open, allowing

me a look at the shambles inside. Before, the trailer had been neatly stacked with Machiko's carefully packed and labeled boxes. Those packed treasures were now nothing more than a pile of debris. There was deliberate malice in the way the boxes had been ripped open, the contents scattered and smashed and torn to bits.

"It's a mess, isn't it," Halvorsen commented.

Speechless with rekindled anger, I could only nod.

"But there's no sign of a computer here anywhere," Halvorsen continued. "If it was here, they got it. That's what I told the guys at the roadblock to look for, a stolen computer."

As we stood there surveying the damage, a woman came up behind us. Although much older than Kimi, her clothes looked as though they had come off the rack in the same St. Vincent de Paul store—work shirt, faded jeans, dusty, run-down boots.

Rita Brice was well into her fifties with naturally silver hair and the icy blue eyes of a born Scandinavian. Deep laugh lines crinkled up from the corners of her eyes, across tanned and weathered cheeks. The eyes weren't laughing now.

"How's Kimi, Andy?" she asked, addressing Detective Halvorsen with easy small-town familiarity. "Any word yet?"

"They're taking her to Spokane for surgery."

The blue eyes narrowed at Halvorsen's answer. "What about her mother?"

"She'll probably be all right. They're keeping her in Colfax for observation."

A car door slammed and the deputy came hotfooting it toward us at a fast trot. "Got a message for you from the sheriff, Detective Halvorsen. He says Cap Reardon just called in to say whoever cut the lines musta used a helicopter."

"What?" Halvorsen demanded.

"Sheriff Coffee says they used a helicopter. He says for you to call in as soon as you can and he'll give you the details."

Halvorsen sprinted away toward the car, leaving me standing there with Rita Brice. "Who are you?" she asked.

"Detective Beaumont," I replied. "With the Seattle Police Department." I offered her a business card.

"What happened to your hand?" she asked.

"Slammed it in a door," I replied, grateful that at least I now had that much of an answer when somebody asked the question.

She stuffed the card in her hip pocket. "What's a Seattle detective doing out here?"

"You haven't heard about Kimi's father?"

Rita frowned. "What about him?"

"He was murdered the night before last. I'm the detective on that case."

A white pallor slipped under the tanned skin of her cheeks. "What's this all about? Why would anyone do such a thing?"

"That's what we're trying to find out."

For a time we said nothing. I could see Halvorsen through the windshield of the K-car, talking animatedly on his radio.

Finally, Rita said, "Do you want to see the barn? I

let the other horses out, but Sadie's still in there. I'll have to have help to move her."

"Please," I said.

We said nothing more as I followed her to the sagging barn. When we first entered the shadowy building, it smelled the way you'd expect it to smell, of hay and manure and horses, but toward the back of the barn, there was another smell as well, the distinct metallic odor of blood.

Rita led me to a stall at the far end and I peered inside over the wooden railing where a mutilated horse lay dead on the floor, sprawled in a blood-soaked layer of straw. A cloud of flies hovered busily on and around the dead animal.

"It must have been terrible for Kimi," Rita said quietly. "To have to watch. Sadie was like her child." She pointed toward the far corner of the stall. "That's where I found her."

Near the wall was another blood-soaked layer of straw. "Those bastards!" I muttered.

Rita Brice nodded and wiped her eyes.

I had seen enough. As we turned away from the stall, Halvorsen came rushing to meet us.

"Can you beat that? A goddamned helicopter. That's what they used. I couldn't figure out how they managed to be all over the county at once."

"One of the linemen called his supervisor in Spokane this morning after it got light enough to see. He said he noticed a place near one of the poles where the wheat was all beaten down. Sheriff Coffee sent somebody out to check and sure enough, they found evidence that a helicopter landed there.

They stopped off at two more sites on the way back. Same thing."

He had been talking excitedly. Suddenly he stopped and his face fell. "Damn!"

"What's the matter?"

"Those roadblocks won't ever catch a damn helicopter."

The three of us walked out of the barn together. Outside, away from the smell of death, the world was serene, peaceful, and awesomely quiet.

"You didn't hear anything?" I asked Rita. It seemed to me that a terrified horse would have made a helluva lot of noise.

Rita Brice shook her head. "I sleep with the television set on," she said. "My husband snored, and I still haven't learned to sleep when it's quiet."

"And you don't have a dog?"

"I don't like dogs," she answered simply. "They chase horses."

Halvorsen walked straight to the car. "We've lost them," he said. "We'd better go see the mother."

I nodded in bleak agreement while Halvorsen re-lit the short stub of his cigar before starting the car. "So did they get what they were looking for or not?"

"Who knows?"

Halvorsen was my kind of cop—action first, bullshit and paperwork later. We had lost one round fair and square, but he was ready to get up and get back in the game.

Rita Brice went to the house to change clothes before heading to Spokane where she, along with a police guard, would stand vigil with Kimi at Sacred

Heart Medical Center. We left her place, drove back out to the highway, and turned left to drive toward Colfax.

"I've got a bad feeling about all this," Halvorsen said quietly.

"Like what?"

"Helicopters, cut telephone lines, what they did to her. This sounds like big-time shit to me—professionals, the mob. It's the kind of crap I wanted to leave behind me when I came back home to work. And if we're dealing with name-brand muscle here, then whatever or whoever it is has to be big. Something to do with drugs unless I miss my guess. Is it possible either the father or the daughter were involved in dealing drugs?"

"No way," I said. "Tadeo Kurobashi was broke, dead broke. He was losing both his business and his house. And his daughter shovels horseshit for a living. That doesn't sound like any high-flying drug dealers I know."

"I still think it's drugs," Halvorsen insisted.

Colfax Community Hospital, situated on a hillside at the edge of town, was small but modern enough to have gotten on the no-smoking bandwagon, so Halvorsen snuffed out the smoldering remains of his cigar in a sand-filled ashtray near the hospital's main entrance. A nurse directed us to the proper room.

Machiko Kurobashi, looking more frail than ever, lay flat on the bed, wearing a hospital-issue gown. Both eyes were black. A jagged cut on her lower lip had been neatly stitched shut. Her left arm, bandaged and in a sling, was strapped firmly to her chest while the fingers of her other hand stroked a gnarled wooden piece of what had once been her cane. Her glasses were gone, and I assumed they too had been smashed by her attacker.

She gave no sign of recognition when I walked into the room. Only when I came close enough that she could focus on me clearly, did her eyes widen in alarm and her free hand go to her mouth. I'm sure she thought I was coming to give her more bad news about Kimi.

"Kimiko okay?" she asked plaintively, reaching out and grasping my hand with her thin, clawlike fingers.

"I don't have any news of her, Mrs. Kurobashi," I said gently. "They have taken her to Spokane. That's all I know."

She nodded and let go of my hand. Peering behind me, she caught a glimpse of someone else and frowned.

"It's Detective Halvorsen," I explained. "From the sheriff's department. We must ask you some questions."

Machiko Kurobashi closed her eyes. I wondered if she was listening or not.

"Do you know the men who did this to you?"

"No."

"You had never seen them before?"

"No."

"Or heard their voices?"

"No, but if I hear again, I know."

"Do you think he was someone from Micro-Bridge, someone who worked with your husband?"

She shook her head. "Maybe, maybe not."

"What did he look like?"

"One was big," she answered firmly. "Big and mean. Other, with stocking on face. Smaller and not so mean."

"Did they say what they wanted?"

"Computer. Kimiko's computer."

"What computer, and why did they want it?"

She shrugged.

"Where was it? Did Kimi keep the computer at home or at work?"

Machiko shook her head emphatically.

"If she didn't keep it either place, where was it?"

"In trailer. New computer. Surprise from Tadeo."

I felt a quick catch of excitement in my throat. "A surprise? A gift? Did Kimi even know she had it?"

"No."

"It was a present for Kimi from her father?"

The eyes opened and looked full at me, bright and alert. "From father and mother," she corrected firmly. "Graduation present."

Her answer almost made me smile. Machiko Kurobashi was down but she most definitely was not out. Anyone who thought otherwise would be vastly underestimating her.

"From both of you," I agreed.

She smiled. Faintly, but a smile nevertheless.

"But the computer's gone now," I said. "They found it and took it." I expected that news to have some visible impact on her, but she lay there looking at me, comprehending but showing no sign.

"Do you know why they want it so badly?"

Machiko Kurobashi smiled at me again, almost

serenely this time. "No matter," she said, waving her hand in dismissal.

"No matter!" I exploded, unable to contain my impatience. "What do you mean, 'No matter'? The people who wanted that computer put you in the hospital and your daughter in surgery."

"Computer sick," she explained. "Need medicine. If man not have medicine, computer not work."

"What does she mean, the computer's sick? The virus?" Halvorsen caught on fast.

"Must be," I said. Turning to Machiko, I asked, "You mean the computer you were giving Kimiko also has the virus?"

She nodded. "Tadeo smart man. He fix."

"Fixed so it wouldn't work?"

"Yes."

For once in my life, I couldn't think of the next question. Halvorsen had to manage for both of us.

"Why?"

"Tadeo worry someone try to steal. He fix. Medicine in safe place. Only Kimiko can use."

"But where is the medicine? How is she supposed to get it?"

Machiko answered with still another noncommittal shrug. A nurse came in and motioned for us to leave. I started for the door, but Machiko spoke to my back. "Where is sword?" she asked.

Her question, as firm and resolute as the tempered steel in the weapon itself, stopped me cold. I turned around to look at her. The nearsighted eyes were gazing vaguely at the whole half of the room.

"Where?" she repeated.

"It's in the crime lab," I answered slowly. "George Yamamoto is in charge of it."

She grimaced at the mention of George's name. "I want sword," she said quietly. "For Kimiko."

Of course she wanted it for Kimi, I thought. Why shouldn't she? Knowing what I did, I was afraid the sword would be the sum total of Tadeo Kurobashi's legacy to his daughter. "I'll see what I can do," I told her.

I only hoped Kimiko would live long enough to inherit it.

CHAPTER 9

A YOUNG HISPANIC-LOOKING DOCTOR WITH A CHART IN his hand was standing near the nurses' station when Andrew Halvorsen and I left Machiko Kurobashi's hospital room.

"How's it going, Rico?" Andy said to him.

The doctor, Enrico Rodriguez, looked up from the chart, saw Halvorsen, and smiled. The two of them evidently knew each other. "Not bad, Andy. This your case?" He closed the chart, impatiently drumming his fingers across the metal cover.

Halvorsen nodded. "Sure is, and this is Detective Beaumont from Seattle P.D."

"Seattle?" Rodriguez frowned. "Have we been annexed?"

"I'm working a case we believe may be related to this one," I explained.

"Is that so?" Dismissing me, the doctor turned back to Halvorsen. "What can I do for you, Andy?"

"Will the daughter live?"

Rodriguez shook his head. "It's way too soon to

tell. She was still hanging in there when they got to Spokane. That's good for starters."

"And Mrs. Kurobashi?" I asked.

Rodriguez turned and looked at me before deciding, finally, to answer. "She's not that badly hurt. She's got some cuts and bruises all right, and a couple of cracked ribs. She sprained her wrist when he knocked her down and broke her glasses. I've called her optometrist in Kirkland. He's sending a new pair over by Federal Express. They won't be here until tomorrow, but conceivably, we could release Mrs. Kurobashi this afternoon."

"Don't," I said. The word slipped out of my mouth before I could stop it.

Dr. Rodriguez looked at me quizzically. "Don't?" he asked, raising one disapproving eyebrow. "Don't what?"

"Don't release her."

I knew from the deep frown on Rodriguez's face that I had stepped in it all the way up to my armpits. I had done the unthinkable—called into question a doctor's unquestionable, God-given judgment.

I backpedaled as fast as I could, hoping to undo the damage. "What I meant to say is that if you kept her here, we could probably make arrangements for a guard—"

Dr. Rodriguez cut me off. "Let me remind you, this is a hospital, not a jail. We treat sick people here. We don't hold them under guard, and we don't keep them any longer than absolutely necessary. Furthermore, let me assure you that this hospital is fully capable of protecting patients while they are here. Once we release them, then they're your problem."

With that, Dr. Rodriguez slammed the metal chart down on the nurses' station counter and stalked off.

"Rico doesn't like being told what to do," Andy Halvorsen observed.

"I noticed," I said.

For the next two hours, accompanied by a telephone company lineman supervisor, we went from one deserted field to another, locating and examining the helicopter flattened areas near the site of each cut phone line. We scoured each area in hopes of finding some shred of evidence that would help us identify the persons responsible, including collecting the cut ends of the wire for sampling later. Other than that, we came up empty-handed.

About two o'clock, we gave up and went back into town to find something to eat. Colfax is far too small to boast its own set of Golden Arches. Big Macs are imported from Pullman, seventeen miles away. Halvorsen led me to the Wheat & Barley, a reasonably upscale eatery, where the two of us dined finger-food fashion, with thick hamburgers and mountains of french fries, on the largess of the City of Seattle. After lunch, we holed up in Detective Halvorsen's Spartan shared office.

When the spoils of statehood were being parceled out here in Washington, Pullman got what was then called the Normal School, and Colfax got the Whitman County Seat. I'm sure it looked like a good deal at the time. For my money, it still is. I would choose Colfax and county government over living with a town full of kids any day of the week.

Rather than an aging relic, the Whitman County Courthouse was a modern stucco building crowned with a rampart of high-tech antennas. Crammed into a tiny office, we grabbed phones and let our fingers do the walking as we tried to learn where the wire-snipping helicopter had come from and gone to.

Using a series of information operators, we worked our way through major and minor flying services all over the state, everything from slick yuppie charters to down-at-the-heels crop-dusting outfits. To no avail.

Well into the afternoon, Andy received a call from Rita Brice, who phoned from a waiting room in Sacred Heart Medical Center to say that Kimiko had survived the surgery but was not yet out of the woods. She was still in the Intensive Care Unit and still listed in critical condition.

I know all about hospital euphemisms. *Critical* is one degree worse than *guarded*. *Critical* still has the potential to go either way. Both terms are a hell of a long way from satisfactory.

When Halvorsen passed the news along to me, I didn't allow myself the luxury of a spoken reply. Instead, I picked up the phone and dialed another flying service. By that time we were down to calling seat-of-the-pants outfits in podunk, off-the-wall towns. It was after five and I was almost ready to give up, but that one last call yielded a slender lead.

The number I had dialed belonged to the St. Helens Flying Service in Woodland, Washington. The woman who answered the phone did so with the frantic hello of someone who has spent hours waiting for a call that doesn't come. I heard her sigh of disappointment when she realized mine still wasn't the voice she wanted to hear, that the call she was expecting still hadn't come.

"My name is Detective Beaumont," I began.

"A detective! Oh, my God! What's happened? Where is he? Is he all right?"

I hate conversations where I feel as though I'm not playing with a full deck, particularly when I'm the one initiating the call. "Is who all right?"

"My dad, David Lions, who else?"

Who else indeed! I didn't know David Lions from a hole in the ground.

"Excuse me, but I'm afraid I don't know what you're talking about. I don't know anyone named David Lions, and I certainly don't know where he is."

"Didn't you say you're a detective? Aren't you with the Spokane police."

"No, I'm with the Seattle police, not Spokane's."

"But the helicopter's in Spokane. They called and told me it was there. How'd he get to Seattle?"

It was getting worse, not better. "Hold on a minute," I said. "I'm not at all sure what's going on here. I'm a Seattle police officer investigating a case, and I've been contacting charter services to see if anyone can provide information that would help us."

The woman was instantly contrite. "I'm sorry. It's just that I'm so worried. He's been missing since this morning, you know."

I felt a quick catch of excitement in my throat. "Miss . . ."

"Lions," she supplied. "Dana Lions. My father and I own the flying service together. He flies the planes. I do the books and handle the reservations."

"Miss Lions," I said calmly. "You say your father is missing?"

Across the room, Andy Halvorsen put down his phone and listened intently. Dana Lions hesitated. "Not really. It's just that now nobody can find him."

"Tell me exactly what happened."

"He left late yesterday afternoon to pick up a charter in Seattle and ferry him to Spokane. He had flown another trip earlier in the day, so he planned to stay overnight and come back this morning. We haven't heard from him since."

"Maybe he rented a room somewhere, and he's still asleep."

Dana Lions took a deep breath. "I already checked the Ridpath. That's where he usually stays, but he's not there. Besides, he wouldn't still be asleep at this hour." She paused. "Dad doesn't need much sleep."

She stopped. I had a feeling there was something else, something she wasn't saying, but I had no idea what it was. I waited for her to continue.

"He came back from Vietnam in '71 and started the business in '75. After St. Helens blew up in 1980, he got the idea of doing scenic flyovers so tourists could take pictures. We did fine for a while, but in the last few years he's had some problems."

"Problems?" I asked. "What kind of problems?"

"Post-traumatic-stress syndrome."

Those few words gave me a hint of what she hadn't been saying earlier.

"Periodically, if he gets a pocketful of money, he goes a little haywire."

"And you think that's what's going on here?"

"When the guy called in yesterday to make the

reservation, I asked him for a credit card number. We always do that in case of cancellations and no-shows, but he said he'd be paying cash and that he'd throw in a little extra. We need the money real bad right now, so I took it. I hope to God it wasn't anything illegal, was it?"

I sidestepped her question by asking one of my own. "Didn't you say you knew your father had landed in Spokane?"

"We talked to them about noon when we still hadn't heard from him." Dana Lions gave me the name and number of an official at Spokane International Airport. "Will you let me know what you find out?" she asked.

"Certainly," I said, allowing my voice to sound far more convincing than I should have. If David Lions was somehow tied in with the severed telephone lines, he and his little company and his worried daughter were in big trouble, far worse than that caused by a few unpaid bills.

"Just a few more questions," I said. "Did the man making the reservation leave a name?"

"Smith. Charles Smith. I have it written down right here. Dad was supposed to meet him at the Renton Airport."

"Did he?"

"As far as I know."

"Did your father file a flight plan?"

"Always. You can get a copy of it from the FAA. But why do you want it? I told you, the helicopter's already safely on the ground in Spokane."

"Right," I said. As we finished talking, she gave me her home number in Kalama, and I told her how to locate both Andy Halvorsen and me if she needed to, reassuring her one more time that we'd notify her instantly if we learned anything more about her missing father.

"Looks like you hit the jackpot," Halvorsen said as I held down the switch hook long enough to get a dial tone. Reading from my notes, I dialed the number at Spokane International and talked to a man named Kyle Preston.

"Do you have a helicopter there that belongs to an outfit named St. Helens Flying Service?"

"Sure do."

"I want you to post a security guard out by that helicopter," I said. "No one is to go near it or touch it, is that clear? And if anyone tries to take off in it, detain them until we can get there."

"Wait just a damned minute! Who the hell do you think you are, ordering me around like this?"

"My name's Detective J. P. Beaumont with the Seattle Police Department, and I've got a Whitman County sheriff's department detective named Andrew Halvorsen with me. We're on our way."

"What's going on here? This Lions character has been doing nothing but causing trouble all day long. First thing this morning that SOB puts down here and walks off without paying his landing fee, without saying how long he'll be here or kiss my ass. Nothing. It's like the world owes him a goddamned living. We're not running this place just for the hell of it, you know."

"Did you actually see him get off the helicopter?"

Kyle snorted derisively. "Are you kidding? You think I've got time enough to give every harebrained pilot around here the damned red carpet treatment? We've got an airport to run. We leave the greeting committee bullshit to the local chamber of commerce."

Without giving him the opportunity to make any further objections, I hung up the phone. Halvorsen picked up his phone and dialed a number.

"Hi, hon," he said a moment later. "Did I wake you?" A sudden brittle tension had crept into his voice and a slight tic appeared over his jawline, a mannerism that I hadn't noticed before. "Sorry. Look, Monica, something's come up. Right now I'm on my way to Spokane. Can you get a ride to work?" He paused. "I know. I'm sorry, sweetie, but it's important."

He grew quiet before a sudden verbal onslaught that I could hear angry echoes of clear across the room. Whoever Monica was, she sounded pissed as hell.

Finally he said resignedly, "But, hon, I'll be back in plenty of time to pick you up . . ." A dial tone buzzed in his ear. Monica had hung up on him. Halvorsen threw the phone back in its cradle.

"Come on," he muttered. "Let's get the hell out of here."

We rode toward Spokane in silence, with Halvorsen brooding and driving like a bat out of hell, alternately smoking and chewing on a new cigar. I left him alone. Whatever was going on between him and Monica was none of my business. Besides I had plenty to think about on my own.

No matter what, I couldn't shake the conviction that St. Helens Flying Service and David Lions were somehow involved in what had happened to

Kimi and Machiko Kurobashi. To an outsider, the connection might seem remote, but I'm no believer in blind coincidence. Cops don't think that way. If things appear to be connected, they probably are.

It all boiled down to one major question and several lesser ones. Who the hell was Charles Smith, David Lions' cash-paying passenger, the mysterious client who had chartered a helicopter to fly across the state? Had he disrupted telephone service and assaulted two innocent women along the way? If so, what did he really want? And did he already have it?

"You have any friends or acquaintances at the Federal Aviation Administration?" I asked.

"Huh?" Halvorsen returned, still lost in his fog of anger.

"Do you have any connections at the FAA?" I repeated. "Someone who could locate the flight plan for us."

Halvorsen seemed relieved to have something else to think about. Shaking off his black mood, he put out the cigar and picked up the radio. He talked to someone at the Pullman-Moscow Airport, some deer-hunting/fishing buddy from the sound of it. The information we needed came back to us in less than ten minutes.

David Lions' flight plan, as filed before he left Renton Airport south of Seattle, was to fly to Vantage, halfway to Pullman, land on a landing strip there, and wait for another passenger. Estimated time of arrival in Spokane had been 6:00 A.M.

"So they got into Spokane right on time," I said, after we had heard the information. "No one thought anything was amiss, except for the daughter."

"Who didn't have any idea that the trip was going to take that long."

"So did Lions know about it or not? Was he in on it from the beginning, or was he someone who got sucked in along the way?"

Halvorsen punched in the button on the car's cigarette lighter. "No way to tell that until we talk to the man himself."

"If we can find him," I said.

It was well after dusk when we parked in the parking garage at Spokane International Airport. We had been told that Kyle Preston would be waiting for us, and he was.

"I posted the security guard just like you told me," Kyle said, leading us toward the asphalt runway. "It's over here. Nobody's touched a thing, but what the hell's going on? My understanding was that Lions primarily flew scenic tours—sight-seeing, picture-taking kinds of things. That copter looks like it's been used for crop dusting. It's still got stalks of wheat sticking to it."

Halvorsen and I stopped short and exchanged glances, while Kyle Preston waited impatiently. "Are you two coming or not?" he demanded. "I thought you were both in one hell of a hurry to see this bird."

"We'd better call the crime lab first, don't you think?" Halvorsen asked.

I nodded, knowing then for sure that Dana Lions' missing daddy was in a whole shitpot full of trouble.

CHAPTER 10

THE CRIME-SCENE TEAM, TWO CRIMINALISTS FROM the Washington State Patrol Crime Lab in Spokane, spent several hours going over the St. Helens Flying Service helicopter while Detective Halvorsen and I paced around outside on the runway like a pair of expectant fathers.

It had been an exceedingly frustrating day. When we started out, we had been only hours behind our quarry. Now, with every passing moment, we were losing more and more ground. The jetways at Spokane International had offered Kimi's and Machiko's attackers instant escape hatches to any destination in the country. Any destination in the world, for that matter.

So far, our inquiries into the whereabouts of David Lions had come to nothing. Everyone we interviewed at the airport assumed that he had been piloting the aircraft when it set down on schedule at six o'clock that morning, but no one actually remembered seeing him get off. Charles Smith, the name used by Dana Lions' cash-paying customer, also drew a blank, but that was hardly surprising. He had doubtless used an alias when he booked the reservation. Without any kind of physical description, we had no idea who or what we were looking for.

A stiff fall wind was blowing east off the Cascades. Shivering against the chill, Halvorsen and I were almost ready to retreat into the terminal when Gary Richards and Helen Driver emerged from the helicopter, bringing their considerable gear along with them.

"That's about all we can do for tonight," Richards said, standing to one side while Helen strung crime scene tape across the door of the helicopter. "We'll come look it over again tomorrow in daylight just in case we missed something important. According to Kyle Preston, they'll have a security guard here all night."

"Find anything?" Andy asked.

"Plenty of fingerprints," Richards responded, "some wire snippers and this."

He held a glassine bag up to the halo of light from one of the runway's mercury-vapor lamps. I looked but it seemed to be nothing but an empty bag.

"What is it?" I asked.

"One hair," he replied. "One long dark hair. Black, I'd say, but it's hard to judge color in this light."

Halvorsen glanced in my direction. "Kimi's?"

I nodded.

Richards noted this exchange. "I thought you two might be interested in that. There are some other bits of trace evidence as well, but we'll have to analyze all those before we know what we're seeing. Where can we find you guys tomorrow in case we need to? Are you staying right here in Spokane?"

I started to nod yes and ask directions to the nearest hotel, but Halvorsen interrupted. "No, we're headed back to Pullman tonight. You can reach us through my office in Colfax tomorrow."

I couldn't believe he was serious. Pullman was a good seventy-five miles away, and it was verging on eleven. I personally had already done more than enough traveling for one day. The last thing I wanted to do was take another seventy-five-mile jaunt in a cramped Colfax County K-car. Unfortunately, we were supposedly conducting a joint investigation, and Halvorsen was driving.

Helen Driver and Gary Richards left then. We were almost to the car when Kyle Preston caught up with us, bringing with him a lady from Budget Rent-a-Car.

The lady's name was Pamela Kinder, and we had missed her in our earlier survey of airport personnel because she had been out playing bridge when Halvorsen had called and left a message on her machine.

Preston suggested we go back to his office and get in out of the cold. Forty-five or so and not at all bad-looking, Pamela Kinder took a seat next to Kyle's desk, crossed her well-shaped legs, and gave us a winning smile.

"I wish I'd known you guys were looking for this Lions character this morning when I rented him the Lincoln. I smelled a rat, but I couldn't prove it."

After a day of massive effort with very little to

show for it, having Pamela Kinder show up at the last minute with that kind of information was absolutely mind-boggling, a cosmic joke. "Are you sure it was him?" I asked. "Do you know the man personally?"

"Not personally, but I remember the name. Believe me, I checked his ID very carefully," Pamela Kinder said. The certainty in her voice was more than a mere statement. Something about David Lions had bothered her, triggered her curiosity.

"Why?" I asked.

"Why did I check so carefully? Because he looked like a bum, like he didn't have two nickels left to rub together. I wanted to be sure I wasn't renting our vehicle to someone using fake or stolen ID. I made sure the picture on his driver's license matched his face, and I double-checked the signatures as well."

"What do you mean, he looked like a bum?"

"He acted sort of spacey, although I couldn't smell anything on him. And he looked like he had spent the night in a field somewhere. He still had straw sticking to his clothes, but his Visa card worked when I called to verify his credit."

"What did he say?"

"Hardly anything. The guy who was with him, though, was a real conversationalist."

"You mean he wasn't alone?"

"No. He had some jerk with him. Tall, dark, and handsome. Obviously considers himself God's gift to women. He tried to hit on me. At six o'clock in the morning, mind you. Asked if he came back later, could he take me out to breakfast."

"What did you tell him?"

"What I always tell creeps like that—that my husband was on his way to pick me up."

"Was he?"

"My husband?" Pamela Kinder laughed, a hearty, throaty laugh. "Hardly. Ralph's been dead for almost six years."

Halvorsen was too impatient to enjoy Pamela Kinder's sense of humor. "Did you notice anything unusual about either one of them, anything that would help us identify them?"

"The straw. I already told you about that. And the other guy, the creep, was wearing gloves. Leather gloves, inside the terminal." Remembering Machiko's story, Halvorsen and I exchanged glances, but we said nothing, allowing Pamela to continue. "People sometimes do that, but usually not until after the weather gets cold. It's still way too early. I wondered if maybe his hands were disfigured—burned maybe, or deformed. He mostly kept his hands in his pockets like he was self-conscious about them."

She paused. "And he's from Chicago," she added.

"Chicago? How do you know that?" Halvorsen demanded.

"I heard him talk. Believe me, I can tell a Chicago accent when I hear one. I grew up in Downer's Grove just outside of Chicago. He sounded like my Uncle Bill."

"Did they give you any idea where they were taking the car?" I asked.

"No. I offered them maps. Lions said they didn't need any."

"Do you have any idea where they were going?"

Pamela shook her head. "The car is due back in on Saturday afternoon. Of course, for an extra charge, they don't have to return it here."

"Can you give us a description of the vehicle?"

She handed over a piece of paper. "I can do better than that. When Kyle told me what was going on, I stopped by the counter and made a copy of the rental agreement. It has a complete description of the car, including license numbers and all that."

Andy took the paper out of my hand. "What say I put out an APB on this," he said.

"Put a hold on that Visa number as well," I told him. Halvorsen nodded and hurried away. I started after him, but Pamela Kinder stopped me.

"So this was important, then?"

To outsiders, homicide cops must appear rude at times. When we finally manage to glean some vital tidbit of information, our first instinct is to grab it and run without so much as a by-your-leave or a thank-you. A detective's total focus on finding a killer seldom allows time for social amenities. Pamela Kinder was a nice lady, one who had made a special trip to the airport in the middle of the night in order to help us. Now she seemed disappointed that we weren't acting more grateful.

I was instantly contrite and abjectly apologetic. "It's very important, Mrs. Kinder," I mumbled. "Thank you for taking the time to come down and give it to us."

And so, exercising astonishing self-control, I sat back down, focused my complete attention on Pamela Kinder's once more smiling face, and proceeded to pick her brain. By the time Halvorsen returned from sending out the APB, I had ascertained that Pamela Kinder had little else she could tell us. She had also made it clear that, this morning's encounter with the creep notwithstanding, she wouldn't have minded taking me home with her to continue the discussion.

Unfortunately, Halvorsen was still driving.

Once Pamela left, Detective Halvorsen hustled us out of the terminal as though it was on fire. To say he was anxious to get on the road would be drastically understating the case.

"How does it look?" I asked.

He shrugged. "The APB? It's being broadcast right now, but nobody's very hopeful. Everybody thinks they're long gone, and as for the credit-card thing, Lions won't be dumb enough to try using it again."

"Let's get a room somewhere here in Spokane. In the morning we can stop by the hospital and—"

"I already said, we're going back to Pullman."

"That was before we picked up a major lead. What the hell are you thinking?"

"I'm going home."

"But what about Kimi? We still haven't talked to her."

"You know as well as I do that even if she's out of Intensive Care, they're not going to let us talk to her in the middle of the night, and probably not tomorrow morning either. We've already got a guard posted outside her door. Hanging around here in Spokane isn't going to do us a damn bit of good."

By then Halvorsen had driven us out of the airport complex and onto the freeway. When he started signaling for a right-hand turn at the Pullman exit, I made one more futile attempt at dissuading him.

"Look, turkey, I'm dead tired. What's the problem with spending the night here?"

"I don't want to," Halvorsen replied tersely. Saying that, he lit up a new cigar and turned on the flashing lights. End of discussion.

If it weren't for the badge in his pocket, Andrew Halvorsen would probably have lost his driver's license years ago. He was a maniac behind the wheel. It was a long, wild ride through the moonlit Palouse that night, with him speeding down the straightaways and braking on the curves. Somewhere along the way, a deer leaped across the road in front of us, missing the front fender by inches.

"Jesus Christ, Halvorsen! Slow this mother down before you kill us both. What the hell's the hurry?"

"Monica gets off at one," he said. "I told her I'd be there to pick her up."

"Monica?" I asked. The afternoon phone call in his office was so long ago that I had almost completely forgotten about it. "Who the hell's Monica?"

"My wife," he answered. "Our car's in the shop and she gets off work at one. I told her I'd be there to pick her up."

"But where?"

"At the University Inn in Moscow. That's where she works."

Most of the time I pride myself on being a patient man. Patient and reasonably even-tempered. But that just about corked it. Here we were, driving hell-bent-for-leather through the middle of the night and almost getting killed besides and all because

Andrew Halvorsen had agreed to pick up his dingbat wife after work.

"You mean to tell me she couldn't get a ride home with somebody else?"

The tip of Halvorsen's cigar glowed dull red in the instrument lit darkness. "She probably could," he said. "That's why I'm going to pick her up."

We lapsed into silence. I was too ripped to talk and too busy hanging on. It was 12:45 when we pulled into the parking lot at the University Inn in Moscow, Idaho. It doesn't take a mathematical genius to know that seventy-five miles in sixty minutes is too damn fast!

It was time for last call for drinks. I sure as hell needed one. Instead of stopping to register, I followed Halvorsen into Chasers, where a few late-night revelers, closing-crowd lounge lizards, were still hanging on. The cocktail waitress was a blonde with an electric tan and a long slit up the side of her skimpy skirt. She was true cocktail-waitress material—lots of leg, lots of cleavage, too much makeup, and not enough brain.

"See you made it back," she remarked coolly to Andy as she took a quick swipe across our table with a damp cloth.

If this was Halvorsen's Monica, she was giving him a less than ecstatic greeting. He deserved better— both of us did, considering the way he had driven to get us there. Sure enough, when she came around to my side of the table, I could see her name tag pinned to the collar of the low-cut blouse. And the name tag wasn't all I could see. Halvorsen introduced us.

"What'll you have?" Monica asked, giving me an

appraising glance. The way she asked the question, it didn't sound as though she just meant drinks, and the way she looked me up and down while she was doing it was deliberately inviting. Monica Halvorsen may have been married, but that didn't mean she had quit shopping around.

I glanced in Andy's direction. The nervous tic I had noticed earlier in the day reappeared on his jaw-line.

The term *pussy whipped* has fallen into disuse in recent years, but call it what you will, Andrew Halvorsen was suffering from a hell of a case of it. Monica couldn't have been much more than twenty-five or -six—barely half his age—and Halvorsen's ego wasn't wired for that kind of voltage. I could smell the smoke from blown fuses as he watched her watch me. And here I was stuck working with the poor bastard. No wonder he had been so damned eager to get home.

Monica Halvorsen walked away from the table, stopping by another one along the way to drop off an order of drinks. She stood with her hip slung to one side, the cocktail tray resting casually on her arm while she threw her head back and laughed at some wry comment from a rowdy table of late-night customers. Young late-night customers.

Andy Halvorsen never once took his eyes off her. That kind of jealous obsession is painful to see, especially when it isn't reciprocated.

"What about tomorrow morning?" I asked, dragging his attention away from his wife and back to the case.

"What? Oh, I'll be in the office by eight. I'll check

and see if anything's come of the APB, then I can call you here and let you know what's going on."

"All right. You don't think I'll have a problem getting a room?"

"The vacancy sign was still lit when we drove up."

Monica returned with our drinks. Halvorsen hadn't ordered anything, but from the looks of the glass Monica brought him, he was probably drinking straight Seven-Up or tonic. It was just as well. He was still driving a Whitman County car.

"How much?" I asked, as she set my drink on the table.

"Five-fifty for both," she said.

"Wait a minute. You don't have to . . ." Halvorsen began, reaching for his wallet, but I already had the money out and on the table. I didn't want anything left open to the slightest misinterpretation. I included a tip, one small enough to keep Halvorsen from getting the wrong impression.

The MacNaughton's, when I tasted it, was particularly welcome. It had been a long, long day.

Monica collected glasses from two recently vacated tables, and took them back to the bar, where she stood leaning against the counter chatting easily with the bartender.

"What do you think?" Halvorsen asked.

At first I thought he was asking about the case, but then when I saw his eyes were once more glued to Monica's behind, I knew the Kurobashis were the furthest thing from his mind.

"She's very pretty," I said.

"I think so too," he said.

"How long have you two been married?" I asked.

"Three months last week," he answered. "We had to wait until my divorce was final."

Electric tan, too much makeup, and a homewrecker besides. My already low initial opinion of Monica Halvorsen dipped a few more points.

"I wish she could get a job somewhere else, but this is all she's ever done, and we need the money. Child support and alimony. Barbara seems to think she's got a God-given right to stay home with the kids and sit on her butt."

That was as much as I wanted to hear. My months of helping care for the children of Ron Peters, an ailing fellow police officer, had taught me that there's a whole lot more to taking care of kids than sitting on your tail, but I didn't have guts enough to tell him so.

I polished off my drink in one long gulp and set the glass on the table. "I'm going to go see about a room," I told him.

As I walked away, I couldn't help thinking that Andrew and Monica Halvorsen may have made their three-month anniversary, but I was willing to bet money they wouldn't make six.

CHAPTER 11

I TOOK A DECREPIT CAB, POSSIBLY MOSCOW, IDAHO'S only cab, from the University Inn to Colfax and was sitting in Andy Halvorsen's courthouse office at 8:15 the next morning when he called Sacred Heart Hospital in Spokane for a status report. Kimi Kurobashi was still in Intensive Care, and the doctors said it would probably be several days before we could talk to her.

Rita Brice, bleary-eyed from too little sleep and looking as though she had spent the night in her clothes, showed up in the office doorway a few minutes later to tell us that she was on her way to Colfax Community Hospital, where Machiko Kurobashi was about to be released. Because she had nowhere else to go, Machiko would stay with Rita at Honeydale Farm.

Rita said that her ex-husband had called to offer the use of two of his ranch hands during the crisis, both to help out with the work and to keep an eye on things. For an ex-husband, he sounded like an all right kind of guy.

The short night's stay in Pullman with Monica seemed to have done wonders for Andrew Halvorsen's state of well-being. He was back on top of things. The nervous tic was gone from his face. He was bright, with a quick grasp of what was going on and what needed to be done, and it was a pleasure to observe him working with his head screwed on straight.

Shortly after Rita left, Halvorsen turned to me. "What about you?" he asked.

I shrugged. "There's not much sense in me hanging around on this side of the mountains. Kimi's in good hands at the moment, and, thanks to the Brices, so is her mother. I think I'd better get back to Seattle and see what's going on there."

Halvorsen nodded. "Sounds like a plan."

With a freshly lit cigar in hand, he drove me back to the Pullman-Moscow Airport, where I caught the next plane out, riding home on what was probably the same frayed Metro-Liner I had ridden in on the day before. Scrunched into the too-small seat, I had nothing to do on the way back to Seattle but think.

I kept rehashing what Halvorsen had said the day before, about Kimi and Machiko's attackers being name-brand muscle with Cosa Nostra connections. Everything we had learned since then seemed to lend credence to that theory. The creep from Chicago who had tried to pick up Pamela Kinder hadn't been wearing gloves because his hands were deformed. He was a man with something to hide, a scumbag who probably knew his fingerprints were on file somewhere, along with a couple of outstanding arrest warrants.

Chartering helicopters is an expensive proposition. Whoever was behind it either had money to burn or else they had some damaging piece of information on David Lions, information with enough blackmail potential that the charter pilot had been forced to go along with the program.

Last but not least was Pamela Kinder's comment about the Chicago accent. I'm sure there are lots of law-abiding citizens living in Chicago, but with all due respect to them, Elliot Ness didn't spend his career busting mobsters in Hoboken, New Jersey. That was reaching, though, and try as I might, I could see no connection between Tadeo Kurobashi and the Mob.

Waiting in line to pay the garage parking charges at Sea-Tac Airport, I used my car phone to try calling Big Al down at the department. Margie, our clerk, said that Detective Lindstrom was down at Industry Square meeting with Bernard Rennermann and Thomas Blakeslee. Obviously, Big Al hadn't been sitting on his hands in my absence. I told Margie I'd try to catch him there on my way into town.

Locating Big Al turned out to be no trouble at all. A white Reliant with the usual police department markings was parked near a building one building over from the one where Tadeo Kurobashi's body had been found. Bernard Rennermann's digs were next to the elevator on the ground floor.

A young receptionist took my name and called the information into an inner room. A moment or two later, Bernie himself appeared at a door down a short hallway, mopping perspiration off his brow with what looked like yesterday's handkerchief.

"Oh, Detective Beaumont. You're here too. I didn't know you were expected."

"I wasn't," I replied. "I managed to get here anyway."

He stepped aside and let me into the room. It was a spacious conference room whose main piece of furniture was a long, rectangular oak table. The padded captain's chair at the far end was empty. Big Al Lindstrom sat on one side of the table, glaring sullenly at a smug little man who was seated opposite him, a man I assumed to be Thomas Blakeslee.

Somehow I had imagined Blakeslee, the bane of Tadeo Kurobashi's existence, to be different—bigger, larger than life. Instead, he was a stunted, bald-headed little twerp with thick glasses who smoked unfiltered Camels like a damn chimney.

Two chain-smokers in as many days! Doesn't anybody read those Surgeon General's warnings?

Thomas Blakeslee had managed to get himself at cross purposes with Big Al Lindstrom, whose hackles were definitely up. As I came in the door, Al glanced briefly in my direction and nodded, but immediately he turned his full attention back on Blakeslee.

"This is my partner, Detective Beaumont," he said. "Now, would you please answer my question?"

"What was it again?"

"Did Mr. Kurobashi know that you were the new tenant who would be taking over this space?"

"I wouldn't know about that. You'd have to ask Bernie here. He might have told him."

"I didn't," Rennermann blurted, again wiping his

damp forehead. "You asked me not to, remember? So I didn't."

"Why didn't you want Kurobashi to know that you were moving in?"

Blakeslee shrugged. "It would have been awkward, that's all. Besides, Tadeo had lost the lease. It was none of his business what happened to the space after he moved out."

"Except that he lost the lease because he lost the patent infringement lawsuit against you."

"Business is business," Blakeslee said off-handedly.

He was a cold-blooded, mean-spirited little rat. No wonder he had provoked Big Al's ire. Lindstrom may look big and tough, but there's not a cruel bone in his body. Never has been. Meanness offends him.

Blakeslee thumped a mound of ashes into the large cut-glass ashtray on the table in front of him. "Look," he said, "I wanted the space, all right? My lease at the old place was running out in a few months anyway. I had to look for a new location. Then, when I found out that Tadeo was leaving, I decided why not? After all, we were in pretty much the same business. He laid out the manufacturing plant here almost identically to what I've been using in my place. Hell, he's the one who organized that plant years ago when he was working for me, except this one is brand-new, totally upgraded."

"What about the equipment?" Lindstrom asked.

"I'll be bringing my own, of course."

"And what happens to the MicroBridge equipment?"

Again Blakeslee tapped his cigarette, a gesture I

recognized as a delaying tactic. "As the major creditor, I expected to buy it at the auction. For ten cents on the dollar, I should have been able to pick up all the equipment, the hard assets, and customer lists, and I wouldn't have had to pay a dime out of my own pocket."

"It sounds as though that deal is off," Big Al interjected.

Blakeslee shrugged again. "From what I hear, there's not much left, although I may still bid on some of the equipment."

"Do you have any idea what Mr. Kurobashi was working on at the time of his death?"

"None whatsoever."

"And you're not interested in finding out?"

"Not particularly. My dear Detective Lindstrom, RFLink provides me with a more than adequate livelihood."

"Particularly if your major competitor is no longer in business."

"That's right."

"Or dead," Big Al added.

"Are you accusing me of something unlawful here, Detective Lindstrom? If so, I'm afraid I'll have to request that my attorney be present. I agreed to come here and talk to you of my own free will, but it seems to me that your questions are going beyond the pale of what's acceptable and what isn't."

I had heard enough to see what kind of a tack Big Al was running on, and I happened to have some information that he didn't.

"Mr. Blakeslee," I put in, "would you have any idea

why Tadeo Kurobashi would feed a virus into his entire office computer system, including the new computer he was giving his daughter?"

"How would I know? Everybody always told me he was a genius, but he never showed me anything I couldn't have done better myself and in half the time," Blakeslee replied.

"Or why he would send most of his important company records to the shredder?"

"Like I said, even when he was working for me I didn't understand him. I have no idea, unless . . ."

"Unless what?"

"Unless he had something to hide."

"What might that be?"

"I don't know."

"How much did you win?" Big Al asked, returning to the fray.

"Excuse me?"

"The judgment you won against him. How much was it and when is it due?"

"A total of 350 K. It was all due and payable the first of last month."

"Will the judgment be voided by the bankruptcy proceedings?"

"No."

"So his estate will still have to come up with that much money?"

"That's my understanding."

"Did he actually steal your patents, Mr. Blakeslee?" Big Al asked.

Blakeslee tapped his cigarette and smiled enigmatically, a vulture claiming his prize.

"That's no longer a matter open to debate, Detective Lindstrom. A jury said he did. That's what counts." He pushed his chair back and stood up. "I must be going now, if you don't mind. I have a luncheon appointment."

Disgustedly, Big Al waved him out of the room. Bernard Rennermann hurried after his departing guest and soon-to-be tenant.

"I'm glad I'm a cop," Big Al said. "At least with pimps and pushers, you know where you stand. These guys are absolute cutthroats. That asshole doesn't give a shit that Kurobashi is dead. All he cares about is how soon he can move in and pick the rest of the meat off the bones. And Rennermann's no better. The whole time Kurobashi was fighting to keep his head above water, that lousy little creep was wheeling and dealing with the guy who was pulling the rug out."

"Did you ask him where he was three nights ago?"

"Who? Blakeslee?"

I nodded.

"He claims he was at a board of directors meeting for RFLink, that he was there from dinnertime until well past midnight. He gave me the names and numbers of several people he says were there with him. I haven't had a chance to check any of them out yet."

"But you're going to."

"You'd best believe it. I don't trust that squirrelly little son of a bitch any further than I can throw him. What about the women? Are they going to be all right?"

"Machiko was supposed to get out of the hospital

today. Kimi is lucky to be alive. The last I heard, she's still in Intensive Care."

"Those bastards!" Big Al muttered under his breath. He stood up and stretched. "Been home yet?"

"No."

"Ralph Ames came by the department looking for you early this morning. I told him that I'd have you call as soon as you showed up. Meantime, I have a lunch date. You're welcome to come along."

"Who with?"

"Mrs. Oliver, Kurobashi's secretary. She called this morning and wanted to see one or both of us. I'm meeting her for lunch."

"Where?"

"An ex-gas station over by Sears."

"A what?"

"A converted gas station called the Pecos Pit Barbecue over on First Avenue South not far from here. She said to meet her there around eleven and it's almost that now. Are you coming or not?"

"I'm in," I said, "but why meet her there when her office is right across the parking lot?"

"I asked her that myself since I figured I'd be finishing up with Rennermann and Blakeslee about now, but she insisted that she didn't want me coming by the office."

"She's still holding down the fort then?"

"That's right."

We took both cars and, once we reached the neighborhood, had to look around some before we found places to park. Pecos Pit Barbecue may have been a converted gas station, but it appeared to be fairly popular.

Mrs. Bernice Oliver, dressed in a heavy black sweater and an old-fashioned black sheath dress, a mourning dress, was standing in line with a bunch of hard-hats and other hungry working sorts. It was only ten after eleven, but there were already fifteen people and one outsized malamute pup waiting in line to be served. The line snaked its way through a collection of outdoor picnic tables and ended up in front of a serving counter/window that had been built into the front wall.

Bernice Oliver was only five people back from the window when we got there. She motioned for us to come stand beside her. "So you're both here. Do you like your barbecue hot or medium?" she asked. We both requested medium. She directed us to go locate a sunny table where she joined us a few minutes later bringing with her a cardboard tray laden with three paper bags, three sodas, and a stack of napkins.

"I hope you don't mind that I just ordered for all of us," she said. "It would have taken a lot longer if you two had to go to the back of the line."

The barbecue beef sandwiches were huge, mouthwateringly delicious, and impossibly messy. I would hate to have ordered hot, because the medium made my eyes water and my nose run. And I didn't escape the meal without a wart-sized blob of barbecue sauce landing square in the middle of my tie.

Eating the sandwiches required full concentration, and none of us attempted to speak until our sandwiches were completely gone. Mrs. Oliver finished first.

"Mr. Kurobashi used to bring me here for lunch

sometimes," she said. Taking one of the remaining napkins from the stack, Mrs. Oliver wiped her eyes. Her tears had nothing to do with the spiciness of the food.

"I wanted to come here today because . . ." She stopped and shook her head. "Just because . . ." Her voice trailed off.

"That's understandable," I said.

"But also to give you something," she added. She reached into her purse and pulled out a piece of paper. "You asked me the other day if I knew who Mr. Kurobashi might be going to see on a ferry. I couldn't think of anybody then, but this morning I was going through last week's messages, the carbon copies, and I came across this."

Big Al was still working on his sandwich, so she handed the paper to me. The blue ink had copied badly, so it was difficult to read. The telephone number itself was almost totally illegible.

"Clay?" I asked. "I can't make out the last name."

"Woodruff. He called last Friday. I was so upset at hearing his voice that I almost didn't give Mr. Kurobashi the message."

"Who's Clay Woodruff?"

"I *thought* he was Mr. Kurobashi's friend," Mrs. Oliver said disdainfully.

"Was?" I asked. "What happened?"

"I met Clay when we all worked at RFLink. He was young then, but he was already director of marketing. He and Mr. Kurobashi became very close. They both loved computers, used them at home and in the office the way other people use pencils. That was years ago, you see, long before everybody had one."

I nodded, not wanting to interrupt her, but trying to urge her to go on.

"Anyway, when Mr. Kurobashi came up with that new product design, it was really innovative, really exciting. The two of them went to see Blakeslee and offered it to him. It could easily have doubled the sales of RFLink, but Blakeslee turned it down. Clay said that was crazy and that if Blakeslee was that stupid, he was quitting, so Blakeslee fired him on the spot. He fired Mr. Kurobashi as well. I quit right after that."

"It sounds like Blakeslee was a turkey and the other two stuck together like glue."

Mrs. Oliver nodded. "That's how it seemed at the time. Right away, Mr. Kurobashi began putting together money to start MicroBridge. Blakeslee had made him sign a noncompetition agreement, but since he had been fired, Mr. Kurobashi figured it wasn't enforceable. Blakeslee's lawyer must not have thought so either, because nothing ever came of it, but after MicroBridge came online, Blakeslee sued for patent infringement."

"And won," I said.

"He shouldn't have," Mrs. Oliver said bitterly. "And he wouldn't have, either, if Clay had done his part."

"Which was?" I prodded.

"Show up to testify. He dropped off the face of the earth for a while after he left RFLink. He's a composer, and he told Mr. Kurobashi at the time that he was sick of the business world and that he was going to concentrate on his music. When the patent infringement thing came up, Mr. Kurobashi didn't worry about it very much, because he was sure Clay would testify. Except he didn't."

"Why not?"

"I don't know. Before the trial, Mr. Davenport tracked him down. He had to hire a private detective to do it. That's very expensive, you know. But when it came time for the trial. Clay couldn't be found. Mr. Davenport said that Blakeslee must have bought him off. That was why I was surprised when he called on Friday, acting all friendly like, as though nothing had ever happened. Such nerve!"

"So you gave Mr. Kurobashi the message. Did he return the call?"

"I don't know. I didn't pry into Mr. Kurobashi's affairs, but he may have."

"Where does Clay Woodruff live?"

"At the time of the trial, I remember Mr. Davenport saying Clay was living in a hotel over on the peninsula somewhere."

"Which peninsula, Kitsap? Olympic?"

"Over there somewhere," she said. "Across the water."

"Can you get us a better copy of this phone number?"

"I wrote it down on the back," she said.

I turned over the paper and looked at the number. The last four digits began with a nine. "This is probably a pay phone."

Mrs. Oliver shrugged. "That's the only number he gave me."

Big Al had long since finished with his sandwich and had been listening quietly from the sidelines.

"How did Mr. Kurobashi feel when this Woodruff character didn't come testify? Was he angry?"

"Not angry. Hurt. To be treated like that by a friend when he had counted on him so heavily. I mean, he had borrowed money everywhere, even mortgaged his house."

"And Woodruff let him down."

She nodded. "And that's what makes me think Mr. Kurobashi must have talked to him."

"Why?"

"Because the last thing he said to me as I was leaving on Friday was that he just didn't know who he could trust anymore."

Abruptly, Mrs. Oliver stood up to leave. "I'd better be going now. I don't like to be gone more than an hour. People still expect someone to answer the phone, you know."

"Could I ask you one more question, Mrs. Oliver?" Al Lindstrom asked.

"Certainly." She sat back down and waited attentively.

"Why didn't you want us to meet you at your office?"

"I suppose I'm just being silly, but several times during the last few weeks, Mr. Kurobashi said he felt like someone was spying on him. Maybe he was just being paranoid, but with everything that's happened, I'm not so sure."

"But you still can't tell us what exactly he was working on?"

"No. I know he thought it was important, but he kept all his notes about it locked up in his own computer and written in Japanese. He said he didn't want someone wandering into his office and reading things over his shoulder."

"Not even you?"

"Not even me," she replied.

I tried to tell if there was any resentment in her voice when she said it, but I couldn't. If Mrs. Bernice Oliver was angry with Tadeo Kurobashi for keeping secrets from her, it certainly wasn't showing.

She stood up again. Pausing long enough to wipe a few remaining bread crumbs and sesame seeds from her lap, she stepped over the rail at the end of the picnic table bench and walked back to her car, hurrying to answer the last few phone calls in her dead boss's dead business.

Big Al shook his head as he watched her walk away. "I still haven't figured out what makes that old dame tick, have you? Do you think he was banging her?"

"Who, Kurobashi?" It was almost impossible to think of the angular Mrs. Oliver in a sexual context, but luckily for the human race, we don't all have exactly the same tastes.

"Maybe," I said, "but then again, maybe not. And I sure as hell don't have balls enough to ask her."

"Me either," Big Al admitted ruefully, "so I guess we'll never know."

CHAPTER 12

BIG AL AND I SAT IN THE WARM AUTUMN SUN AT THE rough picnic table at the Pecos Pit Barbecue for the next forty-five minutes, while outdoor diners milled around us. We chewed on leftover hunks of ice in Styrofoam cups and brought each other up to date on what had been happening at opposite ends of the state.

"Did you ever talk to the people from the shredder company?" I asked.

"Not yet. They were out of town yesterday when I stopped by on my way home. I thought I'd try to see them today."

"And what about Davenport?"

"I had an appointment for yesterday, but he stood me up. His secretary rescheduled me for later on this afternoon."

"I'll go along, if you don't mind. He may be able to shed some light on this Woodruff thing. If nothing else, he might know where to look for him. Mrs. Oliver's saying he lives in a hotel on one of the peninsulas isn't a whole hell of a lot of help."

"We can always get the location of the pay phone from the phone company," Big Al said.

"I know, but if we can get it from Davenport it'll save time."

When we finally left the Pecos Pit, it was to drive to 1201 Third Avenue, Chris Davenport's shiny new building. According to the rave review of one prominent architectural critic, the building is "a perfect rendition of art deco style." I'd call it more an architectural rendering of tutti-frutti, with its towering confection of green mirrored glass and matte-finished pink granite. The multi-humped roof line looks like it came straight from the set of the 1930s *King Kong*, but of course that movie was made in black and white.

Once inside, we found that the old-fashioned marbled lobby looked like a time traveler from that same era. We fumbled around for several minutes before we were able to locate the bank of elevators.

Chris Davenport's office on the forty-fifth floor was suitably high in the building, definitely not low-rent squalor. When the elevator door opened, we found ourselves in a spacious and highly modern reception area done in the current fashion of dusty rose and subtle grays, rich-looking but soothingly quiet.

"Bankruptcy must pay pretty good wages these days," Big Al said under his breath.

"For attorneys," I returned.

As far as female help is concerned, law firms always seem to recruit the pick of the crop. A young receptionist with big boobs, a tightly belted knit dress, and a tiny waist announced our arrival over an intercom. Behind the receptionist's desk, mounted on the cloth-covered wall, was a large brass plaque listing the names of the partners, thirty-four by actual count. Davenport's name, in position nineteen, showed that despite his youthful looks, he had been around for some time.

Another nubile young secretary appeared, seemingly out of nowhere, to lead us to Davenport's office. She directed us through a door around the corner from the reception counter. The door opened on a private stairway leading down to the next floor. That's when we discovered that the firm—Rice, Baxter, and Wheeler—leased two entire floors.

Davenport may not have been high enough in the pecking order to rate an upstairs office, but his did have a western exposure window with a magnificent view of the shipping traffic on Elliott Bay.

As we were shown inside, we found Davenport seated at his huge polished desk intently studying the inside of his mouth with a small, hand-held mirror. Like a kid caught doing something he shouldn't, he quickly stowed the mirror in a desk drawer and stood up, rubbing the outside of his cheek, offering his other hand in greeting.

"Sorry," he said, with an apologetic, metallic grin. "My orthodontist tightened the bands this morning. It hurts like hell."

"Aren't you a little old for braces?" Lindstrom asked. I detected a trace of Norwegian humor behind the question. If Davenport caught it, he ignored it completely, and he didn't appear to be offended by the question. By then he was probably used to it.

"In our family, the girls were the ones who got

braces," he explained. "They all had to be pretty enough to land husbands. That's why I'm having my teeth fixed now."

My own private opinion was that it would take a whole lot more than straightened teeth to turn Chris Davenport into Prince Charming, but I remained silent. Somebody on the team had to play it straight.

Davenport motioned to the window. "Great view, isn't it?"

It was the same view of Elliott Bay that I see every day from my windows in Belltown Terrace, but, remembering the manners my mother had drummed into me, I went over to the window, looked out, and politely agreed that it was indeed a magnificent view. As I turned back to the room, I noticed the wall behind the visitors' chairs had two framed diplomas on it as well as a series of wife-and-kiddie-type photos.

I stepped close enough to the wall to read the text on the two diplomas. One was a Bachelor of Arts from Loyola and the other was a Juris Doctor from Northwestern. Neither was *Summa Cum Laude* or *Magna Cum Laude*, which didn't surprise me when I remembered Mrs. Oliver's derisive assessment that bankruptcy was all Davenport was good for.

The lawyer noticed my interest in his sheepskin display. "Good Catholic family," he said. "We boys all went through the Jesuit mill."

"Law school instead of braces?" I asked.

He nodded. "Yup. That's how it works."

Davenport seated himself behind his desk and began doing a series of annoying finger aerobics that revealed, despite his otherwise open and relaxed air, that Christopher Davenport wasn't nearly as happy to be spending time with us as his outward show of geniality implied.

Big Al had lowered himself into a complicated low-slung chair where he shifted uncomfortably, like a rhino stuck in the mud. "We don't want to take too much of your time, Mr. Davenport, but we do need to ask you a few questions."

"Fire away," he said.

Since Big Al had set up the appointment, I was content to take a backseat and let him run the railroad.

"We're still trying to piece together Mr. Kurobashi's activities and whereabouts on the day he died," Big Al said.

Davenport nodded. "That makes sense. It's hard for me to believe he's dead. And the news reports of what happened to his wife and daughter—" He broke off, shaking his head. "It's shocking. Appalling."

"I couldn't agree with you more," Big Al said. "When was the last time you saw him?"

The attorney opened his top desk drawer and pulled out a leather-bound appointment book. He paged back through several days, then stopped and ran his finger down the page.

"Here it is. Friday, one-thirty. He came by and we went over what all he needed to bring to the hearing on Monday."

"The bankruptcy hearing?"

"Yes. I told him everything we'd need in court on Monday."

"And he agreed to bring whatever was needed, financial records, and all that?"

"Of course."

"So you're saying that you as his attorney were not in possession of those records?"

"That's right. We always reviewed them in Tadeo's office. He insisted that we do it that way."

"Do you know anything about an arrangement to have the company records moved or destroyed?"

Davenport let out a disgusted sigh. "As far as I know, they're still there. Somebody called me with a wild rumor that Tadeo had sent everything to the shredder."

"Who?" I asked.

"Who what?"

"Who called you with that rumor?"

Davenport looked at me for a long moment before he answered. "Mr. Blakeslee was the one who called. As head of the creditor's committee, he was all in a lather over it."

"And where did Blakeslee get his information?" Big Al interjected.

"From that slimy Rennermann character, the Industry Square property manager. He claimed to have gotten the scoop from one of the cops on the case. I told him I was sure it wasn't true, but I haven't been able to go by and check for myself. Mrs. Oliver told me that you cops aren't allowing anyone inside."

Big Al and I exchanged glances. We had caught Mrs. Oliver in a little white lie. "In other words, you can't go inside because of the investigation?"

"That's what she said. I told Blakeslee not to worry, that I'd have things straightened out as soon as possible, with the new owner."

"Who is?"

"Machiko Kurobashi. In name only, of course. Until the bankruptcy proceedings are completed."

I was stunned. "Machiko? Are you sure? What could she do with it?"

"Yes, I'm sure. In the corporate minutes she's listed as both a major stockholder as well as an officer. But she's certainly not qualified to run it, and Tadeo didn't expect her to. He thought that with his wife holding the company, his daughter would finally come on board and take control. Now, though, with the bankruptcy proceedings, it's just a formality. At least this way I'll have someone qualified to sign off on things. Thank God, she's all right."

"Did Kurobashi have any enemies as far as you know?" Big Al asked.

"Other than Mr. Blakeslee? No, not that I know of."

"What about Clay Woodruff?" I asked.

"What about him?"

"Would he qualify as an enemy?"

"I don't know how to answer that."

"What do you mean?"

"They were friends once, had worked together at RFLink. Tadeo claimed that Woodruff had been present when he offered to sell his new product design to Blakeslee, that Woodruff knew Tadeo had done all the design work on his own computer at home during off hours. And that testimony would have been invaluable, but Woodruff didn't testify. Without him, Tadeo's version of the meeting was totally inadmissible."

"Why didn't Woodruff testify?"

"I couldn't find him. I sent process servers out after him, but by the time they located him, it was too late. The case had already been decided."

"And Tadeo lost his patent infringement case."

"You bet we lost. The whole case hinged on him."

"And it put Tadeo out of business."

"That's right. Tadeo felt that Woodruff had let him down, and of course he had. I think someone paid Woodruff to drop out of sight at the critical time."

"Who?" I asked.

Davenport shrugged.

"Would Blakeslee have done it?"

"He wouldn't be above it," Chris Davenport replied.

It was conjecture on the attorney's part, but it was worth following up on nonetheless. I nodded in approval as Big Al made a note of it.

"Who was the judge?" I asked.

"Kelley," Davenport answered. "Judge Chip Kelley. He's good. Tough but good."

"I know Judge Kelley," I said. "Tell us what you know about Bernice Oliver."

Davenport shook his head. "A kook, if you ask me. When I found her there working, I tried to tell her to go home, that the company's broke and nobody's going to pay her, but she was adamant, said no matter what, she'd stay and keep on working until they disconnect the phones at the end of the month."

"Why would she do that?" I asked.

Davenport shook his head. "I don't have any idea."

"Was there any hanky-panky going on between her and Tadeo?"

Chris Davenport grinned as though he found the very idea quite amusing. "Bernice Oliver? She doesn't seem like the type. Besides, Tadeo never struck me as being that desperate, if you know what I mean."

"When you talked to Mr. Kurobashi on Friday did he mention being in touch with Woodruff?"

This time Davenport frowned before he answered. "No. Why should he be in touch with Woodruff? I'd be surprised to hear there was any further contact between those two. Tadeo was a stubborn man, gentlemen, and once someone crossed him . . ."

"Like his daughter?"

"So you know about that? Yes, exactly. Once he wrote someone off, that was it."

As long as I was sending up a series of trial balloons, I figured I could just as well let go of all of them. "What about connections to organized crime?"

Davenport looked incredulous. "Tadeo and organized crime? Totally preposterous! You can't be serious."

"Do you have any idea what Mr. Kurobashi was working on just prior to his death?"

"No, not really. He was a secretive man. Small-time entrepreneurs often are. They invent something or discover something and then want to keep it all to themselves. They'd rather go out of business than have to give up control to an investor."

"Were there investors willing to step in and save MicroBridge?"

Abruptly, Davenport stood up, took an open briefcase from the credenza behind him, and began placing a series of file folders into it.

Questioning witnesses is very much like panning

for gold. You have to sort through a lot of water and sand before you see the glimmer of a trace of gold in the muck at the bottom of the pan, and this was nothing more than a glimmer, but a sudden need for physical action is often indicative that the questioning is coming too close to real nuggets of truth. If that was the case here, Christopher Davenport didn't want us any closer.

"There could have been," he said eventually, as he snapped the briefcase shut and spun the numbers on the combination lock. "But Tadeo wouldn't let me try to find any. Instead, he borrowed money on his own home to keep the company afloat. He kept it going far longer than anyone expected, but in the end it was like holding his finger in a dike. I tried to get him to see how unwise that was, to cut his losses. As I told you, Tadeo was a very stubborn man."

"Is it possible that Mr. Kurobashi might have stumbled onto some important discovery or process that he thought would turn things around?"

"It's possible. He hinted around about that some, but that's all. That's the other thing you have to understand about entrepreneurs. They're always incurable optimists who think the next thing down the pike is going to save their ass."

"What about the sword?"

"A sword? You mean like in Knights of the Round Table?"

"No," Big Al said, consulting his notes. "They call it a *tanto*, a samurai short sword, very old and very valuable. It looks more like a large knife than what we think of as a sword. Did he ever mention it to you?"

"Never."

"And you never saw one in his office, didn't know he owned such a thing?"

"No, I didn't, but you say it was valuable? How valuable?"

"Very," I replied.

"It's strange Tadeo never brought it up when we were going over the financial difficulties. If nothing else, it sounds like an asset that at least would have bought him a little more time."

I was listening intently to everything Davenport had to say, but in the back of my mind, I was still thinking about the wild card in the deck—Clay Woodruff.

"Where does Woodruff live?" I asked.

"Port Angeles," Davenport answered without the slightest hesitation. "In a place called the Ritz Hotel. He owns that and the tavern under it."

Glancing at his watch, a Rolex, Davenport grabbed the briefcase and swung it off his desk. "I'm sorry. It's late and I really must go. If you need more info, we'll have to arrange another meeting."

"Bum's rush again," Big Al said good-naturedly when we were once more in the elevator. "So what now?"

It was late, almost four. "I'll tell you what. You go check on the DataDump folks, and I'll head back to the department and do the paperwork."

Big Al's jaw dropped three inches. "You've got to be kidding. Since when do you do paperwork?"

"Since right now. When I finish, I'll go grab something at Vito's."

"How come?"

"Because that's where Chip Kelley hangs out."

Allen Lindstrom shook his head in mock disbelief. "You sure as hell won't get any argument from me. If you're doing paperwork, I'm by God taking you up on it. I'm outta here." And with that, he took off and left me standing on the sidewalk outside 1201 Third.

When I got back to the department, the fifth floor was relatively quiet. Working slowly, I hunted and pecked my way through the necessary forms and reports. Watty stopped by my desk just as I was finishing up. Naturally, with someone watching me, I screwed up.

"Get out of here," I said, handing him the stack of papers. "You always fuck up my typing."

He scanned through the reports. "How does it look?"

"Beats me. My best guess is that this Woodruff character over in Port Angeles could shed some light on all of it if we could just talk to him. I tried calling the number Mrs. Oliver gave us, but no one answered, and there's no listing for the Ritz Hotel."

Watty sighed and rubbed his chin. "Sounds like somebody'll have to take a run over there."

"That's about what I figured."

"By the way, George Yamamoto stopped by today. He wanted me to let you know that he's having a memorial service for Tadeo Kurobashi at four o'clock on Saturday afternoon."

"He is." So George Yamamoto was going ahead with a memorial service for his friend despite Machiko Kurobashi's express wishes to the contrary. "Where will it be?"

"In Waterfall Park at Main and Occidental. George said both he and Kurobashi lived right around there after the war."

While we talked, Sergeant Watkins had stepped back a pace or two. I stood up to leave as well, taking my jacket off the back of my chair. I tried to put it on, but the sleeve hung up on the splints. In order to untangle it, I had to reach up the sleeve with my other hand.

With Watty standing there watching my clumsy efforts, I felt like I was making a damned spectacle of myself. So I was already defensive *before* he opened his mouth to ask the question.

"When do you go back to the doctor to have those bandages changed? They look like hell."

"When I get around to it."

That kind of curt answer wasn't at all what Watty deserved, but he shrugged it off and walked away leaving me shamefaced and once more painfully aware of the constant throbbing in my fingers.

In the busy days since Monday, except for the inconvenience of zipping my pants or starting a car or putting on my socks and shoes, I had managed to stop focusing all my attention on my damaged hand. The steady pain had receded into the background of my consciousness along with the nagging worry of not knowing exactly how the accident had happened. But Watty's question had brought it all back to the forefront.

My reaction was strictly out of frustration and reflex. Without considering the consequences, after Watty left, I slammed my hand into the desk and then stood there in shock, almost doubled over by the pain. Amazed and humbled by the pain. I've been shot before without having it hurt that much.

Slinking out of the office, I climbed down the four flights of stairs to the ground level. From past experience, I suspected that my face was probably gray with pain, and I didn't want to have to explain it to whoever might be in the elevator.

I made it to the car and sat there for several minutes waiting for the pain to subside enough so I could start the car. What should I do? Go to another doctor? Which one? Where?

I gave up having a family physician when I gave up having a family. The times I've gotten hurt since, it's alway been on the job. The medics have dragged me down to Harborview Hospital and the Emergency Room folks have glued me back together. But I couldn't very well turn up at that same ER and say please fix this, because the questions on the form would be a nightmare: When did it happen? How did it happen? Who treated it initially?

It was a helluva lot easier to handle the pain than it would be to bluff my way through the goddamned form. Defeated, I reached through the steering wheel and used my left hand to turn the key in the ignition. Ignoring the pain as best I could, I headed for Vito's up on Madison, a restaurant and bar with the dubious distinction of being called the drinking man's annex to the King County Courthouse.

Vito's may not be the closest watering hole to the cop shop and the courthouse, but it's far and away the most popular. It's where the lawyers and judges and detectives all go to hang out and rub elbows and tip a few when work is over for the day.

Judge Chip Kelley and I go back a long way. When I was starting out on the force, he was a flunky in the King County prosecutor's office. For years, since long before he was a judge, Chip Kelley has carried an invisible but unbreakable lease on a table in the far back corner of Vito's bar. I recognized his unique laugh the moment I stepped through the door into the darkened room.

It was the middle of the after-work rush. The place was crowded, but Kelley and two of his compatriots were at the usual table, cackling together over some ribald joke. Kelley stopped laughing when he saw me.

"I'll be damned! If it isn't the old lonesome stranger himself, J. P. Beaumont. Long time no see, Beau. Sit down. What the hell happened to your hand?"

Without waiting for a response, Kelley stole a vacant chair from an adjoining table and shoved me into it, summoning the cocktail waitress with his other hand. "You still swilling that rotten Mac-Naughton's?" he asked.

The other questions hadn't merited answers. This one did. I gave the waitress a grateful nod while Kelley ordered another round for the whole table. Everybody else was drinking martinis.

"Hey, Beau, you know these two guys?"

I did, but he introduced us anyway. Chip Kelley was on a roll.

"So what brings you to this joint? I thought you ran more to the Doghouse these days."

"I came to see you," I said. "It's easier than trying to make an appointment."

The drinks came and he tipped his glass in my

direction. "*Salut*. Here's to not having to make appointments. So what can I do for you?"

One of the reasons I don't hang around Vito's anymore is that Chip can drink me under the table any day of the week and still sound sober as a judge, if you'll forgive the expression.

"I understand you were the judge in a patent infringement case that went to trial several months ago."

Kelley nodded. "Probably. Seems like a couple of those turn up every year. And if it's still in the appeals process, I may not be able to comment."

"Let me ask you about it in theoretical terms then, no names."

"All right."

Observing Vito's long-standing and inviolable rules of order and without ever leaving the table, the other two men drifted tactfully into a quiet discussion of golf scores, leaving us with as much privacy as if we had physically moved to another room.

"Go on," Chip urged.

"Let's suppose that this guy invented something on his own time while he was working for somebody else, and suppose he offered it to his employer. The employer didn't want it, in fact refused it outright, but when the poor schmuck who invented it began developing and marketing the product on his own, the former employer filed suit saying that the patent really belonged to him, that the guy had done the work while working as an employee on company time."

"So?" Chip asked.

"So eventually the poor schmuck loses in court. Damages, court costs, the whole ball of wax are awarded to the former employer. But supposing there was a witness to that same conversation between the schmuck and the employer, a witness who could testify to that effect, that the product had been offered to the employer and subsequently turned down, and that the development didn't happen during work hours."

"So what's the problem?"

"At the time of the trial, the witness was nowhere to be found."

Kelley considered the situation for a few moments. Finally he shrugged. "I don't know all the extenuating circumstances here, but off the cuff I'd say that without the witness, the schmuck would be SOL. With the witness, the case would probably go the other way. I would have dismissed it with prejudice so the ex-employer couldn't jack him around anymore. I take it this missing witness has now been found? Is he willing to testify?"

"I can't say."

"Well then, I don't know what the exact judgment was, but there may be nothing to stop the schmuck from reopening the case and filing a countersuit of his own."

"Yes, there is," I said.

"What's that?"

"He's dead."

"Oh." My answer had a visibly sobering effect on Judge Chip Kelley. "Maybe the heirs can file a suit, then," Kelley suggested after a moment. "It's been done."

"That's all I needed to know." I finished my drink and pushed back my chair.

"Hey, you can't go yet. You've only had one. Aren't you going to have something to eat?"

"I'm too tired to eat, and one drink is more than enough. Thanks for the help."

Ignoring Chip's squall of protest, I made my way out the door into the clear fall evening. It was a long way from Moscow, Idaho, to Vito's, and it had been a long, long day. All I wanted to do was spend a quiet evening at home in my recliner.

Dream on, you fool. I should have known better.

CHAPTER 13

MY HAND STILL HURT LIKE HELL AS I RODE UPSTAIRS IN the Belltown Terrace elevator. My plan was to go to bed early and try to get some sleep, but I knew that idea was screwed the minute the elevator door opened and I smelled the garlic.

Ames was inside my apartment and up to one of his culinary shenanigans. Several times now I've accused him of being a closet Italian with heavy investments in a multinational garlic-growers cartel. He denies it, but whenever Ralph Ames starts dabbling in the gourmet kitchen he helped design for me, he goes crazy with the garlic.

I stood outside the door for a moment, wondering if there was any way I could gracefully get out of dinner by pleading a combination of illness and fatigue. Then I heard voices. Not only was Ames cooking dinner, he had invited company.

Ralph popped his head out of the kitchen when he heard the door open. "There you are. I was hoping you'd get here in time to eat. Come on out to the kitchen. I want you to meet a friend of mine."

Plastering a reasonable facsimile of a smile to my face, I went into the kitchen disguised as Mr. Congeniality himself.

The place was in total uproar. Generally speaking, Ralph Ames is a very precise, well-contained individual, but he lets his hair down completely when he cooks Italian. His preferred method is to start with enough boiling water to deliver several babies. He continues from there, cutting and chopping with increasingly wild abandon. The majority of the ingredients end up in the pots, but debris tends to fall where it may and stay there.

Once the cooking is over, Ames has the enviable ability to turn out the lights in the kitchen, shut the door on the chaos, and go into the dining room, where he eats with obvious enjoyment, without giving the least thought to the disaster area he's left behind. My whole problem with cooking is that I hate cleaning up, and I never forget, not even for a minute, that the mess in the kitchen is sitting there, waiting for me. Waiting and congealing. I still don't have nerve enough to leave one of my cooking catastrophes for Florence Cooper, my cleaning lady, to straighten up.

Tonight Ames' culinary masterpiece was linguini primavera. The pasta had boiled over on the stove, leaving a huge dark brown stain across and around the burner. Both the pasta and the sauce had evidently progressed through a series of smaller pots to larger ones, so that the whole counter was littered with empty but nonetheless dirty cooking utensils.

And at the far end of the kitchen sat a man I didn't know, a man with a glass of wine in his hand.

He didn't sit so much as he lounged, his back against the partially opened kitchen window. He appeared to be about Ralph's and my age. His short gray hair was tightly permed into a frizzy halo. He wore a yellow silk shirt with the top two buttons unfastened, revealing an expanse of tanned chest as well as a single gold chain. His shoes were expensive and polished to a mirror shine. On his face was a look of bemused detachment as he observed Ralph's frenetic meal preparations.

Ames stopped in the middle of the room, waving a slotted spoon in one hand. "Beau, I'd like you to meet an old college chum of mine, Raymond Archibald Winter, III. This is my friend and client, Detective J. P. Beaumont."

Winter put down his wineglass, held out his hand, and grinned a white-toothed, wolfish grin. "How do you do, Detective Beaumont. My friends call me Archie. Any friend of Aimless is a friend of mine."

"Aimless?" I asked, puzzled.

"That's what we used to call old Ralphy here when we were in school together. He was always too damn serious. We tried to lighten him up a little, you know?"

I almost choked, stifling a hoot of laughter. "Did it work?"

Winter grinned again. "Not at all. At least not for him. Did for me, though. You should have turned the tables and called me that, Ralphy. I've been through at least a dozen careers since I left law school. Never gets boring that way, though. I'm still having fun."

Ralph Ames frowned as he stirred the bubbling pot of linguini. He seemed to be taking a dim view of his friend's teasing. He certainly didn't encourage it. "The mail's in on the table," he said. "Dinner will be ready in about fifteen minutes."

"Time enough to shower?" I asked.

"As long as you get a move on."

Suddenly I found myself looking forward to dinner. Anybody who could get away with calling Ralph Ames "Aimless" or "Ralphy" couldn't be all bad. With a cheery wave in Archibald Winter's direction, I said, "I'll be right back," and ducked out of the kitchen. I paused long enough to collect the mail, then headed for the shower, shuffling through the letters as I went.

They were mostly department-store bulk flyers with a small core of first-class mail, most of them bills. At the top of the stack was an envelope from Swedish Hospital. The next one came from a place called Orthopedics Associates with a street address on Madison. With a happy but silent "Eureka," I ripped open the envelope from the hospital. It was a bill all right, inarguably exorbitant, with a computer printout detailing emergency room charges, X-rays, and splints. The second one, equally outrageous, was from a doctor I had never heard of before, someone named Herman Blair, for professional services rendered.

Never in my life have I been so happy to receive two outrageously expensive bills. After smashing my hand on the desk, it had continued to throb without a hint of letting up. I was beginning to have a niggling worry in the back of my mind that maybe the problem with my hand was something more serious than I had supposed. That thought combined with the ongoing pain had finally convinced me that I would see a doctor the next day, no matter what. Now, thanks to the bills, I at least knew which doctor to call for an appointment.

Taking the telephone number from the top of the billing statement, I went to the bedroom phone and dialed. It was after five. Naturally, the doctor's office was closed, but his answering service took the call.

In theory, answering services are supposed to protect doctors and other important people from being pestered by insignificant people—patients in this case. The lady on the phone was determined to give me the brush off. I was equally determined not to be brushed. After all, I had been searching unsuccessfully for Dr. Blair for the better part of a week. In the end, my inherent stubbornness paid off.

"Give me your number," the woman snapped at last. "I'll see if the doctor can call you back."

He did. Within minutes, but he, like his answering service, was none too cordial.

"You know, Mr. Beaumont, you were supposed to be in my office early Tuesday morning to have those bandages changed and get the hematomas drilled. What happened?"

"I was out of town on a case," I said lamely. "Get what drilled?"

"Your subungual hematomas. That's what's causing all the pain. Drilling will relieve it. I couldn't do it the other night. They hadn't filled up that much yet."

"Filled? With what?"

"With blood. It's pooled under your nails just like I told you it would, remember?"

I didn't remember, but I said, "Right," and tried my best to make it sound convincing.

"So how bad is it?" Blair asked, after a pause.

Real men don't eat quiche, and they don't whine to their doctors, either. "Not that bad," I said.

"Can it wait until morning? Otherwise you're looking at another emergency room charge."

"It can wait."

"Be at my office at nine sharp tomorrow morning. We'll take care of it then. Meantime, take a couple of aspirin if you need to. By the way, who's your regular doctor?"

"I don't have one."

"A man your age ought to," he said. "See you tomorrow. Nine o'clock."

"Yes," I replied meekly. "I'll be there."

Feeling like I'd been thoroughly put in my place by Dr. Herman Blair, I climbed into the shower, got dressed, and finally ventured out into the dining room to see if dinner would be any less demeaning.

Somehow, the very word *Sotheby* exudes an aura of staid men wearing understated suits and conservative ties. Raymond Archibald Winter, III, with his yellow silk shirt and expensive gold chain, didn't at all resemble my idea of a Sotheby's oriental artifacts guru. He looked more like the Hollywood stereotype of a big-hitting movie producer.

He may not have looked the part, but Winter was obviously knowledgeable in the area of ancient Japanese artifacts. He spoke of them with the easy assurance of someone whose expertise is unassailable.

"It's a genuine Masamune all right," he said, holding a newly filled wineglass up to the light and gently swirling the golden liquid. We were drinking some kind of French wine whose name I couldn't pronounce and didn't recognize. I had one glass. It was very dry and seemed dangerously close to champagne. I worried about doing a repeat performance of Sunday's boondoggle.

"You've seen it then?" I asked.

Winter nodded. "Ralph here finagled an appointment with George Yamamoto this afternoon, right after he picked me up from Sea-Tac. Mr. Yamamoto was kind enough to show us the sword. Extraordinary, finding it this way. It's like having a long-lost Michelangelo turn up in some little old lady's attic."

He paused long enough to take a sip of wine. "I wouldn't say the sword is priceless. Everything has its price. But it is exceedingly valuable, and it certainly shouldn't be sitting on some shelf in George Yamamoto's property room. He's aware of the sword's value, of course, and he seems to be taking some extra precautions, but we all know that evidence rooms aren't nearly as secure as they ought to be."

"Not nearly," I agreed.

"You see," Winter continued, "we're talking about a museum-quality piece here, one that had long been thought lost. By rights it ought to be in a vault somewhere, preferably one that's climate and humidity controlled."

"You know about it then?" I asked. "I mean, about this piece in particular?"

I had declined a second glass of Winter's wine and had switched back to my usual regimen of MacNaughton's and water. I congratulated myself on learning from my mistakes for once. At least I was reaping some small benefit from my champagne-induced disaster.

"Let's just say the sword was thought to exist, was believed to exist. I'm relatively sure it's part of a set that belonged to a family named Kusumi, an old and much-honored samurai family, who evidently refused to relinquish their weapons and sword furniture when ordered to do so in the mid eighteen hundreds. And I can see why. As far as sword makers go, Masamune was the master. I certainly wouldn't have wanted to part with it."

"I know about Masamune," I said. Arching one eyebrow, Winter regarded me quizzically over the rim of his glass.

"Do you know about things samurai?" he asked.

"Not really. Only enough to be dangerous. Tell me more."

"My guess is that no one outside the immediate Kusumi family knew that the set still existed. The sword itself is over seven hundred years old, but I imagine the rosewood box dates from the time during the mid nineteenth century when the Kusumi family decided to conceal their treasures rather than give them up.

"You see, even though the handle design was lovingly copied on the cover of the box, the inlay work isn't nearly the same quality as that on the sword. In addition, a box like that would never have been part of traditional samurai sword furniture."

"How do you know this particular set belonged to that particular family?"

"There is still written record of the set being designed and forged by Masamune for Yoshida Kusumi. The record, in the samurai archives of the University of Tokyo, includes a complete description of the handle design, but the set itself didn't come to light until two years after the end of World War II, when a number of pieces were discovered buried in radioactive rubble at Nagasaki. Only the metal pieces remained. If there were other boxes like the one here in Seattle, they were destroyed in the firestorm that swept the city after the explosion."

"Nagasaki?" I blurted, remembering Machiko Kurobashi saying that she was originally from Nagasaki.

Winter looked at me questioningly. When I offered no explanation, he went on. "It's a miracle that the swords themselves weren't totally destroyed as well, although they were badly damaged. Once they were discovered, an extensive search was instituted to find any possible heirs, but as far as I know, no surviving family members were ever located. After undergoing decontamination, all the remaining pieces were reconditioned as much as possible and ended up at the Tokyo National Museum at Ueno.

"The curators there suspected that a matching *tanto* or short sword had existed at one time, but they assumed it had been lost if not earlier, then certainly at the time of the bombing."

"You're convinced then, that this is part of the same set?"

Winter nodded. "Of course I'm sure. I've seen the other surviving pieces in Japan. They're not in nearly as fine shape as this one, but it's clearly the same set. I have only one question. Why the devil is that *tanto* sitting in Dr. Yamamoto's evidence room?"

"It's part of a murder investigation," I explained. "It may not be *the* murder weapon, but it certainly was used to manipulate evidence at the scene, and that makes it part of the official investigation."

Winter waved his hand impatiently. "I understand that, Detective Beaumont, but how did it get here, to the States? How did it get from wartime Nagasaki to Seattle, Washington? Where has it been for the past forty plus years? And how did the dead man, this Kurobashi fellow, come to be in possession of it?"

I was struggling manfully to get a mound of slippery linguini to stay on my left-handed fork long enough to make the treacherous journey from plate to mouth. It wasn't working. I am not and never have been the least bit ambidextrous. Finally, disgusted with my clumsiness, I dropped my fork onto my plate and left it there. It was impossible for me to talk and manage the fork at the same time.

"Kurobashi's wife—" I stopped and corrected myself. "Kurobashi's widow is named Machiko. I have no idea what her maiden name was, but she did mention that she was originally from Nagasaki."

"I see," Winter said, nodding thoughtfully. "So

the sword could have been hers all along. Do you suppose she'd be interested in selling it?"

I remembered what Machiko had said about wanting the sword back, wanting it for Kimi.

"I wouldn't know about that," I said. "Once she gets it back, I believe her intention is to give it to Kimiko, her daughter, although it may not be that important to Kimi. According to her, she never saw the sword before the night of her father's death, never even knew it existed."

"Strange, wouldn't you say?" Winter asked.

"What do you mean?" I asked, although I had already reached the same conclusion myself.

"Why keep it hidden all this time? Even from close family members." Winter shook his head before adding, "Not only that, Ralph mentioned something about the Kurobashi family being in dire financial straits, that they were being forced to file bankruptcy proceedings. Keeping the sword hidden doesn't make sense when you consider how much the sword would have brought if they had sold it."

"How much would that be?" I asked.

Winter took a slow sip of wine before he answered. "It could be as much as several million," he said deliberately. "Especially if some of the museums get into a bidding war over it. But you still haven't told me how the sword came to be in this country in the first place."

"I don't know," I replied. "We'll need to ask Machiko about that."

"Where is she?"

"Over in eastern Washington."

"Do you think it would be possible for me to talk to her?" Winter looked at me appraisingly. "After all, if the mother does decide to put the sword on the market, I'd very much like to be involved. I can assure you, it would be beneficial for all concerned."

What he said made sense. Any way you sliced it, Machiko and Kimi Kurobashi were probably going to be in a bind for money. If they did decide to sell the sword, simply being represented by Sotheby's, one of the world's biggest and most respected dealers in fine arts, would automatically up the ante.

"I'll speak with her about it," I said. "She may be interested, but I don't know."

I picked up my fork and tried again. Winter paused with his own fork halfway to his mouth, watching my struggle. "What did you do, slam your hand in a door?" he asked.

"You must be psychic," I said, and let it go at that.

Before Ames had a chance to get in his two cents worth about my hand, Andrew Halvorsen rescued me from the table with a perfectly timed telephone call.

"They caught him," he announced triumphantly. "I just got word from a detective back in Schaumburg, Illinois."

"Caught who?"

"David Lions. He tried to buy a television set at a place called Woodfield Mall. They say it's close to the airport. The Visa people alerted the store as soon as they called in for credit approval. Lions made a run for it, but a security guard happened to be walking past in the mall. Lions practically fell into his arms."

"A television set?" I asked. "What the hell would he want with a television set?"

"Beats me. It was one of those big-screen color jobs, too. At least that's what the dick from Schaumburg told me. He called a few minutes ago looking for a rap sheet. I told him we didn't have one."

My first thought was for Dana Lions, David Lions' daughter, waiting at home in Kalama. By now her father had probably already called, asking her to post his bail.

"Have you talked to the daughter yet?" I asked.

Halvorsen paused. "No, not yet. I thought I'd let you do that since you were the one who talked to her to begin with."

"Gee thanks," I muttered. "That's big of you."

Minutes later, I was on the phone with Dana Lions, giving her the bad news. She took it stoically, like someone who has been through it all before, like someone far too familiar with the ropes when it comes to bailing a family member out of scrapes with the law.

"Thanks for calling and letting me know, Detective Beaumont. I'll phone back there right away and see what's what."

I was still sitting beside the telephone looking at my hand and feeling it throb when the phone rang. It was Dana Lions. Again.

"It's not my dad," she said, relief bubbling in her voice. "They arrested somebody else."

"Somebody else? Who?"

"I don't know, but the man they arrested is black. My father definitely isn't black."

"But he was using your father's credit card?"

"That's right. The guy finally admitted that he bought the card from someone selling stolen cards at the United Terminal in O'Hare. I don't understand, Detective Beaumont. What does it all mean?"

I had a pretty good idea what it meant, but I didn't want to go into it right then. Dana Lions was still nurturing a small spark of hope for her father. I refused to douse it with bad news until absolutely necessary.

"You'll let me know if you hear from him?" I asked.

"Sure will," she said.

I considered calling Halvorsen back to let him know what Dana had learned, but I decided against it. My hand was still throbbing like mad. Instead of having another drink of any kind, I took the aspirin Dr. Blair had recommended.

By this time, Ames and Winters had left the dining room and returned to the kitchen. Despite his silk shirt, Winters was soon up to his elbows in soap suds as he tackled the trail of cooking pots Ames had left in his wake.

They were both talking and scrubbing away, happy as two little clams. They didn't look as though they needed or wanted any help. I thanked Ames for dinner, wished them both a good night, and excused myself. Before I crawled into bed, I called Machiko Kurobashi at Honeydale Farm.

I more than half expected her to be in bed asleep, but she listened carefully to my halting explanation of who Archie Winter was and what he wanted. When I finished, her response wasn't what I expected, either.

"Have him call," she answered gravely. "We talk."

"I'll do that," I said.

Padding barefoot back down the hall to the almost clean kitchen, I handed a scrap of paper to Archie Winter. "Here's Mrs. Kurobashi's number," I said. "I told her what you wanted, and she said you're welcome to call."

With that, I returned to the bedroom and crawled into bed.

CHAPTER 14

I MAY HAVE BEEN IN BED, BUT I HARDLY SLEPT. I LAY there listening to the droning voices of Ames and Winter. At one Winter left to return to his hotel. At two, Ames turned off the music and went to bed in the guest room. By four in the morning, the throbbing in my hand had me wide awake and pacing the floor, wondering if I could last the five interminable hours until Dr. Blair's office opened. During that dark time, the long hours between then and sunrise, I managed to convince myself that the good doctor's telephone diagnosis of sub-whatever was incorrect and that I was really developing a bad case of blood poisoning.

Early morning is a good time for really creative worrying. I never did go back to sleep.

I was sitting alone at the dining room table and drinking my third cup of coffee when the phone rang at seven. It was Ron Peters, calling for the first time since he and Amy had left to go on their honeymoon. Amy had insisted that the girls and their baby-sitter, Mrs. Edwards, go along on the trip. She said that since they were all going to live together as a family, a trip to the Oregon Coast would be a good way of getting started. That wasn't my idea of a perfect honeymoon, but from the animated sound of Peters' voice, they were having a great time.

"Did I wake you?" Peters asked.

"No. I was already up and drinking coffee."

"I should have called earlier—in the week, I mean—but we've been having too much fun. By the way, how are the fingers? Heather wanted me to ask. She's been worried sick about it."

Heather knew about my fingers, too? Did every goddamned person in the whole world know about my fingers but me?

"They're giving me a little bit of trouble," I admitted reluctantly. "As a matter of fact, I have an appointment to see the doctor today."

"I hope it's nothing serious," Peters said.

"Naw," I replied, with as much casual unconcern as I could muster despite the hours of worry. "I'm sure it isn't. When are you coming home?"

"Saturday night at the latest," he replied. "The girls have to be back in school by Monday. We've kept them out a full week as it is. It'll take all day Sunday to get squared away, to get ready for work and school."

"Call me when you get in."

"Will do. Anything doing at work?" Peters asked.

Ron Peters had been kicked upstairs. His new position in the media relations department had him rubbing shoulders with nothing but polished brass, big shots, and members of the press. I could hear the frustration in his voice and knew he missed the real world of the fifth floor and the easy camaraderie that goes along with being a detective.

"We're working the Kurobashi case," I said.

"I read about that one," Peters returned. "It was big enough that it made the regional section of the *Oregonian*. It sounds interesting."

For the next few minutes I forgot about my fingers while Peters and I discussed the case. Talking things over with him always helps clarify my own thinking. He agreed with my conclusion that things didn't look very good for David Lions.

"Have you talked to anyone who's working on the Lions case in Illinois?" Peters asked.

"Not yet, but that's a good suggestion. I should do it now. Call Schaumburg before the rates change."

"I'll let you go then," Peters said. "Take care of yourself, and those fingers too. Heather feels terrible about it, even though we've all told her it was an accident. She's afraid you're mad at her."

"Tell her not to worry. She's still my favorite toothless kid."

Peters laughed. "Right. I'll do that."

Minutes later I was talking to a lieutenant named Alvin Grant in the Detective Division of the Schaumburg, Illinois, police department. He knew all about the phony David Lions.

"He's gone. His lawyer came in and bailed him out."

"Did he tell you how he came to have the card?" I asked.

"Sure. Said he bought it for fifty bucks from some dude at the airport."

"Did he say what this guy looked like?"

"It wasn't the real David Lions, if that's what you're thinking," Grant said. "We talked to Dana Lions and got a complete description of her father. I talked to a Detective Halvorsen from out there in your neck of the woods as well. Believe me, this character isn't your David Lions. No way."

"What did he look like?"

"The one who sold the card? Fairly tall, good-looking, dark. Wore gloves." From Grant's description the guy sounded a whole lot like Pamela Kinder's self-styled God's gift to women.

"While he was in custody, we managed to convince the little puke that he needed to do a composite drawing of the guy who unloaded the card," Grant continued. "He had to finish before we let him out. I offered to FAX it to Halvorsen, but he said the resolution on their machine isn't very good. So I'm sending it FedEx. He said you might want a copy as well."

"I do," I said. "Send it the same way. To my attention at Seattle P.D. They'll see that I get it."

On my way to Dr. Blair's office, I called Big Al on the car phone to tell him I'd be late. At 8:15, a full forty-five minutes early, I was sitting in the waiting room of Orthopedic Associates, conscious of nothing but the throbbing pain under my bandage. A brusque, businesslike nurse took me into a treatment room at 8:55 and expertly removed the bandages and splints, clicking her tongue in disapproval at the grimy condition of the bandage.

She left the room briefly, and for the first time, I got a look at my fingers. They were ugly, more purple than black and blue, and wildly swollen. The nails were blackened by the pools of blood trapped beneath them. The nurse came back in and caught me examining my nails.

"Pretty bad, aren't they? Wait a few days until the swelling goes down. They'll look like a matched set of pancake turners."

There's nothing like a little cheer and comfort from a lady in white.

When Dr. Blair finally appeared, he looked a whole lot more like Santa Claus than some of the department store models I've seen lately, but personality-wise, he was anything but jolly, and certainly no better than his surly nurse. He studied my fingers through thick bifocals.

"What's the matter with them?" I asked.

"Nondisplaced ungual tuft fractures," he said.

"What's that?"

He looked up at me, briefly meeting my gaze. "They're broken," he said with no trace of a smile. He turned to the nurse. "Bring me a paper clip, would you please?"

"A paper clip?" I yelped. That didn't sound very medicinal to me. "What are you going to do?"

"Drill 'em," he relied casually. "Like I told you on the phone. It's the blood under your nails that's causing the pain."

He turned to a small cupboard beside me, reached into a drawer, and brought out a cigarette lighter.

"What's that for?" I asked warily.

Dr. Blair didn't answer. The nurse returned to

the treatment room and silently handed him a paper clip. He straightened it with utmost concentration. Once it was flat, he held it with a hemostat and began heating the straightened end with the lighter. When the end of the paper clip was glowing red hot, he took hold of my hand and pressed the hot metal to one of my blackened nails. I winced, expecting some pain while the paper clip sank easily through the nail as though it were melting plastic.

When the hole went all the way through, the trapped blood squirted into the air. "It doesn't hurt because the blood cushions the pain," he explained.

I couldn't help wishing he had told me that *before* the operation rather than after it. I may be a homicide detective, and legend has it that homicide detectives are all tough macho types, but I was feeling more than a little queasy by the time he finished burning through the third nail.

When he was done with the last one, Dr. Blair retrieved the splints and began to rebandage my hand. "Just how much do you drink, Detective Beaumont?" he asked.

"I beg your pardon?"

"How much?"

"No more than anybody else."

"When I talked to you on the phone last night, you sounded as though you had never heard that these hematomas needed to be drilled. And a few minutes ago, you seemed surprised to find out that the fingers were broken. We went over all of that Sunday night. In fact, I gave you a piece of paper, a form with written follow-up instructions on it."

"I don't remember seeing it," I said.

"You stuck it in the pocket of your tux."

I remembered the tux then, a rental that had been returned with the other wedding party duds on Monday morning. The Belltown Terrace concierge had handled the transaction.

"No wonder I couldn't find it," I said. "The paper must have gotten sent back to the rental company."

Dr. Blair wasn't paying much attention to my excuses. Finished with the bandage, he said, "Take off your shirt, loosen your belt, and lie down here on the table. I want to check something."

"Look," I objected, "I broke my fingers, not my ribs."

But you don't argue with doctors, or at least I don't. Obligingly, I lay down on the table and he poked me in the gut.

"Did you know your liver is enlarged?" he asked after a few moments of prodding.

"My what?"

"Your liver's down three centimeters. How long's it been like that?"

"I never knew it was," I said.

"You don't have a regular doctor?" he asked again.

"No."

He picked up a pad of paper and jotted a name and phone number on it. "This fellow's an internist who works right here in the building. His name is Dr. Wang. Go see him. Today. He'll need to do a complete workup on you. In the meantime, how long ago did you have a tetanus shot?"

"I don't remember."

"If you don't remember, it's been too long. I'll send the nurse back in to give you one, and then you go on upstairs to see Wang. I'll call ahead and make sure they work you in."

I sat still long enough for the shot, but I didn't go see Dr. Wang. Instead, I went out to the parking garage, sat in my car, and brooded. I've never liked being *told* what to do, and Dr. Herman Blair was one bossy son of a bitch. I was offended by the way he had treated me. He had acted as though my forgetting his damned follow-up form was some sort of major crime.

I was offended, but worried too. More pissed than worried. Where the hell did some goddamned finger doctor get off telling me that my liver was enlarged? Enlarged liver? Me? Bullshit! Except for my hand, I was healthy as a horse.

And even as I sat there, I began to notice that my hand didn't hurt nearly as much as it had. Ugly as it had looked, Dr. Blair's drilling and blasting must have done some good. In fact, now that I thought about it, my whole hand was feeling much better.

And so, thumbing my nose at Dr. Blair, and to prove both to him and to myself that he was dead wrong, I started the car and drove to work. Let Dr. Blair put that in his pipe and smoke it.

Big Al was on his phone and waiting on hold when I came into our cubicle.

"What'd the doc say?" he asked. "How're the fingers?"

"They're broken," I said.

He looked at me and shook his head. "I knew that, for Chrissake! The doc told us that in the emergency room the other night. What the hell do you think I am, deaf or just plain stupid?"

I sat down at the desk and thumbed through the collection of inter-office junk mail that had collected in the in basket during my absence. Whoever Al was waiting for came back on the phone. While that person talked, Big Al nodded from time to time. Eventually he scribbled a note on a piece of paper and pushed it across the desk to me. On it were printed the letters MS.

I looked at the note and tried to make sense of it. Ms. who? The note meant nothing to me. Finally Al hung up the phone.

"What's this?" I asked.

"That's what's the matter with Bernice Oliver's husband. MS—multiple sclerosis. He's had it for years, and he's gradually getting more and more crippled up."

"Who were you talking to?"

"Some lady at RFLink. Mrs. Motormouth. I called to find out when Mrs. Oliver left there, and this woman was an hour-long fountain of information. She's been with Blakeslee for years. She told me that Mrs. Oliver gave her two weeks notice the same day Tadeo Kurobashi got his walking papers. It evidently created quite a stir around there at the time. Interesting, don't you think?"

"It's something to check into. What about Data-Dump?"

"They weren't open last night, either, and there's no answer on the phone this morning. What say we drive out there right now and have a look-see?"

"Sounds like a plan," I said.

DataDump was located in a tired one-story building off N.W. 65th on Cleopatra Avenue. From the looks of it, the building contained both business and living quarters. The door was locked. An orange-and-black closed sign was tucked in the corner of one window.

We looked around for vehicles, expecting to see DataDump's mobile shredder parked somewhere nearby, but there was no sign of it. In fact, there were no visible vehicles of any kind parked near the modest storefront building. Inside, however, we could hear the steady patter of a droning television game show.

There was a bell beside the door. Big Al rang it with a heavy hand. We waited a minute or so before he rang it again, even more insistently. This time, the television set switched off and the curtain behind the front window rustled as someone peeked out at us.

A moment later, the door was flung open. "Who are you and what do you want?"

The woman at the door was probably only in her thirties, but she looked world-weary and bedraggled. Her long hair was lanky and unkempt with a streak of gray running through it that was far too plain to be a dye job. She wore a faded bathrobe and scruffy slippers. Her mouth had a hopeless downturned cast to it. "Can't you read the sign? It says we're closed."

"We're police officers," Big Al said.

"Cops!" She jumped as she spat out the word and would have slammed the door in our faces if Big Al hadn't caught it and held it open. Police officers weren't the lady's favorite people.

"Are you the owner of DataDump?" Big Al asked.

She nodded.

"We'd like to talk to you then, if you have a minute."

She stepped aside, letting the door open a little wider but not inviting us inside. "What about?" she asked glumly.

"A company called MicroBridge."

Her eyes dilated at the word. It takes real fear to make eyes do that in broad daylight.

"What about it?"

"You had someone working at a place called MicroBridge on Sunday night this last week, didn't you?"

"My husband, Dean."

"Would it be possible to talk to him?"

"He's gone."

"Do you know where he is or when he'll be back?"

"No." We were getting answers, but we weren't getting much information, and we wouldn't either, not as long as she was scared to death. Somehow I had to relieve her fear enough so we could see what was behind it.

"Do you mind telling us how you got the Micro-Bridge job?" I asked.

"He called," she said.

"Who did?"

"The owner. A guy named Kurobashi. He called Friday night after we were closed and left a message on the machine. Wanted us to do a job on Sunday. Offered to pay double."

"Double?"

"You heard me, mister. That's what I said." She seemed to have summoned a fresh supply of courage from somewhere deep within her. She looked me squarely in the face. "Dean didn't kill nobody," she announced flatly.

With that, she turned her back on us and walked away, moving to a battered desk across the room. She seated herself behind it.

"Might just as well come on in," she said wearily. "No sense standin' around in the doorway."

"What do you mean, 'Dean didn't kill nobody'?"

"That guy was already dead when Dean found him. He didn't do it. You've got no right to chase after him."

"We just want to talk to your husband," I said quietly. "To ask him some questions."

"Sure you do," she said, sounding unconvinced. She plucked a cigarette from an open pack of Marlboros on the desk, lit it, and dropped the match into a heaping, stale-smelling ashtray. She took a long drag on the cigarette, and her face hardened.

"Don't you go fuckin' with me, mister. I'm nobody's dummy. It's just like he said would happen, that you'd come here lookin' for a way to pin it on him."

"You're saying that your husband didn't kill him, but that he saw the dead man?"

"That's right."

Big Al had extracted his notebook from his jacket pocket and was starting to jot down the information. "What's your name please?" he asked.

She jerked her eyes in his direction. "Chrissey," she answered. "Chrissey Morrison." There was a note of defiance in the way she said her name.

"Did your husband say what time it was when he

found the body?" I asked, trying to keep from saying anything that might sound accusatory.

"No."

"When did he tell you this—after he got home?"

She nodded.

"What time was that?"

Chrissey Morrison shrugged. "Midnight, one o'clock. I don't know for sure. I was asleep."

"He told you, but he didn't report it to the police? Why not?"

Tears sprang to Chrissey's eyes. "He was scared, that's why."

"Scared of the dead man?" I asked.

She turned and looked at me. The defiance drained away, leaving her haggard and hollow-eyed. "Of you," she answered.

"Of me? Or you mean of cops?"

She nodded. "Of cops. Of *all* cops. Dean already done some time. He was scared shitless that if he reported it . . ."

"What was he in for?"

Regaining control, she blew a languid plume of smoke into the air. "Drugs," she answered casually.

And suddenly I knew where I had seen that worn, dispirited look before, in the wives and girlfriends who follow their menfolk to prison and who live as outcasts in the small towns outside the prison walls, their own lives on hold until the husbands are released.

Chrissey Morrison was a survivor, but there was no dignity in it, no victory. Dean was out now, and they were trying to go on, but his past still cast a shadow over everything they did. I didn't know Dean Morrison, but I felt sorry for his wife.

"Tell us exactly what Dean told you," I urged.

"He was there late afternoon and evening. Musta started about five o'clock or thereabouts. He said about nine or so he finished and come back to the office after runnin' the shredder and found him like that, on the floor with a big old ashtray upside his head." She paused. "From the way he was layin', Dean knowed right away he was dead."

"What happened then?"

"Dean said he started to call the cops, but changed his mind and came home. He didn't want to get involved, figured they'd find a way to blame him for it. When I told him he should report it, he got mad as hell. He jumped in the truck and took off. I ain't seen him since."

"Do you have any idea where he is? We just want to talk to him, to ask him some questions."

"No. He hasn't called or nothin'. I thought maybe he'd be back today, bein's it's our anniversary and all, but he ain't. Maybe he won't never come back."

"We could put out a description of the truck," I offered. "We could probably find him that way."

She cringed visibly at the prospect. "Don't do that. Please don't do that. He'd think you were arrestin' him and I don't know what would happen. He didn't do nothin'. Just let him come home on his own."

"Did he tell you anything else about MicroBridge? Did he see anyone there? Talk to anyone?"

"He said a woman come in while he was there, a young gal. He said he thought she was the dead guy's daughter. Before he was dead. Dean said they started out talkin' real nice like and ended up fightin' somethin' terrible."

"Did he tell you what they were fighting about?"

"No. He said later on he thought he heard a car drive away while he was out in the truck. He figured that was her leavin'. When he come back to the office to drop off the bill and the bags, that's when he found the body."

"After the daughter left?" Big Al asked.

Chrissey nodded. My mind caught hold of the word *bags*. I didn't remember seeing any.

"What bags?" I asked.

"The bags of confetti. Our shredder makes confetti out of all them records and files and floppy disks that people want to get rid of. We always bring the bag back to the owner so he can be sure it's properly disposed of. That way there's never no question about what happens to it."

"How big was this bag?" Big Al asked.

The woman looked at him. "Not bag," she corrected. "Bags. Musta been several. Dean always takes along a big roll of them fifty-gallon trash bags. I don't know how full they was, or how many. Depends on how much got shredded."

"You're sure he said 'bags' plural?" I asked.

"That's right. Said they was too heavy to carry, so he dragged 'em back in from the truck on a cart, a little handcart. When he finished, he called to the guy, but there was no answer. He said he looked around the rest of the buildin' but couldn't find nobody else, so he come back to leave the cart and the bill there in the office. That's when he found the body."

"What did he do then?"

"Ran, I guess. Took off. He was so scared he left the cart right there where it was, and the bill too. Ran back to the truck and drove away. He went to a tavern a few blocks away and sat there and had himself a couple beers to calm himself down. Then he got to thinkin' that maybe you cops would come lookin' for him, so he went back, thought he'd get the bill and the cart, but the door to the dock was closed and locked. He couldn't get back inside."

I glanced at Big Al. Bernard Rennermann had said the door to the loading dock was open. Not only that, Big Al and I had been all over the MicroBridge plant the morning Tadeo Kurobashi's body was found, and neither one of us had seen a trace of a cart with trash bags full of shredded confetti. Or an ashtray either.

"Tell us about the confetti. What's it like?"

"Like confetti. Everybody's seen confetti."

"I know what it looks like, but it wasn't there when we got there. Why would someone take it? Could they put the pieces back together and tell what was on it?"

She shook her head. "No way. It'd be like a million-piece jigsaw puzzle."

Chrissey Morrison watched us disinterestedly, with the air of someone too tired to care and too broken to lie. I decided to press the advantage.

"What did your husband get sent up for?"

Her gaze became brittle. "I already told you. Drugs.

He got rehabilitated in jail. Been straight ever since he got out."

"Did he ever steal anything, Mrs. Morrison?"

"No." Just as I expected, her answer was too quick, too definitive, too defensive.

Playing for time, leaving her to squirm, I ran my finger along the marred edge of her wooden desk for several long seconds. "Would it be safe to assume that you and your husband don't make a lot of money in this business?"

"We make enough to get by," she said. "We pay our bills."

"But it's not easy, is it?"

She studied me warily as if trying to sniff out whatever trap I might be setting for her. "No," she answered finally. "It ain't."

"What if your husband happened across something very valuable, an ancient sword that was just lying there free for the taking? Would he have picked it up?"

"He didn't say nothin' about somethin' like that." Her voice was tight, verging on panic.

"A sword was found with the body," I said, "so we know he didn't take it."

"Then why're you askin' me about it?"

"What do you think would have happened if he had seen it, though? Would he have taken it?"

"I don't understand . . ."

"Would he?" I insisted. "If he had seen it, would he have picked it up?"

She dropped her eyes. "A fancy sword? Probably. Dean'd know how to fence somethin' like that. He got sent up for drugs because that's the only thing they charged him with."

I looked at Big Al. He was nodding.

She stood up, her face slack with despair. "You better go now. I don't want to talk no more. If he calls me, maybe I can make him turn himself in."

When she said that, I realized that Chrissey Morrison still thought her husband was under suspicion.

"Chrissey, listen very carefully. As I told you, we know your husband didn't take the sword, and we're pretty sure he didn't kill anybody, either."

She stared at me blankly. I still wasn't getting through. Chrissey Morrison was a whole lot more loyal than she was smart.

"Are you listening to me?" I demanded.

She frowned. "If Dean didn't take nothin', and if he didn't kill nobody, then why're you hasslin' me like this?"

"You're sure he didn't say anything at all about a sword being there with the body?"

"No, goddamnit, an ashtray. Don't you listen to nothin'?"

"But no sword."

"I already tol' you."

"Maybe you didn't understand me the first time. This sword we're talking about was with the body when we found it, so if your husband didn't see one, then the killer may still have been there at the same time your husband was. And that's why we have to talk to him the moment he shows up. He may have seen or heard something that would help us."

"You mean you don't think he did it?"

She had finally gotten the message. "No, but he may have seen whoever did." I handed her one of my cards with my home number scribbled on the back. "Will you have him call us?"

She crushed the card in her hand and nodded wordlessly. For the second time, tears welled in her eyes.

We got up to leave. I paused in the doorway. "When you see your husband, you might tell him from me that he's damn lucky to be alive."

"I'll tell him," she whispered. "I sure enough will."

CHAPTER 15

"TELL ME JUST THIS ONE THING," BIG AL SAID, AS WE climbed into the car for the return drive to the department. "How the hell does someone who got sent up for drugs manage to get licensed and bonded to run a shredding company?"

"Don't ask," I responded. "You don't want to know and neither do I."

"Are you going to head on over to Port Angeles today?" he asked.

Baseball teams have designated hitters. In Big Al's and my partnership, I'm the designated traveler. Allen Lindstrom lives to eat, and he's especially partial to his wife's brand of home cooking. He doesn't like to go anywhere if he can't be back in time for dinner. Other than Ralph Ames, I've seldom met a bachelor whose dinners were worth going home for. Mine certainly aren't, so if traveling is optional, I go and Big Al stays home.

"That's the plan," I said, except the plan didn't work according to schedule. Going to Port Angeles to see Clay Woodruff that Thursday afternoon got shoved aside by something else.

Before we made it all the way inside the garage at the Public Safety Building, we were dispatched back out and sent to one of the city's better-known crack houses over on East Yesler. There, sometime during the night, in a filthy apartment that reeked of urine and vomit and human feces, a young hotshot drug addict named Hubert Jones had OD'd on heroin. He had fallen onto a bare mattress on the floor in one corner of what passed for a living room—a dying room in this case—and had been left lying where he fell. It was morning before any of his drugged-up pals bothered to call in a report.

The dead man's driver's license revealed that he had turned twenty-one just two months earlier. When we started asking questions about him and about what had happened during the night, nobody in the house knew anything, heard anything, or saw anything.

These were people who had fried their brains on drugs but whose bodies hadn't yet given up the fight. From what we could ascertain, Hubert Jones had died alone in a room filled with at least two dozen partying zombies, none of whom had bothered to notice. With cretins like that for friends, Hubert Jones had no need of enemies.

It's hard for cops to get emotionally involved in cases like that. It's hard to care. We all get them, though, and far too often. With anti-drug hysteria running at a fever pitch, police jurisdictions all over the country, hounded by the press, are under tremendous pressure to *do* something. Exactly what, nobody's sure.

And so, when another case crops up, we go through the motions. We ask all the usual questions and write down the usual non-answers. We visit the grieving next-of-kin, usually and painfully the parents, and do what we can, with our questions and our forms, to make sense out of the tragedies of their children's amputated lives. Sometimes we find out who's at fault; more often, we don't. When we're finished, we go home or else we move on to the next case. After a while, all OD's look alike, and it's hard to give a rat's ass. You're just grateful as hell that it isn't your own kid being packed off to the morgue.

On that particular day, Hubert Jones' squalid death took precedence over Tadeo Kurobashi's murder, over my going to Port Angeles to talk with Clay Woodruff. More than the critical forty-eight hours had passed since Tadeo's death, and the odds against our actually finding his killer were going up exponentially.

By the time we finished the next-of-kin visit, it was quitting time, and quit we did. Hubert Jones' wretched life and meaningless death sure as hell weren't worthy of our working overtime. All I wanted to do was go home and put my feet up.

My emotional battery had just about run down. The days of almost round-the-clock work and concentration had drained me, and I found myself filled with a vague sense of uneasiness. It wasn't anything physical. Thanks to Dr. Blair, my hand was feeling much better. There was, however, on the periphery of my mind, the nagging knowledge that I hadn't done as I'd been told and gone to see Dr. Wang.

Sitting in the recliner, I noticed how quiet the apartment was. Far too quiet. Ames had left a message on the answering machine saying that he and Winter were driving over to eastern Washington to visit with Machiko Kurobashi at Honeydale Farm. I missed the kind of creative uproar that seems to accompany Ralph Ames wherever he goes. And I missed having Peters' kids popping in and out unannounced in hopes of snagging some forbidden treat. And I missed having someone there to talk to. And I was restless as hell.

About six, I picked up the phone, dialed the Mercer Island Police Department, and asked to be put through to the chief. The words *police chief* didn't used to make me think of sex. Ever. But that was before I got to know Marilyn Sykes. Before I *really* got to know her.

Mercer Island is one of Seattle's suburban neighbors, an independent bedroom community in the middle of Lake Washington with its own city government. Marilyn Sykes, the Mercer Island police chief, and I have a sometime thing going. Like me, she works too much and plays too little. She answered the phone in her office on the second ring.

"It's six o'clock. Why are you still working?"

"Do you have any better ideas?"

"Actually I do. What are you having for dinner?"

She laughed. "Lean Cuisine. Again. As usual."

"How about leftover linguini primavera?"

"At your house? If you've got leftovers, that must mean Ralph Ames is still in town."

"In Washington, but not in town."

"Is that a hint?"

"An invitation," I corrected.

"Are you sure you're up to it? How are the fingers?"

The damn fingers again! "Now that they've stopped hurting, they're fine," I answered. "Believe me, I never felt better."

"So I don't need to bring over a pot of chicken soup?"

"No. Your toothbrush."

"I'll be there in twenty minutes," she said.

And she was. That's one of the reasons I like Marilyn Sykes. She doesn't require engraved invitations or lots of advance notice.

We never did get around to the linguini. When I woke up at six o'clock on Friday morning, Marilyn was plastered against my back, one hand wrapped around my middle, snoring softly. I felt the soft swell of breast against the skin of my shoulder blade and the arousing tickle of her pubic hair against my butt.

We've been around one another enough now that I no longer wake up in a blind panic, trying desperately to figure out who's in bed next to me. I know upon waking and without looking that it's Marilyn, and I'm grateful to have her there. We've never discussed the fact that she snores. I probably do too.

I lay there for a while, delighted to notice that my fingers weren't throbbing. Between Marilyn's capable ministrations and Dr. Blair's red-hot paper clip, I was feeling a whole lot better. A gentle euphoria slipped over me as I relived the previous evening's activities. Neither Marilyn nor I had anything to apologize for in the screwing department. On that score alone, I felt downright terrific. In fact, the more I thought about it, the more I thought Dr. Blair must have had his wires crossed. It wasn't possible for someone who felt this good to be sick. Enlarged liver, my ass! Enlarged something else.

Marilyn stirred in her sleep. A hand grazed my chest.

"Awake?" I asked, turning to face her.

"Mmmmmm," she answered.

I couldn't tell if that meant yes or no. "Which is it?" I asked.

"Depends on the question."

She snuggled comfortably against my chest, nuzzling into the curve of my neck. Totally un-police chief like behavior.

"What time do you have to be at work today?" I asked.

"Eight. I told them last night that I might be running late."

"Oh no, you won't. I have to be at work at eight, too. Do you want breakfast?"

"Not exactly," she said.

"Me neither," I said, easing myself on top of her. She pulled my face down to hers and gave me a lingering kiss. A demanding kiss.

When I drew back from her lips, Marilyn's eyes were open, and she was smiling. "Good morning," she whispered.

"Don't talk," I said, and buried myself inside her, which is why, without ever having breakfast, I was ten minutes late to work and Marilyn Sykes was twenty. The good thing about being chief of police is that not many people have nerve enough to ask a police chief where she's been or what she's been doing, and even if they had asked, Marilyn Sykes is the type who probably would have told them.

I wasn't that lucky. Big Al was waiting for me, and so was Sergeant Watkins.

"You working banker's hours these days?" Watty demanded.

Watty and I have had numerous run-ins of late, particularly since my series of hassles with Paul Kramer, one of the newer detectives on the squad. I'll admit, I haven't been busting my butt to mend fences, but then neither has Watty.

"Doctor's orders," I answered with a tiny white lie, and Watty didn't question it. With a disgusted shrug of his shoulders, he walked away.

"I've got a message here for you," Big Al said. "George Yamamoto wants to see you right away."

"Where are you going?"

"To see Captain Powell."

"What about?"

"Maxwell Cole is doing a feature on Hubert Jones' mother. He wants to interview one of the detectives. Powell says I'm elected."

"Thank God for small favors," I responded.

Maxwell Cole is a longtime acquaintance of mine, a crime reporter turned columnist, whose profession naturally puts him at odds with cops in general and me in particular. We can't be in the same room together without setting off explosions. Powell probably figured, and rightly so, that any interview Maxwell Cole did with me would not reflect favorably on the Seattle Police Department.

Counting my blessings, I dashed down the stairway and into the crime lab to talk with George Yamamoto. As soon as I saw him, I knew something was wrong. George was sitting alone at his desk, staring at his phone. I knocked on his door frame twice before he heard me and looked up, his narrow face drained and haggard.

"Come in," he said, motioning wearily. "Come in and close the door."

"What's the matter, George? You look beat."

He cocked his head to one side. The slightest hint of a sardonic smile played around the corners of his lips. "Beaten? Maybe I am. Isn't that Ralph Ames a friend of yours?"

"Yes."

"A good poker player?" Yamamoto asked.

I shrugged. "I wouldn't know about that. I don't play poker."

George nodded wisely. "I do. He's a good bluffer. I believe I've just been blackmailed, Detective Beaumont, and unless I'm sadly mistaken, your friend Ralph Ames is behind it."

"Ames? Blackmail? No way." I almost laughed aloud, but George's coldly humorless expression stifled the urge.

"There are many degrees of blackmail, Detective Beaumont, and this is probably fairly benign, but it's blackmail nonetheless."

"Jesus Christ," I groaned. "What the hell is going

on? I don't understand any of this. And how you got the crazy idea that Ralph Ames is behind it—"

"He is," George interrupted. "Ames and that Winter fellow."

"What could Ralph Ames or Archie Winter possibly have on you?"

"Not them," Yamamoto said quietly. "Machiko."

"This doesn't make sense."

"Ames and Winter came here yesterday wanting to see the sword, and I showed it to them. Winter has solid credentials. He agreed with me that the sword is a genuine Masamune. Now, this morning, I have a call from Machiko Kurobashi telling me that if I don't release the sword to her at once, she'll go to the media with the story."

"What story?"

"Conflict of interest. The newspapers will lap it up. She'll tell them how I'm keeping the sword because of the long-standing feud between us."

"But how can she get away with that if it's not true?"

George Yamamoto leaned back in his chair, his fingertips templed in front of his nose. "But that's where you're wrong, Detective Beaumont. It is true. I thought the sword was Tadeo's. One of the reasons I didn't want to release it to her is that I didn't think she deserved to touch it. Now Winter tells me the sword is rightfully hers. Her maiden name was Kusumi."

I nodded. "I thought as much when Winter was talking about it the other night, when he told me that the other matching pieces had been found in the ruins of Nagasaki."

"What exactly do you know about Machiko's background?" George asked.

"Not much. Only what you told me, that she came to this country as a war bride, an occupation bride really, and that she married Tadeo after her first husband died."

"She was a whore!" George Yamamoto declared vehemently, slamming his fist into his desktop. "Machiko Kurobashi was a no-good worthless whore!"

For a long moment it was silent in George Yamamoto's small private office. In the outer lab, beyond the closed door, humming voices droned and telephones rang faintly. No one beyond the confines of his private office seemed aware of the outburst.

"You don't know that for sure, do you, George?"

He nodded. "Yes, I know it for sure. I told you before about Tomi, my sister. When Machiko showed up out of nowhere and took Tadeo away, I wanted to find out about her. I had friends who were able to check into her background. They told me she was working the streets in Tokyo when she met and married her first husband. I reported what I had found out to Tadeo, but he said it didn't matter. He married her anyway."

George swung around in his chair and stared angrily out his office window, a dingy pane of water-splotched glass overlooking Third Avenue.

"I've run this department for years without a hint of scandal," George said slowly, "and as long as I give her back the sword, that will continue to be true. No scandal. No problem. She claims she needs to borrow it for a day or two."

"And if you don't let her have it?"

"She goes to the papers."

"It does sound like blackmail," I conceded, "but she can't prove it."

"She won't have to. Newspapers don't require proof."

"Does she know about the memorial service?"

George nodded his head. "I told her. She didn't say anything about it."

"But she isn't coming?"

"No."

Dozens more questions swirled in my head, but they could wait. Between asking then and asking later, I chose later. George was having a tough enough time as it was. I got up, walked to the door, and opened it.

"Will you be coming to the memorial service?" George asked.

"What time is it again?"

"Four o'clock. In that little place called Waterfall Park at Main and Occidental."

"I'll be there," I said.

George nodded. I left the room, closing the door softly behind me. Unfortunately, George Yamamoto regarded even a hint of scandal as a serious assault on his personal honor.

When I got back upstairs, there was a Federal Express envelope lying facedown on my desk. I opened it and shook out the contents—a single piece of paper, a copy of the composite drawing of a darkly handsome man in his mid-thirties. I picked up my phone and dialed Andy Halvorsen in Colfax to see if he had received his copy. He had.

"Just a few minutes ago. In fact, I was about to

call Pamela Kinder in Spokane to see if she can pick this guy out of a montage of pictures. I've spent half the morning on the phone with Alvin Grant, that detective in Schaumburg. He's excited as hell."

"Excited? What about?"

"When he saw the composite, he thought it looked familiar. He worried it all night, and this morning he finally figured out where he knew that face from. He came up with both fingerprints and a mug shot. He's sending us copies of the prints, and he's pulling strings to get the latent prints they lifted off Lions' Visa card run through Cook County's Automated Fingerprint Identification System. He'll call and let us know what happens with that."

"So who is it? Anybody we know?"

"You and I don't know him from Adam, but Grant does. His name's Lorenzo Tabone. He's a small-time thug, not too bright, who's suspected of doing occasional contract work for somebody named Aldo Pappinzino."

"Never heard of him either. Who's that?"

"A major Mafia don. Runs a branch of the mob that's headquartered in Chicago."

"And how exactly does this Alvin Grant propose to catch him?"

"He says they've got a stakeout on the place where Tabone lives, and Grant thinks it just might work. Tabone's got no way of knowing we're on to him. It was nothing but an accident that the security guard caught the guy with the Visa card, and having Grant recognize him is more blind luck, more than we could have hoped for. By the way, Grant's got a real hard-on for these characters, for anybody connected with the Pappinzinos. Anything he can do to help, he's up for it."

"How come?" I asked. If somebody volunteers and says he's covering my backside, I want to know how he got there. I've learned the hard way not to accept allies on blind faith alone.

"Grant's best buddy from high school, a guy he went through the police academy with, got taken out by a Pappinzino hit man. The guy was doing a drug surveillance for the DEA. Got shot in the back of the head execution-style while he was sitting in his car. The guy who did it got off on a technicality. You know how it works."

I did indeed.

Halvorsen sounded different somehow. He had evidently worked back East long enough that even talking to Alvin Grant on the telephone had injected a hint of Chicago accent into his eastern Washington twang.

"So what are you doing?"

"Me? Like I said, I'm going to go see Pamela Kinder. After that, I'll go by Sacred Heart. I may be able to see Kimiko. The doctor said it's a possibility. How about you?"

"We spent most of yesterday working on another case, but we picked up a lead to a friend of Kurobashi's who lives over in Port Angeles. If I can get away this afternoon, I'll go over there and talk to him."

"Sounds good," Halvorsen said. "Let me know if you find out anything, and I'll do the same."

Big Al came back from his ordeal in Captain Powell's office in a blue funk.

"What's Max up to this time?" I asked.

"He's trying to come up with a reason why it's all our fault."

"That Hubert Jones OD'd?"

"That's right."

I laughed. "If anyone can pull that one off, Maxwell Cole is it. Want to go have lunch?"

Allen Lindstrom nodded. It was time. We went to the Doghouse. Big Al had lunch; I had breakfast.

"You know," Big Al said thoughtfully, chewing his way through a Bob's Burger, "you ought to try getting up a little earlier in the mornings and start having breakfast before you come to work. Molly says it's a whole lot better for you."

I smiled and nodded and ate my bacon and eggs without bothering to tell Big Al what I had been doing that morning that had caused me to miss breakfast.

I didn't figure it was any of his business.

CHAPTER 16

BY THE TIME I WAS READY TO HEAD ACROSS THE GREAT water to Port Angeles, it was after four. I probably should have taken a departmental car, but between driving a Porsche 928 and a Dodge Diplomat, there's really no contest. However, I did stop by Captain Powell's fishbowl long enough to get a verbal okay from him.

"If you put a dent in that little hummer of yours while you're over there," Powell warned, shaking his finger in my face, "you'd better not plan on vouchering it."

"No problem," I told him, fool that I am.

Lemmings rushing to the sea have nothing on Seattlites bent on escaping the city and going across Puget Sound on sunny Friday afternoons. With my usual finesse and timing, I managed to be stuck smack in the middle of the worst of the traffic. At the ferry terminal I bought a ticket to Winslow and maneuvered the 928 into the proper line.

The ferry *Walla Walla* is a huge, cavernous affair.

When it was ready for loading, row after row of cars started their engines and drove onto the car decks. For a while, it looked as though I would make it, but I didn't. Loading stopped three cars away, leaving me near the head of the line for the next ferry—an hour later. The Washington State Ferry System is nothing if not implacable. No amount of whining, pleading, or dashboard pounding would fix it. And so, I sat there in my car, doing a slow burn, with nothing to do but think.

Halvorsen's report of his conversation with the detective in Illinois had had a disquieting effect on me. It had stayed in the back of my mind and nipped away at me all afternoon. Now, sitting there trapped in the ferry line, I let out all the stops and stewed about it in dead earnest.

In order to find a killer, a cop sometimes has to put himself in the place of either the victim or the killer, and sometimes both. In this case, I had thought I was coming to grips with Tadeo Kurobashi, with who he was and what made him tick. But now, Alvin Grant's talk about Lorenzo Tabone and Aldo Pappinzino showed me that there was a giant blind spot in my perception of the dead man.

Tadeo Kurobashi's connection with a Chicago-based Mafia boss was something that didn't fit and didn't make sense, something I couldn't get a handle on. Had Kurobashi been involved in the drug trade as Andy Halvorsen had suggested? Even as I asked the question, I discarded it. Nothing in Tadeo Kurobashi's life had hinted at drugs. To all appearances he had been a hardworking entrepreneur, brought to his knees by a conspiracy of less than honest competition.

And if the mob was involved, as they evidently were, what did they want? Was the Mafia branching out and going high-tech these days? Had Tadeo invented some kind of electronics wizardry valuable enough to the criminal element that they were willing to kill in order to lay hands on it? If so, what was it and had they already gotten it? Sitting there in the line with the setting sun glaring in my face, my frustration level went up yet another notch or two.

I wished I could be in two places at once. Kimiko Kurobashi, unwittingly or not, probably held the key to everything I didn't know, and by now, Detective Halvorsen should have finished interviewing her. What had she told him, and would it help us find her father's killer? As my need to know went over the top, I reached for my car phone, dialed the Whitman County sheriff's department, and asked to speak to Detective Halvorsen.

"Sorry, he's sick. He's gone home for the day," the dispatcher told me.

"Home!" I yelped. "I thought he was on his way to Spokane."

"I know he was planning to, but he called in sick early this afternoon."

"Do you have his home number?" I asked.

"I'm not allowed to give it out."

Of course he wasn't allowed to give it out. I *had* the number myself, in my jacket, in the backseat. It just wasn't easily accessible. I found it though, and a minute or so later, Halvorsen's phone was ringing. It had rung seven or eight times, and I was about to hang up when he finally answered.

"Hello?" He sounded funny—distant, hesitant.

"Andy? This is Beau, in Seattle. Are you all right?"

"She's gone," he managed. His words were slurred. He sounded drunk.

"Gone?" My heart rose to my throat. Kimiko dead too? Had someone gotten to her in the hospital, or had she fallen victim to some unforeseen medical complication?

"How can that be?" I demanded. "I thought she was getting better, that the doctors said she was going to be okay."

"Doctors? What doctors?"

"Kimiko's doctors, goddamnit. Halvorsen, are you drinking or what?"

"Who said anything about Kimiko? Monica's gone. She left me. Went home to her mother. I can't believe it. How could she? I mean, she's why I divorced Barbara. I gave up my kids because of her."

Monica was gone, not Kimiko. My relief was almost overwhelming. "So Kimiko's all right? Did you talk to her?"

"No, I came home to tell Monica I was on my way to Spokane and found her packing to leave. I tried to talk her out of it, but she wouldn't listen. Wouldn't even talk to me."

The poor bastard doesn't know when he's well off, I thought. I said, "That's too bad, Andy. I'm sorry to hear it. What are you going to do?"

"Beats the hell out of me. Wait here, I guess. See if she changes her mind and comes back."

I didn't tell him not to hold his breath. Going to her mother's was probably nothing but a smoke screen. My guess was that Monica's shopping around had zeroed in on somebody more to her liking and closer to her own age.

The next ferry had pulled into the Colman dock and was disgorging its load of vehicles. Around me, people were returning to their cars, starting their engines.

"Look, Andy," I said. "I've gotta go. The ferry's here and I'm going to have to hang up. Don't try to do anything tonight. You're in no condition, but tomorrow get your ass to Spokane and go to work. It'll be good for what ails you, take your mind off your troubles."

"You're probably right," Andy Halvorsen mumbled, but he didn't sound convinced. I replaced the phone in its holder, started the car, and rumbled up the gangway onto the car deck. Front and center.

It's an eighty-seven-mile trip from Seattle to Port Angeles, part of it by ferry and the rest on narrow two-lane secondary roads that meander through the forests of the Kitsap Peninsula, Bainbridge Island, and the Olympic Peninsula. It sounds rural, and it is, but it's also full of traffic, particularly on Friday nights. I didn't make very good time.

The various port and sawmill towns that dot the Washington coastline—Port Angeles, Port Townsend, Raymond, Sequim—are as similar as peas in a pod. I've always maintained that you could get drunk in one, wake up in another, and never know the difference.

Port Angeles is built on two levels. The upper one is the town proper. Regular houses are there along with churches, grocery stores, and the trappings of small-town life and business. The lower one is a duke's mixture of tourist traps and lowbrow hotels, taverns, cafes, and restaurants that cater to freighter crewmen, sawmill workers, derelicts, and, occasionally, legitimate tourists. The shops do a land-office business in used books and made-in-Washington gewgaws.

The first person I asked for directions, a teenager pumping gas at a Texaco station, had never heard of the Ritz Hotel. I had expected an establishment with that kind of name to have a certain amount of stature in town and to be something of a landmark. The second person I asked, a grizzled drunk with a rolling gait and a pint bottle of vodka stashed in his hip pocket, nodded and pointed.

"Right up there, fella. Right over Davey's Locker. You got a quarter for a cup of coffee?" I tossed him a quarter, knowing full well he'd put it to bad use.

Davey's Locker turned out to be a tavern on the street level of a long, narrow, two-story frame building whose blackened shingles were rotting with age. The street outside was empty, so I parked directly in front. The tavern, its front windows painted an opaque blue, took up the entire bottom of the building except for the width of a steep, dilapidated stairway that led up from a single door in one corner of the front of the building. Gilt letters stenciled on the glass proclaimed somebody's small joke on the world—THE RITZ HOTEL. Ritz indeed! It looked like an over-the-hill flophouse. A condemned over-the-hill flophouse.

To my surprise, the battered door wasn't locked. I pushed it open and looked up a steep flight of scarred linoleum-covered stairs. Both the walls of the stairway and the ceiling as well had been covered with what looked like old egg crates. I recognized the wall covering as a poor man's version of make-do soundproofing. A single naked light bulb hung from a twisted brown cord high above the stairs.

Attached to the wall on the downstairs landing was a pay telephone. The number was printed on the face of the phone, but when I reached for my notebook to check that number against the one taken from Tadeo Kurobashi's message pad, I realized I had left my notebook on the seat of the car. I stood there wavering for a moment, wondering if I should go back out and get it right then, or wait.

I decided to wait. My life is like that, made up of small and seemingly inconsequential decisions that come back later and nip me in the butt.

"Hello?" I called up the stairs.

Nobody answered, but just then a gigantic burst of music rumbled down the stairs like an avalanche, with bass notes so loud that they vibrated the wooden hand rail I was holding.

"Hello," I called again, but there was no answer. No one could possibly have heard me above that earsplitting racket.

The music stopped momentarily and then started again at the exact same note. It sounded as though an entire symphonic orchestra must be rehearsing in the dim upstairs reaches of the Ritz Hotel.

I climbed to the top of the stairs, covering my ears with the palms of my hands in an effort to filter out some of the music. The noise level reminded me of a rock concert. The music, more classical than rock, was nothing I recognized.

The upstairs landing was soundproofed just as the stairs had been, and so was the long narrow corridor that led from the top of the stairs to the far end of the building. I had expected that the corridor would be lined with a long row of doors leading to separate rooms. Instead, only two doors were showing in the entire hallway, one at the far end of the building and the other directly in front of me. I waited until the next lull in the music and pounded on the door as soon as it was quiet.

The man who opened the door was in his mid to late thirties, six-foot-five at least, with long flowing chestnut hair. I know women who would kill to have hair like his, women who have paid a hundred dollars a crack for permanents and dye jobs in futile attempts to duplicate that look.

In the old days this guy would have worn rope sandals and been called a Jesus freak. Instead, he wore earphones and carried an open laptop computer. I looked beyond him, expecting to see a roomful of people. Instead, I saw a huge room filled with all kinds of computer equipment. Clay Woodruff was an electronics junky. A hacker.

"Are you Clay Woodruff?" I asked.

He nodded. "Whaddaya want?" he demanded, holding one of his earphones away from his head. "Can't you see I'm busy?"

"My name is J. P. Beaumont. I'm with the Seattle Police. May I come in?"

"Come back later. I'm working on a deadline."

He punched a few keys on the computer and closed his eyes to listen. Again a blast of music exploded around me. I waited. He was evidently playing only a short passage on some kind of complicated synthesizer, and I figured he'd stop the music again before long. When he did, I was still standing in the doorway.

"Not enough bass," he muttered loudly when he once more shut off the music. "Ever since those kids messed with my stuff, I haven't been able to get enough bass."

"It sounds like there's more than enough bass to me," I yelled, in order to be heard through his earphones.

Clay Woodruff looked at me in surprise, as though I had materialized out of thin air. "I'm here concerning Tadeo Kurobashi," I added, still shouting.

Woodruff's thick, bushy eyebrows came together in a frown. "What about him?" he asked.

"He's dead."

In one swift motion, Woodruff peeled off his earphones and put them on a table beside the door. "You're kidding. When? How?"

"Last Sunday night, after he came here to visit you."

I pulled out my ID and handed it to him. Woodruff looked at it carefully, then gave it back to me, closed the lid to his computer, and switched it off.

"Let's go downstairs," he said. "We'll talk there."

He closed and locked the hallway door behind him, put the key in his pocket, and then carried the laptop with him, stuffed under one arm like an oversized book. We had to go out on the sidewalk before we could go into the tavern. I stopped at the car long enough to retrieve my notebook, then he led the way into Davey's Locker. "Beer?" he asked.

It was long after hours. I was on my own time and in my own vehicle. "Sure," I said. "Why not?"

Clay sat at a table just inside the door, placing the computer on the floor beside him. He signaled the bartender, holding up one finger on one hand and two fingers on the other. With a nod the bartender translated the prearranged signal into action, bringing over one large pitcher of beer along with two empty glasses and setting them on the table in front of us.

"How's it going?" Clay asked.

The bartender shrugged. "Usual Friday night crowd. No problem."

Clay poured two beers, expertly filling the glasses without running the head over the top. "Tell me what happened," he said.

And so I told him some of it—Kurobashi's death, the vicious attacks on Kurobashi's wife and child—interspersing the telling with enough questions so that in the process of giving out information, I was also receiving it.

Yes, he and Tadeo had worked together at RFLink. Yes, he had been present during the patent discussion between Blakeslee and Tadeo, and when Blakeslee had refused the product, both he and Tadeo had quit outright. No, he had never received a summons to testify in Tadeo's behalf during the patent infringement trial, and yes, he would have been glad to do so had he been notified.

Woodruff told me that he had received a commission to compose an original work for the Houston Symphony, and he had been working on that night and day for months, not accepting phone calls or seeing any visitors. Maybe the subpoena had come then, he said.

Throughout the discussion, Woodruff seemed gravely concerned, particularly when I told him about what had happened to Machiko and Kimi. "Are they going to be all right?"

"Machiko's already out of the hospital. She's staying with a friend of Kimi's near Pullman. Kimi's in Sacred Heart in Spokane. From what I heard today, she's doing much better, but she's a long way from being released."

"I see," he said.

"According to Mrs. Oliver, you called Mr. Kurobashi on Friday."

Woodruff nodded. "That's right."

"Why?"

"I had told Tad that when I finished up with my commission, the two of us would do something together."

"What do you mean? Go fishing? Take a trip?"

"No, no. We were a good team, the two of us. I knew that Tadeo was working on something, had been for years, and I wanted to market it for him. It takes three things to bring off a new product—engineering, money, and marketing."

"What new product?"

Woodruff's eyes became veiled. Until then, his answers had been forthright and easily given. Now he clammed up. He covered his mouth with his hand, letting one finger rest against the side of his nose. I worked my way through college selling Fuller Brush door-to-door. I can tell when somebody stops buying. Clay Woodruff had stopped cold.

"I can't talk about it," he said.

"What do you mean you can't talk about it?"

"I'm doing a favor for a friend," he replied. "Just because Tad is dead doesn't mean I won't keep my word."

I wasn't getting anywhere, so I tried a different angle. "When Mr. Kurobashi came to see you that day, did he seem upset to you?"

"Upset? Hell yes, he was upset. He had lost everything, and all because I didn't testify. Then, out of the blue, I call him up and act as though we're still asshole buddies. He was pissed as hell."

"Were you?" I asked.

"Was I what?"

"Were you still asshole buddies?"

"As far as I was concerned we were," Woodruff replied.

"Why didn't you testify then?" I asked.

Woodruff drew back and looked at me. "I already told you. Because I never got called. I never got a summons. When I explained that to Tad, he understood. When I tried to reach him on Friday, I was calling in the dark. I had no idea that the judge had ruled against him and he was losing his business."

"Tell me about his state of mind that day. Did he give any hint that he was in some kind of trouble or that his life might be in danger?"

"No."

"And this product that you say he was working on. Would it be something that could be of use in illegal activities, something the Mafia might have a vital interest in?"

"No."

"Did you ever know Mr. Kurobashi to have any dealings with criminal types?"

Once more Woodruff's eyebrows knitted together to form a solid bridge across his nose. "You're asking me if I have any knowledge of Tad being involved with organized crime?"

"Yes."

Woodruff's finger moved away from his nose. He rubbed his hand thoughtfully back and forth across his jutting chin. The salesman in me recognized the gesture as a buying signal—decision time.

"Wait here," Woodruff said. "I need to go get something. Want another beer?"

"Fine," I said.

Woodruff picked up the pitcher and filled both of our glasses; then, grabbing his computer from the floor, he excused himself and walked over to the bar. He spoke briefly to the bartender, then he came back to where we had been sitting.

"It's upstairs," he said. "I'll be right back."

"Take your time," I said casually, trying to conceal any show of curiosity about what he was going to get. The bartender came to the table and busily wiped off the damp rings left by the pitcher and glasses.

"So you're from Seattle, are you?" he said. "Here for the weekend?"

"Just tonight," I replied.

"The music starts up at nine," he offered helpfully. "Local group, R and B. Real laid back. People around here seem to like it."

"You mean you don't play Woodruff's music here in the bar?"

The bartender grinned. "Oh, it gets played in here all right. Not necessarily on purpose. For instance, everybody knows that section he was working on today pretty much by heart."

"The soundproofing's not that good?"

"You could say that."

My glass was partially empty, and the bartender filled it with the dregs of the pitcher before hurrying back to the bar, where someone was calling him for a refill. I sat there alone for several minutes watching the denizens of Port Angeles and Davey's Locker perform. They all knew one another, knew who was good at pool and who was lousy, who could hold their beer and who couldn't. A television set in the background was quietly playing a "Star Trek" rerun to an audience of one medium-old lady with a cigarette in one hand and a beer in the other. The place seemed as innocuous as an overgrown living room.

I drifted for a few moments, sipping the beer and contemplating what it would be like to live in a small town like this as opposed to a big city. When my glass was almost empty, though, I began to grow uneasy. It was taking Woodruff a hell of a long time to bring back whatever it was he was going to show me.

I turned and tried looking out the window, but the opaque blue glass barred any view of the street outside. I stood up, walked over to the door, opened it, and looked up and down. In either direction, the sidewalk and the wide one-way street were totally deserted. I stepped far enough out onto the sidewalk to see the windows of Woodruff's apartment above Davey's Locker. They were dark and empty, with no sign of life behind them, and when I tried the door to the stairway that led up to the Ritz Hotel, it was locked with an old-fashioned Masters padlock.

There was a sudden sinking sensation, a lurch in my stomach, telling me that somehow, for some reason, I'd been suckered. I turned toward the 928. My door was still locked, but I could see that the door on the passenger's side wasn't, even though I knew I had locked it. After all, I'm a cop. I *always* lock car doors.

"Damn!"

I hurried around to the driver's side and opened it with my key. I shoved the key into the ignition and turned. Nothing happened. Not even so much as a click.

"Damn," I said again. "Damn, damn, damn."

CHAPTER 17

BY MIDNIGHT I WAS BACK IN LINE WAITING FOR A FERRY. Again. This time, I was on the Winslow side, trying to return to Seattle. The ferry had been pulling away from the dock just as I came roaring down the hill into Winslow. The ferry schedule isn't like horseshoes. Near misses don't count. The score for the day stood at Washington State Ferry System—two; J. P. Beaumont—zip. Had there been a blood-pressure measuring device in my car, I'm sure I would have registered off the charts.

I'm not any kind of mechanical genius, and I make it a point *never* to fiddle around with the complicated equipment under the hood of my flashy 928. I let someone else do it, preferably a tried-and-true Porsche specialist.

On this Friday night in Port Angeles, it had taken Triple A more than an hour to send out some jerk in a tow truck. He tried using a set of jumper cables, turned the key, and nothing happened. Then he had poked around under the hood with a flashlight, finally discovering that the battery cable had been neatly clipped. Whoever did it had made sure that the break in the wire was well out of sight.

So the damage was repairable, but everything took time, and I knew that with every passing moment, Clay Woodruff was slipping farther and farther beyond my grasp. While the tow truck guy was looking for a replacement battery cable, I walked across the street to the Port Angeles Police Department and attempted to swear out a complaint against Clay Woodruff, accusing him of vandalizing my car. The Port Angeles cops treated the whole situation as an enormous joke.

How did I know it was Woodruff who had vandalized my car? Had I actually seen him do it? What was it he had gone to get when he left me waiting in Davey's Locker, and where had he gone when he left there? My complaint that every passing moment was giving Woodruff more time to get away fell on deaf ears. Get away from what? Was Woodruff under suspicion for some crime? Was the Seattle Police Department looking for him for a specific reason? Woodruff had been a law-abiding citizen in Port Angeles for a number of years. Who the hell was I?

I'm a slow learner, but eventually I got the picture—small-town cops stonewalling big-city cop. On the small-town cop's turf. At the city cop's expense. They laughed at first, but finally, reluctantly, they put out an APB, but by then Woodruff was nowhere to be found.

Recrossing the street, I went back inside Davey's Locker long enough to hassle the bartender. I told him his friend was in a whole shitload of trouble, and he invited me to leave. Point/counterpoint. Mexican standoff. I took the hint and left, convinced that the city of Port Angeles had revoked every welcome mat in sight.

Back on the street outside Davey's Locker, beneath the black lifeless windows of the Ritz Hotel, I was forced to kibitz, peering over the tow truck driver's shoulder until he finished installing the new battery cable and had my 928 purring again. By then it was almost ten o'clock, too late to go driving around the Olympic Peninsula looking for Clay Woodruff. Even had I known where he was going, he had a several-hour head start. I never would have been able to catch up.

Much later, sitting in the car at the ferry dock, I tried my best to be philosophical about having lost Clay Woodruff and also about having missed the ferry. My eyelids were getting heavy and I was dozing off when the phone rang, startling me awake. It was Ames, calling from my apartment.

"Where are you?" he asked. "I've been trying to raise you on the phone all night."

"I've been out of range. Right now I'm stuck in Winslow, waiting for the ferry. Why? What's up?"

"The phone's been ringing off the hook all night. Doesn't anybody ever call you at work?"

"Hardly ever. What's going on?"

Ames was his unflappable best. "In order of priority, I suppose the call from Dana Lions is the most important."

"A call from Dana Lions? What about?"

"They found her father." Ames paused. "He's dead."

With those two words my worst suspicions about David Lions and his traveling Visa Card were confirmed. There was no elation in being right, only a grudging acknowledgment that I had seen it coming. I thought of Dana Lions, waiting by her phone in Kalama. At least I hadn't told her so, although maybe it would have been kinder if I had given her some hint, some warning.

"Who found him?" I asked.

"A group of Cub Scouts from Seattle on a camp out over near Lake Kachess. Dana's on her way to Seattle right now. According to what the state patrol told her, he was found just inside the King County Line, and they're bringing the body to the medical examiner's office here."

"How do they know for sure it's Lions?" I asked. "We've already been through one false alarm when everybody thought he'd been found in Chicago."

"His dog tags from Vietnam. They got his name off them."

I remembered Dana mentioning the dog tags then, so there was probably no mistake, and the body really was that of David Lions.

"If Dana calls back, tell her I'm on my way and that I'll meet her at Harborview as soon as I can. What else?"

"A call from Alvin Grant in Illinois. He said it's too late for you to call him back tonight. He says he'll talk to you in the morning."

"Anything else?"

Ames paused. "Well, actually, there was one other call."

"Who from?"

"A Dr. Blair. He sounded a little crusty. And serious. He says that he checked with Dr. Wang and that you didn't do as you were told and go see him. Blair wants to know if you have another doctor in mind. If so, when do you plan on making an appointment? What's this all about, Beau?"

"No big thing," I answered. "Dr. Blair's the guy who took care of my fingers."

"So who's Dr. Wang?"

"An internist, somebody Blair wants me to go see for a second opinion."

"For a second opinion on your fingers? Do broken fingers call for an internist?"

Ames didn't get to be where he is or what he is without being an astute judge of human behavior. He is also a consummate asker of questions. He can sniff out and demolish one of my puny smoke screens from miles away.

"Not exactly."

"What then?"

I hesitated. Unable to find a plausible fib, I was forced to answer without one. "Blair seems to think my liver's enlarged. He wants me to go see this Wang character for a complete checkup."

"Wants? It sounded more like he gave you strict orders to go and you didn't bother."

"I'll go, I'll go," I said irritably.

"When?"

"When I get around to it, dammit. This case has me tied up in knots right now. I'll go when I have time."

I could hear the defensiveness in my voice and it made me even angrier. I hadn't wanted to discuss the subject of my enlarged liver with Ralph Ames in the first place. Now, here he was, in it up to his eye-teeth. I knew that if I tried dropping the subject, old "Aimless" was far too cagey to let it stay dropped. I made the attempt anyway.

"Let's just forget it for the time being," I suggested. "How was your trip to Colfax?"

"Fine, fine," Ames replied. "Archie and Machiko are getting along famously. You might be interested to know that he speaks what I understand to be passable Japanese."

"That would be useful," I said.

"Incidentally, Machiko came back here to Seattle with us this afternoon. She has a meeting scheduled with Dr. Yamamoto in the morning."

My yellow mental warning light came on. Ralph Ames was venturing into dangerous territory, talking casually about an ongoing police investigation over a mobile phone. Cellular phones are notorious for allowing casual eavesdropping under even the best of circumstances. That was without having had an electronics wizard break into the car and do God knows what.

I peered out across the water. The incoming ferry was nowhere in sight. "Wait a minute, Ralph. Let me call you back."

"Call me back?" Ames echoed. "What's the matter?"

"Never mind. I'll call you back in a minute."

I hung up, got out of the car, locked it, and went

loping back up to the terminal building. Inside, I finally located a bank of pay phones and dialed my home number.

"What's going on?" Ames asked, as soon as he answered.

"People listen in on car phone conversations all the time," I muttered irritably. "The Kurobashi case isn't exactly public domain, you know."

Ames laughed. "Are you getting paranoid in your old age?"

"Maybe," I returned. "Now tell me. Why is Machiko seeing George?"

"To ask him for the sword."

"But he can't give it to her. It's part of an active murder investigation. He still doesn't have the print results back from the computer. How on earth could he possibly turn loose of the sword?"

"It doesn't hurt to ask," Ralph Ames replied mildly.

Ask like hell, I thought. George had called it blackmail, not asking, and he had accused Ralph Ames of being behind it. I've known Ames long enough to know there's solid granite concealed under his foppish exterior. I was glad to know, however, that George Yamamoto hadn't knuckled under. At least not yet, he hadn't.

Ames misread my silence for tacit approval. "At least now we know why her husband never tried to sell it," he continued.

"We do?"

"Because of her husband," Ames said. "Her first husband. When Archie told Machiko how much the sword would probably bring at auction, she broke down and told him the whole story. It must be a tremendous relief for her to finally be able to let go of that burden after all these years."

"Goddamnit, Ames. Will you stop talking in circles and tell me what the hell's going on?"

"Tadeo Kurobashi killed Machiko's first husband. With the sword."

Ralph Ames knew good and well what kind of impact that news would have on me. He paused, waiting for my reaction.

"Good Lord. You've got to be shitting me!"

"Not at all. The first husband's name was Lamb. Aaron Lamb. He met Machiko when she was working in Tokyo after the war."

"When she was working as a hooker?" I asked innocently. I'll be damned if I was going to let Ames think he was the only one holding any cards in this particular game.

"That's right. She had evidently lost her entire family and wanted to come to this country in the worst way. Machiko says now that she thought at first that Lamb loved her. Once they were here in the States though, he turned mean and abusive. He beat her constantly. She didn't dare leave or ask for help because he told her that if he divorced her, she'd be deported and sent back to Japan."

"What does the sword have to do with all of this?"

"It was her most prized possession, her only possession. A gift from her grandfather. He told her never to draw it unless she intended to use it, but that if it became necessary, she should use the sword to defend her honor or her life.

"One day Lamb came home drunk. He accused Machiko of hiding money from him. While he was looking for the money, he found the knife. He had never known about it before, had never seen it. Machiko had brought it with her, concealed in her luggage. Lamb came after her with the knife. He had it out of the box and was threatening her with it, demanding to know what else she had hidden away in the house. And that's when Tadeo Kurobashi happened to show up. He was out delivering groceries."

"And killed the husband?"

"Unintentionally. With Machiko's sword," Ames added. "Tadeo was trying to disarm him but in the struggle, Lamb went down, fatally wounded. Machiko was terrified that without Lamb, she'd be shipped back to Japan. Kurobashi was scared, too. It was such a short time after the war. He was afraid he'd be facing lynch-mob mentality, not justice. He didn't think anyone would believe he had acted in self-defense, so he and Machiko disposed of the body. Kurobashi came back for it that night in his grocery truck. They carted the body out to Ballard and dumped it into Salmon Bay, where it was found a week later."

"And no one ever suspected?" I asked.

"Think about it," Ames said. "It was just after the war. Lamb was a lowlife to begin with, a thug, married to a Japanese woman, an ex-prostitute he had brought home with him. The spoils of war, as it were. I don't think anybody cared very much."

"No," I said quietly. "I don't suppose they did." I thought about it for a moment. "So why did the Kurobashis keep the sword hidden all those years?"

"Out of some form of irrational fear that they'd be found out," Ralph Ames answered. "For years it was in the safe at Kurobashi's office. Until last week."

"What happened last week?"

"I don't know, but whatever it was, it made Kurobashi change his mind. He called Machiko late Sunday morning and told her that he had decided to go ahead and sell the sword. He said they would use whatever proceeds they got from it to start a new company."

"Where's Machiko now?" I asked.

"Archie put her up down at the Four Seasons. That's fairly close to the Public Safety Building, where we'll be meeting with Dr. Yamamoto tomorrow."

"The Four Seasons! Isn't that a little steep?" I asked. "How can she afford it?"

"She can't. Archie's paying for it. Cost of doing business and all that."

"Making sure he gets first dibs to handle the sword?"

"That too," Ames replied. "He wouldn't be doing it if he didn't think it would be worth it in the long run for both of them."

I was feeling more than moderately irritable with Ames and Archibald Winter both. Ames sounded smug. Not only had he stepped into my business with Dr. Wang, here he was, along with his high-toned friend, messing around in more of my business, solving a murder, a forty-year-old one at that, an unsolved murder nobody had looked at in years.

"Is Machiko going to go to the memorial service tomorrow afternoon?" I asked.

"I don't think so," Ames replied. "At least she didn't mention it. Our appointment with Dr. Yamamoto is scheduled for eleven. Before that we're meeting with Chris Davenport. He's anxious for Machiko to sign off on some of the bankruptcy proceedings, and I'm not sure that's wise."

"What have you done, Ames, taken another chick under your protective wing?"

"I just don't want to see her rushed into something that wouldn't be advantageous, considering the situation with Archie and the sword."

Outside I heard the deep-throated honking of a horn announcing the arrival of the ferry. "I've gotta go," I said quickly. "Once I get to Seattle, I'll stop by Harborview long enough to see if there's anything I can do for Dana Lions, then I'll be home. See you in the morning."

The few inbound cars were already unloaded and the cars waiting in line behind me were already starting their engines as I reached my vehicle. Barely missing the previous ferry guarantees you a front-row seat on the next one. I drove all the way to the restraining chains at the front of the ferry and settled deep into the Porsche's chilly leather seat for the thirty-minute ride to Seattle. I leaned back against the headrest and closed my eyes, but I didn't sleep. I didn't even doze.

I was still plucked by what I regarded as Ames' and Winter's interference in my case, even though, at the same time, I was dazzled by all the information those two interlopers had managed to glean. If any or all of it was true, then the dynamics of Tadeo and Machiko's marriage were much different from what I had supposed and from what other outsiders had assumed. I found myself examining the Kurobashis' marriage through a prism of new information.

George Yamamoto had seen Tadeo's total absorption in Machiko, had watched it draw Tadeo's affections away from his sister Tomi. He had tried to understand it, finally explaining it to himself as some kind of sexual entrapment, a web of eroticism only a street wise prostitute could weave.

Now I felt certain that Machiko's fascination for Tadeo had been far less complicated than that, far less sinister. I saw it as the simple magnetism that often draws the strong to the weak, the powerful to the helpless. Tadeo had literally wrested Machiko from certain death at the hands of her brutal husband. That act had bound the two of them together in such a symbiotic, mutually dependent relationship that even Kimiko, their well-loved child, had not been able to penetrate it, much less understand it.

What Kimiko had seen as a prison, Machiko had viewed as a haven, a refuge. The father, the villain Kimiko regarded as her mother's ruthless jailer and dictator, had chosen to alienate his daughter, to go without speaking to his only child for nine long years, rather than reveal his own terrible secret, a secret he and his wife had shared and lived with and carried together for more than forty years.

So what had changed? What event had, in a single day, triggered such a fundamental change in Tadeo Kurobashi's life? What had made so great a difference that he had been willing, after all those years, to sell the sword? He must have known that Machiko's sword was indeed two-edged, that it held the promise of bringing them much needed financial relief, but that it also carried the threat of bringing with it questions and an investigation that might reopen that forty-year-old nightmare.

That weekend, something had made such a profound impression on Tadeo Kurobashi that he had been willing to risk revealing the desperate act he and Machiko had kept hidden for so long.

There was only one thing I knew for sure about that Friday. It was the day Clay Woodruff had called and left a message for Tadeo Kurobashi with Bernice Oliver. Was that call the catalyst? Was that what had sparked Tadeo's sudden change of heart, or was it something that happened later at the meeting in Port Angeles on Sunday?

I had no way of knowing, and no way of telling which side Woodruff was, to say nothing of which way he might have pushed Tadeo. Woodruff had claimed that he was doing something for a friend, a final favor. Maybe that had been a lie, something Woodruff threw in to keep me off guard. If so, it had worked like a charm. Clay Woodruff had outfoxed me six ways to Sunday. He had gotten away clean without my having any idea where to look for him.

Frustrated with thinking about how stupid I was, I went back to thinking about Tadeo Kurobashi, struggling to come to grips with this changed vision of him, to understand how this newly revised and heroic version was tied in with a gangster named Aldo Pappinzino in Chicago, Illinois. No matter how I shoved the pieces around on the board, I couldn't see a connection.

The ride from Winslow is a relatively short one. I stayed in the car, watching as Seattle's nighttime cityscape slowly crystallized and emerged from the ghostly glow of cloud-shrouded lights in the distance. In thirty time-warping minutes, I traveled from sleepy rural backwoods to the heart of a metropolis still alive with its late-night diversions, from towering, darkened forests to nighttime skyscrapers whose lights beckoned like so many burning candles.

That ride and that view always have a soothing effect on me, and this time was no exception. As I drove off the ferry, I was no longer nearly as pissed with Ames and Winter as I had been when I had boarded the boat in Winslow. Driving up the hill toward the Medical Examiner's Office, I felt a sudden burst of energy, a second wind. If "Aimless" Ames and his buddy wanted to muck around in forty-year-old murders, let 'em. My job was to deal with the murders in the here and now. Specifically with the murder of Tadeo Kurobashi. Tadeo and, secondarily, that of David Lions. He was mine too. By proxy. Because I said so.

In trying to talk to Dana Lions, I would be in direct competition with other cops from other jurisdictions. Detectives from the King County Police would be there. I was sure they would want me to take a number and get in line.

I had news for them. They were coming into this case from way behind go. They were just beginning to wonder who had killed David Lions. I already knew. All I needed was one tiny smidgen of evidence to prove it.

With any kind of luck, Lorenzo Tabone would have made a slip, one seemingly insignificant mistake, that would give me something to remember him by, something that would buy him a one-way ticket to the gallows, Washington State's still extant but rarely used form of capital punishment.

CHAPTER 18

WHEN I GOT TO THE MEDICAL EXAMINER'S OFFICE, three people were grouped and talking in low voices in the small reception area outside Doc Baker's door. Two were women, one about my age and the other much younger, no more than twenty-five. All three looked up at me questioningly as I came through the door.

"Detective Beaumont," I announced.

As soon as I said that, the younger woman leaped from her chair and hurled herself toward me. She was a tiny woman, only about five feet, but when she crashed into me, I almost lost my balance. I grabbed at a chair to keep from sprawling on the floor.

"Detective Beaumont, thank God you've come." She threw her arms around me and buried her head in my chest as though I were some long-lost relation. "I told them you were coming," she sobbed, clinging to me like a burr.

The man stepped forward with a puzzled frown on his face. "I'm Detective Hal Forbes," he said, "and this is my partner, JoAnne Reece. We're with the King County Police. Miss Lions here was telling us that you're already involved in this case. Is that true?"

I nodded. "Sort of. I'm working the Tadeo Kurobashi case," I said as I pried Dana Lions' arms loose from around my waist, walked her over to a chair, and helped her sit back down.

For the first time, I got a good look at her. She was wearing a bright orange jumpsuit with the words ST. HELENS FLYING SERVICE emblazoned in blue embroidery on the breast pocket. Her hair, so red that it almost matched her uniform, was short and curly. Her vivid green eyes were swollen from weeping.

I took one of her small hands in mine. "Is it your father?"

She swallowed hard, nodded, and said nothing.

"Wait a minute," Forbes said. "Isn't Kurobashi the man who was found dead in his office on Fourth Avenue South sometime this week?"

"That's the one," I replied.

"I remember now," Forbes continued. "And there was something later on about his wife and daughter being attacked over in eastern Washington?"

"You got it." I glanced down at Dana before I spoke again. She wasn't going to like hearing what I had to say, but I went ahead with it anyway.

"I've been working with Detective Halvorsen from the Whitman County Sheriff's Department over in Colfax. He's in charge of the assault case. We believe that Mr. Lions' aircraft was used to create a diversion to cover up the attack on the Kurobashi women."

"No!" Dana exclaimed. She pulled her hands free from mine and covered her face. "My father wouldn't do that. It isn't true. This is all a mistake."

"There's no mistake, Dana," I said gently. "He may not have had a choice, he may have been forced into participating, but he was there, and so was the helicopter."

"Didn't have a choice?" Dana asked. "What do you mean?"

Detective Forbes looked at Dana, but he spoke to me. "Sounds like we're all over the map on this one. Somebody dead here, somebody attacked in Colfax, the body found by Lake Kachess."

I didn't bother to tell him that I had just come back from Port Angeles, where Clay Woodruff had left me in the dust. Why make things more complicated than they already were?

Dana's eyes, bright as emeralds, pierced into mine. "You still haven't said what you meant."

"Just a minute, Dana. We'll come back to that." I turned to the other detectives. "Who found the body?" I asked.

JoAnne Reece opened her notebook and paged through it. "A Cub Scout named Ryan Jacobsen," she said. "He was on a father-and-son hike and camp out. Fortunately the father is an attorney. He made sure nobody disturbed anything."

"Physical evidence?" I asked.

With a meaningful look in Dana Lions' direction JoAnne Reece said, "Maybe."

That led me to believe that some physical evidence did exist, but the King County detectives didn't want to discuss it in front of the victim's daughter.

I'd have to ask them about it later. Meanwhile, I sat down next to Dana and pulled my chair close to hers.

"I'm going to ask you some questions, Dana, questions that may possibly be painful for you to answer."

She seemed to have gotten a grip on herself. "It's all right. Ask me anything. I'll do whatever I can to help."

"Did your father ever have any dealings with the Mafia?"

"The Mafia!" Forbes exclaimed involuntarily, then he fell silent, watching me warily.

"Just answer the question, Dana. Did he?"

She shook her head. "Not that I know of. He had some friends that weren't such nice people, but I never thought any of them were connected to the Mafia. Why?"

"That Charles Smith, your cash-paying customer, had he ever chartered with you before?"

"No. At least I don't remember the name."

"Wasn't it unusual for someone to call for a charter from Seattle? Why didn't he use a company that was closer to him?"

"I don't know," Dana replied. "I've asked myself the same question over and over all week long."

"What about the name Tabone, Lorenzo Tabone? Does that one ring any bells?"

Dana Lions frowned. "It sounds familiar, but . . ." She shook her head. "No, I just can't place it."

"He's from Chicago," I said, trying to jog her memory.

"Wait a minute," JoAnne Reece interrupted.

"What's going on here? I don't understand what we're talking about."

Dana Lions, her brows furrowed, was still thinking. "Lorenzo Tabone from Chicago?" she murmured. "I wonder . . ."

"You wonder what?"

"If that isn't the name of the guy Dad told me about. Only he didn't call him Lorenzo. Bones, I think it was. No, that's not right. Bony. Bony Tabone."

Dana Lions' recognition of Lorenzo Tabone's name sent a shock through my system like a jolt of pure adrenaline or a shot of straight MacNaughton's, take your pick. The other two detectives, deferring to that reaction, faded quietly into the woodwork. Suddenly it was as though there were only two of us in the room—Dana and me. I pulled my chair around in front of her and sat with our faces only inches apart. With every particle of my being, I willed her to remember.

"Who was he?" I demanded.

Dana's lower lip trembled. "Dad flew helicopters for the army. He must have loved it while he was doing it, but he got a general discharge from the service." Her voice was hardly a whisper. "Less than honorable."

"So?" I asked. "What does that have to do with Tabone?"

"It was something that went on while they were over there, in Vietnam. They were in the same outfit, platoon, or whatever. My father didn't talk about it very much, and he never told me exactly what caused all the trouble. I guess I didn't really want to know. But this Tabone guy had something to do with it. Dad always blamed him."

"Blamed who?"

"My father blamed Bony, he called him, for getting him thrown out of the service."

"Was there any contact between them after that?"

"Not that I know of."

"Did you ever see Tabone in person, or did your father show you any pictures?"

"No."

"Would you recognize him if you saw him?"

"No," she said again. "I don't think so."

"Too bad," I said. "I just happen to have a composite drawing of Lorenzo Tabone on my desk down at the Public Safety Building."

I turned to Reece and Forbes. "You two are in luck. Tabone's your man. I'll have prints and a mug shot for you as soon as Federal Express delivers them to me tomorrow morning."

JoAnne Reece stood with her head cocked to one side with an incredulous look on her face. "Come on now, Detective Beaumont. What is all this? You expect us to believe you already know who the killer is? Somebody's sending you prints and a mug shot in the morning mail, just like that?"

I tried not to sound too smug or too impatient. "We know that David Lions was in the Spokane Airport early Tuesday morning. He was there along with a man who matches the description of Lorenzo Tabone. The two of them rented a car together."

"And who exactly is Lorenzo Tabone?"

"He's tied in with a Chicago Mafioso named Aldo

Pappinzino. Maybe Tabone didn't kill David Lions, but if he didn't, he's one of the last people who saw him alive."

"Can I go now?" Dana asked suddenly. I couldn't blame her for wanting to leave. I'm sure our conversation was pretty rough going for her.

"Where are you staying?" I asked.

"I don't know. I came straight here when I drove into town. I need to find a place to stay and I should call my mother. She still doesn't know what's happened."

"Where is she, down in Kalama?"

"She lives in Anchorage. My parents were divorced years ago, Detective Beaumont. I didn't want to call until I knew for sure." She stood up. "I'll be going then."

Dana Lions seemed so small, so crushed, that I wanted to help her somehow, to take on some of the burden and carry it for her. I offered her a ride, but she declined.

"I have my own car," she said. "I'll be all right."

She moved toward the door. I hated to see her go, but I made no effort to follow her. After all, she had told me what I needed to know. My job now was to talk to the King County detectives and exchange detailed information with them. I had to convince them I knew what the hell I was talking about and then make sure they were on the right track.

"Call my home number and leave word on my answering machine where you're staying," I said.

"Let us know too," JoAnne Reece added.

Dana Lions nodded, but she walked out of the room without saying anything more.

I turned back to the others in time to catch Hal Forbes giving JoAnne Reece a questioning look, which she returned with an exaggerated shrug. It was as though they were silently debating whether or not J. P. Beaumont was on the level or if he was actually a stark raving loony.

I wanted to squelch that discussion once and for all. "When I first got here, you said something about physical evidence. What is it, fingerprints?"

"No," JoAnne Reece replied. "Thread."

"What kind of thread? Where from?"

"Wool thread, like from a man's jacket. They found it stuck between his teeth on the left side of his mouth."

"Who found it?"

"Mike Wilson. The assistant medical examiner. He happened to be here doing another autopsy when they first brought Lions in. One of the technicians who went out to pick up the body had noticed it when they were loading him up for transport."

"So how did it get there?"

"Wilson said he'll have to study the thread, but he said it looked to him like there was blood on it. He already sent the thread down to the crime lab. He thinks there was a struggle and Lions must have bitten his attacker."

"Hard enough to draw blood?"

"And put a hole in his jacket," JoAnne Reece replied. "So if you're right about the Chicago Police picking up that Tabone character, if he's our man, he should have a bite mark on him somewhere. What I still don't understand, though, is what all this has to do with the case you're working on."

"Believe me," I told her. "Neither do I."

I spent the next two hours with Detectives Forbes and Reece. By the time I left them, we were all working on the same team and pulling in the same direction. I went home and crawled into my own little bed. Onto is more like it. I fell asleep crosswise on the bed without bothering to take off my jacket or pull down the covers.

It seemed as though my eyes had barely closed when the phone rang. I was sleeping the wrong way on the bed, so it took a while to figure out where the phone was. By the time I found it and picked it up, the answering machine was already playing. I had to wait through the entire long-winded recording before I could find out who was calling.

"Who is this?" I asked, vowing mentally that I'd shorten the damn message before the day was out.

"Lieutenant Grant. From Schaumburg. I wanted you to be the first to know. We've got him. Caught him coming home this morning with a girl on each arm. I don't think the evening ended quite the way any of them expected it would."

"Hot damn! Congratulations." It was good news, stunningly good news. Even on less than three hours of sleep, I didn't stay groggy. I was wide awake, ready to work. "Did you see him?"

"You'd better believe I saw him," Grant replied. "I wouldn't have missed it for the world."

"Listen," I said. "This is important. He doesn't happen to have a bite on his arm or his hand, does he?"

Now it was Alvin Grant's turn to be stunned. "On his wrist. How the hell did you know about that?" he demanded. "That's why he hasn't been home, that and a bruised kidney. He went to an emergency room to have the bite treated, and they put him in the hospital because he was pissing blood. I guess the bite's pretty bad, too. Did you know human bites can be really dangerous?"

"With any kind of luck," I said, "this one will be fatal."

We talked on the phone for a long time. I told Alvin Grant as much as I knew and gave him instructions on how to reach Detectives Forbes and Reece. Grant would need to work closely with them since that was the case with an obvious connection to Lorenzo Tabone, and one with a good chance at extradition.

"But what about your case?" Grant asked. "Where do you fit in?"

"Beats me. As a matter of fact, if you have a chance to question that bastard, you might just ask Tabone what the hell was going on between him and Tadeo Kurobashi."

"I don't think it's very likely that he'll tell me," Lieutenant Grant said with a laugh. "But it doesn't hurt to ask."

I was up by then, totally up and awake and hungry. All was quiet in the guest room. I took off my wrinkled, slept-in clothes, put on a pair of comfortable sweats, and left the apartment where Ames was still sleeping to go in search of food. The deli downstairs is closed on Saturdays, so I walked over to the Doghouse. Wanda was surprised to see me.

"What are you doing here so early, and on a Saturday yet?"

"Feed me," I said.

She grinned and slid a cup of coffee in front of me. "Let me guess. Two eggs, over easy, bacon, hash browns, whole wheat toast, and a crossword puzzle."

"Right on all counts," I said.

She brought me the section of paper with the crossword puzzle in it. Unfortunately, it was also the section that contained Maxwell Cole's column on Hattie Marie Jones, mother of Hubert.

Hubert would have been fine, his mother said, if the cops hadn't harrassed her son and forced him to fall in with a bad crowd. It was during a stint in Juvie that he had gotten involved with drugs, specifically cocaine, more specifically crack. All of that was in the first four paragraphs. I didn't bother to read any further.

I turned instead to the puzzle. The theme was biblical, both passages and characters. For somebody whose days in Sunday school ended a long time ago, I surprised myself by doing all right. Very well, in fact. I knew most of the answers, but writing them down proved difficult.

When I had gone to have my fingers drilled, I had forgotten to ask Dr. Blair how long I'd be stuck in the splints. We had been too busy hassling about my enlarged liver. And I sure as hell didn't want to call him back to ask about it now. He'd climb all over me about not seeing Dr. Wang.

Lost in thought, I didn't notice Wanda standing beside me with my plate in her hand watching as I struggled to write down twenty-three across, Jacob.

"You're sure good at that. I never have been able to work crossword puzzles."

"I'm good at it, Wanda, because my mind is brimming over with useless facts and information."

She looked at me sympathetically and shook her head. "You just eat your breakfast now, and don't you go paying any attention to what that Maxwell Cole writes. He doesn't know what he's talking about, and you shouldn't take it to heart, you hear?"

She put down my plate and walked away. I did as I was told. I ate my breakfast. I did *not* read the end of Maxwell Cole's column. I didn't want to, didn't dare. I was afraid that if I did, I'd go out and find that rotten little son of a bitch and shoot him.

Whoever said, "Sticks and stones will break my bones/But words will never hurt me," didn't know Maxwell Cole.

So much for everything I ever learned in Sunday School.

CHAPTER 19

RALPH AMES WAS UP AND GONE WHEN I GOT BACK TO the penthouse. I was restless, itchy, and frustrated. Maxwell Cole's sniping column had cast a pall on the morning. Like a man who looks at his glass and sees it half empty rather than half full, I could no longer take any pleasure from the fact that Lorenzo Tabone was safely in custody in Illinois. All I could see was that I still hadn't gotten to first base on finding Tadeo Kurobashi's killer.

I was missing something. His death wasn't an act of random violence committed by a total stranger. No, there had to be a pattern, a connection, one that still eluded me.

To give myself something to do, I tried calling Clay Woodruff in Port Angeles. The Port Angeles police had reluctantly verified that the number of the pay phone in the "lobby" of the Ritz Hotel did indeed match the one on Tadeo Kurobashi's notepad. I wasn't surprised when nobody answered. When I called Davey's Locker and spoke to the bartender, he told me Clay had been called out of town. I already *knew* that, you jerk, I thought, as I slammed the phone back in its cradle.

Next I tried calling Andrew Halvorsen. He answered on the seventh ring.

"How're you doing, Andy?" I asked.

"Okay," he mumbled. He sounded groggy, half asleep. "What time is it?"

"Eight-thirty. Are you going to go on over to Spokane today?"

"Yeah," he said. "Sure."

"When?"

"Don't rush me. As soon as I get work-wise. I had a bad night."

"You've talked to Alvin Grant?"

"No, oh wait a minute. I guess maybe I did."

"So you know they've got Tabone in custody?"

"I remember that now."

Halvorsen was so rummy, I wanted to shake him, wake him up. Monica Halvorsen wasn't worth being this screwed up over. "Get your ass out of bed and go to Spokane," I ordered. "Are you going to lie around all morning and feel sorry for yourself, or are you going to go to work?"

"You're an asshole, Beaumont," Halvorsen said, banging the phone as he hung up.

Was he going to Spokane or not? I couldn't tell, but at least he was awake. It was cold comfort. Next I tried calling Lieutenant Alvin Grant. The dispatcher in the Schaumburg Police Department told me that Grant had gone home, and when I called there, his wife said he was asleep.

"Al was up working a case all night," she told me. "He just went to bed a few minutes ago. Can I take a message?"

"Tell him Detective Beaumont called from Seattle. Ask him to call me and let me know how things are going with Tabone."

"I'll do that," she said. "But not until after he wakes up."

Chafing at the bit, I tried pacing the floor only to discover that with the splints on my fingers it was impossible to shove my hands into my pockets. Quality pacing requires that both hands be shoved all the way down to the bottoms of pants pockets. I couldn't do anything right, not even pacing.

But just when I thought I was losing it, the phone rang. Somebody was calling me for a change.

"Detective Boomont?" a woman asked. She stumbled over my name the way telephone solicitors do when they are blindly working their way down some charity's sucker list.

"This is Detective Beaumont," I said, withholding the snarl, waiting for the inevitable pitch before I blew her out of the water. The pitch never came.

"Sorry to call you at home, but this is the number you gave me."

"It's fine," I said, trying to place the unfamiliar voice. "What can I do for you?"

She paused, and for a moment I wondered if she was going to hang up.

"It's Chrissey," she said finally, her voice dropping several levels so I had to strain to hear her. "Chrissey Morrison," she added.

The woman from DataDump. Every object in the room suddenly shifted into sharper focus as my whole body jarred to attention.

"Yes, Chrissey. Is there something I can do for you?"

"Can you meet me?" she asked.

I wanted to ask her what had happened, to find out if anything was wrong, but I didn't dare. Her connection to the telephone seemed so tenuous, so frail, that I was afraid any unexpected comment on my part might scare her away, frighten her into hanging up.

"Where?" I asked, keeping my voice low and reassuring. "Where would you like me to meet you?"

"At the locks, the Ballard Locks," she said. "Over by the fish ladder."

"When?"

"Would an hour be all right?"

I could have been there in ten minutes, five if traffic was light, but I didn't say so. "Sure," I said. "An hour will be fine. I'll meet you there about a quarter after ten."

"Come alone," Chrissey Morrison cautioned, and hung up without saying good-bye. I stood there for some time with the phone in my hand and dial tone buzzing in my ear.

I could think of only one reason Chrissey Morrison would call me. Actually there were two. One was if her husband Dean had decided to talk to me. The other was if I was wrong about Dean Morrison and he was Tadeo Kurobashi's killer after all.

So what to do? Did I follow directions and go alone to meet Chrissey Morrison, or did I call Big

Al or someone else from the department and drag them along as backup?

I tried calling Lindstrom's house in Ballard, figuring I could pick him up on my way over, but there was no answer, and Big Al is far too stubborn a Norwegian to stoop to owning an answering machine.

Watching the clock, I took the time to clean and oil my Smith and Wesson. My gimpy hand made gun cleaning a slow and complicated process. When I finished, I tried Big Al again. Still no answer. I tried Watty as well. He wasn't home either, and it didn't seem urgent enough to go through channels and jangle his beeper on his day off.

Time passed incredibly slowly. I showered and changed clothes. My shoulder holster is right-handed, so I had to tuck the .38 in the back of the waistband of my pants, covering it with my jacket. I knew that if I was going to hit something left-handed, it would have to be at very close range. But I took the .38 along anyway, as a security blanket, my cop's security blanket.

In the car and driving toward Ballard, I called again. Big Al still wasn't home. So I drove to the locks by myself.

It was midmorning and sunny. The locks along with the accompanying fish ladder are a popular attraction in Seattle, particularly on sunny Saturday mornings. I've taken Heather and Tracie there a few times. Heather calls it the elevator for boats and the stairs for fish, both of which are pretty accurate descriptions.

There were any number of people on the walkways

and footpaths, watching while a group of boats, including several pleasure craft and a heavily loaded barge, were lowered from Lake Union to Salmon Bay, a drop of six to twenty-six feet, depending on the tide.

I made my way across the series of zigzagging walkways until I reached the fish ladder area on the far side. There I looked around for Chrissey Morrison, but I didn't see her. I had no desire to go inside the fish-ladder viewing tunnels to see the sockeye salmon and steelhead trout going home to spawn. At the beginning of the run they're not nearly as tattered and battle-weary as they will be farther upstream, but they still remind me too much of my own mortality. If Chrissey Morrison was in there, she'd have to come back outside and find me.

I went over to where a concrete bench had been shoved against the bottom of the bluff. From that vantage point, I had a clear view of anyone stepping off the final walkway. Chrissey showed up, ten minutes later and fifteen minutes late, hurrying across the pedestrian drawbridge as soon as it reopened after the load of boats had gone through. She walked swiftly, as though afraid she might change her mind and turn back.

"Hello, Detective Beaumont," she said when she saw me. This time she pronounced my name correctly.

I nodded in greeting. Chrissey Morrison looked even more haggard and worn than when I had seen her two days earlier at DataDump. She sat down on the bench a foot or two away from me staring intently at the people on the other side of the locks.

"Dean says there wasn't no sword," she said flatly.

"You've talked to him then?"

She nodded.

"Where is he?"

"He thinks it's all a trick, that as soon as you see him, you'll arrest him."

"It's no trick, Chrissey. We need his help."

"I tol' him that. He's over there, the one walkin' back and forth." She nodded across the locks. I saw him then, a medium-built, blond-haired man, pacing nervously behind the group of people at the handrail who were avidly watching boats being loaded for the trip in the other direction.

"Will he talk to me?"

Chrissey Morrison turned and looked at me. "He's here, ain't he?" She waved her arm and motioned to him. Dean Morrison stopped his pacing, nodded, and then headed off for the footbridge. "You wait right here," Chrissey said to me. "I'll bring him."

Nervous crooks make me nervous. Dean Morrison may have been straight as an arrow since he got out, but the fact that he was so obviously agitated by the prospect of talking to a cop made me grateful for the unfamiliar but solid bulge of a .38 grinding into the small of my back. I only wished my usual trigger finger was in reasonable working condition.

Chrissey met her husband at the end of the bridge. Together the two of them walked over to the bench where I was sitting.

"This is him," Chrissey said to her husband. It wasn't a very enthusiastic introduction. I didn't get up, but I held out my left hand. Dean Morrison took it and we shook, guardedly sizing each other up as we did so.

"My wife here says you want to talk to me."

"Yes," I replied. "About the dead man you found the other night at MicroBridge."

"What about him? He was alive when I started to work, and when I went back to give him the bill he was dead. What else is there to tell?"

"Did Chrissey ask you about a sword?"

"Yes, and I didn't see one, neither."

"It wasn't lying there on the floor, next to the body?"

"No."

"What time was it when you found him?"

Dean Morrison shrugged. "Ten or so."

"And then what happened?"

"I got the hell out of there. Fast, man! I was scared shitless. I don't want to get sent back up, no sir."

"Where'd you go?"

"I just drove."

"Where to?"

"I ended up in a place down in Tukwila, the Silver Dollar, and had me a couple of pitchers to calm down. But after a while, I got to thinkin' that you cops might come lookin' for me anyways, on account of the bill, and I went back to get it."

"That's when you found that the door to the loading dock had been locked?"

"Yes."

"What happened then?"

"Well, as I was goin' there, I was still scared, see. I figured if somebody had already found him, I didn't want nobody to see me hangin' around, so I parked the truck two buildings over and walked from there." Dean Morrison paused and looked at his wife.

"Go on," she said. "Tell him. This is what we come for."

"So anyways, I'm almost there, walkin' along the railroad track. All of a sudden, this car comes screamin' away from the loadin' dock and practically runs me down."

"Who was it, do you know?"

"How the hell would I know? It was dark. I was just tryin' to get the hell out of the way so the bastard wouldn't hit me."

"Could you tell what kind of car it was, or did you get the license number?"

Dean shook his head. "No way. He was drivin' too damn fast."

"So the driver was a man?"

"I think so."

"What kind of car was it?"

"Small. Foreign. I don't know what kind."

"Was there anything about it that might help us identify it?"

"I didn't see nothin', except for one thing."

"What was that?"

"The taillights. The car had funny little slanted taillights. Reminded me of one of them barber poles."

"Could you tell what color the car was?"

"No way, man. It was dark back there. I couldn't hardly see nothin'. So after he left, I went up on the dock and tried the door, but it was locked, so I give up and come on home."

"What time was that?"

Dean shrugged. "Around midnight, I guess, maybe later. I didn't check."

The timing element in the story bothered me. If Kurobashi was already dead at ten o'clock, why was the killer still hanging around Industry Square at midnight, two hours later? There had to be some compelling reason for the murderer to risk being caught with the body.

I glanced at Dean Morrison. He was standing there, watching me apprehensively, waiting for my next question. "Did you see anyone else around the office during the course of the evening?"

"Only the woman. Chrissey already told you about her."

"No one else?"

"Nobody."

"How many bags of confetti were there when you finished?"

"Six. Five of paper and one with nothin' in it but floppy disks."

"Can you think of anything else?"

"Nope, that's just about it."

"That's what I need then," I said. "Thanks for your help."

"You mean I can go?"

I nodded. He looked down at Chrissey, as though he couldn't quite believe his ears. She returned the look with a smile of encouragement. They turned and started away.

"One more thing," I said.

Dean Morrison's shoulders sagged as he slowly turned back to face me. "What's that?" he asked.

"Get your butt back to work," I said. "You and your wife have a good little business going, but if you go AWOL in that truck very often, you're going to screw it up."

Gradually a grin spread over Morrison's somber face. "You bet. We'll be open again on Monday." He gave a thumbs-up sign.

DataDump was back in business. Have shredder, will travel.

Dean Morrison reached over and put one arm across his wife's shoulders. The two of them walked away. I watched while they crossed the series of footbridges and then went out toward the parking lot through the gardens. They were struggling, but maybe they'd make it. For all her shortcomings, Chrissey Morrison had a whole lot more going for her than Monica Halvorsen.

I sat on the bench for another ten minutes, giving them plenty of time to leave without worrying about being followed. I was lost in thought. A car with barber pole taillights and a handcart loaded with six bags of shredder confetti didn't make for much of a lead, but it was more than we'd had before. Often it's a whole slew of little things taken together that solve a case rather than one huge mind-boggling revelation.

Spending my Saturday afternoon going from auto dealership to auto dealership trying to spot late-model foreign cars with striped and slanted taillights didn't sound like my idea of a good time, and I didn't much want to hike along a railroad track looking for confetti, either, but I knew I'd do both if I had to, if there was no other way.

The phone in the car was ringing as I turned the key in the ignition. "Hello, Ralph," I said.

"How did you know it was me? Am I the only person who calls you on your cellular phone?"

"Damn near. What's up?"

"I just dropped Machiko off at the Four Seasons and wondered if you'd like to have lunch. I'll buy, and not at the Doghouse, either."

Ames is a good sport about going to the Doghouse with me, but I don't think he'd nominate it for inclusion in the local dining guide, *Seattle's Best Places*. *Seattle Cheap Eats* is more like it.

"Where do you want to go?"

"Meet me at Triples. I'm in the mood for Dijon chicken."

Triples is built right on the water at Lake Union. It's a place where you can park your car or your boat with equal facility. It was almost two, but the Saturday lunchtime crowd lingered over coffee and drinks. We had to wait a few minutes to get a window table.

"So how did the meeting go with George?" I asked.

Ames seemed distant, preoccupied. "Oh, that was fine. No problem. From the way it sounded, I think the two of them may get around to burying the hatchet eventually. Machiko told Dr. Yamamoto the same story she told us."

"About her first husband? How'd he take it?"

Ames frowned. "Relieved I'd say. Like he finally had the answer to a question that had been plaguing him for a long time."

"Forty years is a long time to be asking the same

damn question," I said. "But he did give Machiko the sword?"

"He didn't *give* it to her; he *lent* it to her."

"Lent it! What the hell does that mean?"

"He said they got the results back from the lab. The only prints on it belong to Tadeo Kurobashi. George still needs to have the sword available for possible court room proceedings, but Machiko convinced him to let her have it for the afternoon, complete with the rosewood box. Sentimental reasons I guess."

So George Yamamoto hadn't entirely knuckled under. Somehow he and Machiko had reached an agreement. "Isn't George worried that she'll take off with it?"

Ames shook his head. "He isn't. She gave her word. The two of them evidently came to some kind of understanding. They were speaking in Japanese, so I'm not entirely sure what was said. I offered to post a security bond, but George said that wouldn't be necessary."

"Surely your friend Winter could translate for you."

"He wasn't there. Archie got called to Vancouver, B.C., this morning two hours before our first appointment. He had to go up right away to check out something that's coming on the market. The sword business could be delayed indefinitely."

"What about the other appointment, the one with Davenport?"

Ames frowned. "Not so good. That's the one that's bothering me."

"Why? What happened?"

"Davenport is pushing too hard. It's like he wants all of this completed overnight. It's far too complicated for that. I advised Machiko to take her time and not be pushed into anything, particularly considering what's happening with Winter and the sword. Archie may be able to come up with a program that will give them enough capital to pay off the judgment."

"If that flake of a Clay Woodruff would shape up and agree to testify . . ."

"Who's Woodruff?" Ralph Ames was suddenly on point and sitting a full three inches taller in his chair.

"Woodruff. Clay Woodruff, the guy who ditched me over in Port Angeles last night."

"Who is he?"

"He was supposedly Tadeo Kurobashi's friend, a key witness in the patent infringement trial, but he didn't show up when he was supposed to testify, and Kurobashi lost the case. I talked to the judge, Chip Kelley, who's a friend of mine. He said that if Woodruff would actually testify, there was a good chance Kimiko could countersue Blakeslee and void the judgment against her father. But like I said, Woodruff's a flake. When I tried to talk to him last night, he ditched me and disappeared."

"He's here," Ralph Ames said quietly.

"He's what?" I demanded.

"He's here. In Seattle. When I dropped Machiko off at the Four Seasons on my way to meet you, Woodruff was waiting for her in the lobby."

"Jesus Christ, Ames! Why didn't you tell me that in the first place?"

"You never asked," Ames replied. "You never told me his name."

I was already standing up, pushing aside my chair.

"Wait a minute," Ames said. "Where are you going?"

"To find them, goddamnit. I still don't know which side that slippery son of a bitch is on."

CHAPTER 20

THE WAITER WAS COMING TOWARD US CARRYING A tray laden with our food. I nearly knocked him flat as I rushed by. How Ames managed to pay the bill and still catch up with me before I got out of Triples' parking lot, I'll never know. "I'm coming too," he said, climbing into the car. "Where are we going?"

"The Four Seasons," I said. "Maybe they're still there."

But of course Woodruff and Machiko weren't there, or if they were, we couldn't find them.

"What now?" Ames asked.

"I don't know," I told him.

We went back down the escalator to the hotel's University Street entrance with its brass and glass doors and circular drive. Beside the door a uniformed doorman and three parking attendants were involved in an earnest conversation about the afternoon's University of Washington football game in Husky Stadium.

"Did any of you happen to notice a wild-looking

man come in here in the last few hours? He looks like an unreconstituted hippie—mid-thirties, long brown hair, some gray, wears it in a ponytail. He's a friend of mine. I need to find him."

One of the parking attendants nodded. "You mean the guy in the big green station wagon? Sure, I saw him. He was here, but then he left. Had a little old lady with him."

My stomach turned sour as a solid knot of fear grew in my gut. Woodruff had Machiko, and he had taken her someplace with him. That meant he probably had the sword as well.

"What kind of little old lady?" I asked, more out of habit than anything else. I already knew the answer.

"Tiny. Japanese, I'd say."

The parking attendant was basking at being the center of attention. He went on with his story. "When she went to get into the Suburban, it was too tall for her. The guy had a little stool in the backseat. A footstool. She used that."

"Did you say Suburban?" I asked. "A green Suburban?"

The attendant grinned. "That's right. With a bumper sticker that said, 'Have you hugged your horse today?'"

Two limos filled with members of an arriving wedding party drove into the driveway. The doorman and attendants left off their conversation to go to work.

"I'm a son of a bitch," I said. "What the hell is Clay Woodruff doing driving Kimiko's car, and how the hell did he get it?"

Leaving Ames standing there, I hurried back to the car, punched a number into the phone, and dialed the department. Once I was connected, I asked to speak to the traffic supervisor. "This is Detective Beaumont from homicide. Who's this?"

"Captain Donovan. What can I do for you, Beaumont?" he asked cheerfully.

"I need to have people on the lookout for an old white-over-green Suburban with a bumper sticker that says 'Have you hugged your horse today?'"

"How about a license number instead of a bumper sticker?" Donovan asked. "We prefer 'em, actually."

About that time, I didn't need a stand-up comedian. "I don't have a damn license number. The vehicle is registered to a Kimiko Kurobashi who lives over near Colfax. If you can get the number, more power to you."

"So what do you want us to do if somebody sees it?" Donovan asked. "Detain it? Blow it up?"

"No, call me on my car phone, and let me know where they are. I don't want to spook this guy into doing something crazy. He's got a woman with him, an old woman. I wouldn't want anything to happen to her."

For the first time all trace of humor went out of Donovan's voice. "This sounds serious, Beaumont, like maybe it ought to be going out on an APB."

"No. No APB. Keep it low profile."

"If anything goes wrong, Beaumont, it's your ass not mine."

"Right," I said. "That's not news. And something else. Have someone search along the Burlington

Northern track around Industry Square to see if they can locate some fifty-gallon trash bags filled with confetti."

"As in New Year's Eve?" Donovan asked.

Donovan is one of those people who couldn't get serious to save his life. "As in from a shredder," I growled.

"Okay, okay, Beaumont. We'll look into it."

I put the phone back in its holder, and then sat there without moving. The engine was running and my hands were on the steering wheel, but I didn't know where I was going. Ames climbed in beside me.

"Goddamnit, Ames, this case is driving me crazy! We've got a damn suspect in jail in Chicago, but it's not even our case. For the life of me, I can't see any Chicago connection back to Tadeo Kurobashi."

"Chris Davenport is from Chicago," Ralph Ames said quietly.

"He is? How'd you find that out?" I asked.

"At his office this morning with Machiko. His diplomas are on the wall. Northwestern and Loyola are both Chicago schools."

That took me back a step or two. Why hadn't I made the connection? "Davenport's from Chicago? But then, all kinds of folks are from Chicago. It's not against the law to leave there, you know. People do it all the time."

"His kind of lawyering ought to be against the law," Ames declared grimly. "We have first-year summer interns who do better jobs than he's done for the Kurobashis."

I shifted into gear and started into traffic.

"Where to now?" Ames asked.

"Maybe he's still at his office. I want to have a little chat with him."

Ames glanced at his watch. It was 3:35. "I doubt he's still there," he said. "By now he's probably on his way to the memorial service."

"He's going?"

"That's what he told Machiko this morning when she asked him about it. Davenport said he was planning to attend."

I had merged onto University and made a dash for the left lane in order to turn north on Fourth and head over to 1201 Third. Now, with a glance in the mirror, I jumped the green light and headed for a right-hand turn onto Fifth instead.

"God damn you, Ames, you're one closemouthed bastard. What the hell else do you know that I *ought* to know?"

"Maybe the memorial service is where Machiko is going, too."

"That's where you're dead wrong. She wouldn't go there on a bet."

"How much?" Ames asked.

"How much what?"

"How much do you want to bet? As we were leaving Davenport's office, when Machiko asked him if he was going to the memorial service and he said probably, she said she'd see him there."

"I'll be damned," I said.

I was a man putting together a jigsaw puzzle in the middle of an earthquake, with pieces falling off the table in all directions. Important pieces. Corner pieces. Machiko Kurobashi, who had been dead set against holding any kind of memorial service, was now planning to attend one organized by her sworn enemy. And my friend, old Aimless Ames, had been sitting on a ton of information like a great big bird without feeding me any of it. Maybe Davenport *was* the Chicago connection. Maybe it wasn't Kurobashi at all. I fumbled in my pocket and got out the notebook where I had written down Alvin Grant's home number.

"Call this guy at home. Have his wife wake him up if you have to. Tell him I need to know if he's ever heard of anyone named Christopher Davenport."

Darting in and out of traffic, I turned down the hill on Yesler and raced across the north/south arterials on a series of yellow lights. If my driving scared him, Ralph Ames didn't say anything about it. He had picked up the cellular phone and was punching numbers into it.

When I reached the corner of Main and Occidental, I discovered that the whole half block along Main was reserved for fire department vehicles only. I parked there anyway, leaving the motor running and the flashers on.

Someone was just answering Alvin Grant's phone. "When you get done, park this thing, will you?"

Ames nodded, holding the phone to his ear. He was looking ahead of us toward the pay parking lot off on our right. He was the one who saw it first.

"Wait a minute, isn't that the Suburban?"

I looked where he was pointing, and sure enough there in the middle of the lot sat a hulking green and white Suburban. I could see the outline of the bumper sticker even though it was too far away for me to read the words.

"I'll be damned!" With that, I slammed the car door shut and started inside.

Waterfall Park, as it's called, takes up a quarter of a block. Walled in with red brick, it has a terrace with small outdoor tables, while in one corner a two-story-high waterfall drowns out the noise of city traffic with the roaring rush of flowing water. I headed for the open gate at a dead run, only to almost collide with a man in a heavy motorized wheelchair who was trying to maneuver through the same space at the same time I was.

"Sorry," the man said, but it didn't sound like a man speaking. There was a tinny, canned quality to the voice.

"My fault," I said.

I looked down at him then. He was an older man, probably well into his sixties, whose body was terribly twisted and bent. On his lap sat a computer, a laptop very much like the one I had seen Clay Woodruff using to single-handedly produce a hotel full of music in Port Angeles. Laboriously, the man pressed two keys on the computer. The voice said, "I'll go."

Just then Bernice Oliver came hurrying over. "Sorry it took so long, Clarence. All the handicapped spots were taken." She looked up at me. "Why hello, Detective Beaumont. I'd like you to meet my husband, Clarence."

The last thing I wanted to do right then was hold still for introductions, but there was no way to escape.

"We've already met," I said.

Clarence Oliver once more pushed some buttons

on the computer. It wasn't an instantaneous process, because it took time for him to locate the keys with his badly crippled fingers. As soon as he did though, a motor whirred and the chair moved effortlessly through the gate. Bernice Oliver stood on the sidewalk, watching her husband's slow but smooth progress as he negotiated the corner in front of the waterfall and rolled up the walkway to where a group of people were gathered at the far end of the park.

"He did so want to come," Bernice said to me. "It's the least we could do. I don't know how we would have managed if it hadn't been for Mr. Kurobashi. It's his invention, you see."

"What's his invention?"

"Why the computer, of course. Not the computer, but the program in it. You saw how it works—the voice synthesizer, moving the chair. That's all Mr. Kurobashi's doing. He did it for a lark, and wouldn't take a dime for it, either. I never would have been able to keep Clarence at home this long if it hadn't been for that. I have some help, of course. A visiting nurse comes in for a while every day, but that computer has been such a blessing. That was the worst thing about it. Losing the ability to communicate. The computer changed all that. Such a blessing," she said again, and walked away.

I stood for a moment longer, watching Bernice rejoin her husband and continue on to the others. I remembered Big Al's and my conversation when we had speculated about the cause of Mrs. Oliver's fierce loyalty to her dead boss. I had an answer to that question now, and it had absolutely nothing to do with screwing around. So Tadeo Kurobashi had done another good deed. Then what was his connection to a Mafia clan in Chicago?

The delay at the gate had broken up my headlong plunge into the park, and now I stood there a few moments longer, trying to see who was there and who wasn't. Clay Woodruff was easy to spot. He had come forward to meet the Olivers and was standing in front of them, nodding in agreement to something that had been said.

Ames appeared behind me, rushing and out of breath. "I parked the car in a lot, but I had a hell of a time doing it," he said. "What's going on down here? Almost all the spaces are full."

"What did Grant have to say?"

"You're not going to believe it."

"Tell me, goddamnit."

"Christopher Davenport Senior is Aldo Pappinzino's personal attorney."

"No shit!" I turned and sprinted into the park. I had gone only a few steps when George Yamamoto, seated at one of the tables on the terrace, stood up and raised his hand, motioning for silence. Almost instantly, the people grew still. Someone switched off the waterfall. Outside the confines of the tiny park, we could hear the rush of traffic which had previously been drowned out by the roaring water. From the band shell a block away came a wavering high-school-band rendition of "The Stars and Stripes Forever." Inside Waterfall Park itself, it seemed almost eerily quiet.

There was a woman dressed in black sitting at the table with George. Her back was to us, but George nodded to her before he began to speak. Even from the far corner, his voice carried throughout the park. Everyone fell silent. I had taken several more steps, but I stopped now in order to hear.

"When Tadeo and I were young, this park was nothing but an empty lot. We met here as boys, years before Minidoka. This was where we learned to play baseball, to shoot baskets. I have invited you all here today, to honor our friend. Today I have learned things about Tadeo that I never knew before, things about people he helped, things he did that he never broadcast.

"This is not a formal service, not a religious service. Tadeo was not a religious man. He was a good man. Tadeo did not want a funeral, and so no funeral was planned. This is instead a service of remembrance. His wife, Machiko, is here with us. She had not planned to come today, and many of you may never have met her. If you have a chance, and if Tadeo made a difference in your life, let her know about it. This may be your only opportunity."

He held out his hand toward the woman seated at the table and helped her to stand. She was wearing a long black silk kimono, and it wasn't until she turned to face us that I realized it was Machiko Kurobashi. She nodded to the one hundred or so people who were gathered around, then she sat back down at the table. George Yamamoto raised his hand, and the waterfall once more roared to life.

"I'll be damned," I said.

"It's a good thing you didn't bet," Ames said over my shoulder.

Once more we started toward George's table. He saw us coming and waved.

"I believe you know both these people," George said to Machiko as we got closer. She looked up at us and nodded.

Stumped for something to say, I didn't want to blurt out what Ames had just told me about Christopher Davenport. "I was worried about you," I said finally. "I didn't know you knew Mr. Woodruff."

"Didn't," she answered. "Do now. Good man."

"How is Kimi?"

"Mr. Woodruff see Kimiko in Spokane today. Much better. Get well soon."

"Looks like you were just pushing panic buttons on that one," Ames whispered under his breath.

Machiko began struggling to get up. She had a new cane, a metal three-pronged one, to replace the treasured one made of gnarled wood. I took her elbow and helped her to her feet.

She smiled up at me gratefully. "I talk to people," she said.

I turned to George, and he motioned for Ames and me to sit down. "How did all this happen?"

He shrugged his shoulders. "Believe me, I have no idea. This morning, when she came to my office she said she had changed her mind and wanted to come to the memorial service. I was surprised."

"Me too," I said.

I watched Machiko limp her way through the crowd, stopping now and then to speak to someone. I noticed she didn't shake hands, and she seemed to be carrying herself oddly, with one elbow stiffly bent. Her arm looked almost as though it were still in a sling although no sling was visible. I assumed that it was some lingering aftereffect of her injuries and didn't think much about it.

She stopped briefly by the Olivers. Clay Woodruff was still there, talking animatedly. Machiko listened to what he had to say with a kind of grave interest, then she went on. When she was about halfway to the waterfall, I realized that she was no longer following a random path from person to person. She was moving purposefully, with some definite goal in mind.

At almost the same instant, I saw Chris Davenport. He had obviously arrived late and was standing in the same gate we had all passed through earlier. He too was assessing the situation. Unerringly, Machiko was headed toward him.

She stopped for a moment and seemed to struggle with her sleeve, not the one holding the cane, but the other one, the one I had thought was lame. The arm dropped to her side, and for only the briefest moment, the sun caught the glint of metal.

With a flash of insight, I knew what I had seen, knew what was going to happen.

Machiko Kurobashi had the sword in her hand, and she intended to use it.

"My God," I groaned. "She's going to kill him."

If Chris Davenport was somehow behind all this, then I couldn't quarrel with Machiko's intention. But I had to stop her, no matter what. If the sword became a legitimate murder weapon, it would never be able to accomplish Tadeo Kurobashi's dream. It would go back to the evidence room, not to Sotheby's. For Tadeo's sake, for Kimi's, and most of all for Machiko's, I had to stop her.

I leaped to my feet, sending the metal chair crashing into the brick wall behind me. I vaulted over the low wrought-iron fence that separated the upper level of the terrace from the lower walkways. Machiko Kurobashi was diagonally away from me across the park. She was still a good ten steps away from Davenport when I knocked over the chair, and she turned, pausing slightly, to see what had caused the disturbance.

Meanwhile, Davenport caught sight of her. He waved and moved eagerly in her direction, the phony metallic smile plastered on his chipmunk face.

With both of them moving, they were closing on one another far too rapidly for me to get there in time. I had to do something to stop her.

"Machiko," I shouted. "Machiko Kusumi. Stop."

And she did. Long enough to turn and look at me. Long enough for me to reach her side and grasp her wrist.

"Don't," I said. "Don't do this. You mustn't."

She tried to pull her wrist free from my hand. The sword, visible to me, was still concealed from Davenport behind a fold of the flowing kimono.

"I must," she whispered fiercely. "I must kill him. Let me go. Tadeo do this for me. I do it for him."

Davenport must have been close enough by then to hear her. He stopped in confusion and looked around, searching for an escape route, edging back the way he had come.

But Machiko hadn't given up. With an incredibly strong jerk, she pulled her hand free of mine, brandishing the *tanto* in the air. I knocked it down. Down and away. If it hadn't been for the splints on my hand, I probably would have lost some fingers to the razor-sharp blade. The sword crashed to the ground and went spinning harmlessly across the bricks.

Machiko dropped to the ground too. For a moment I thought I had hurt her, but she knelt there sobbing hopelessly. I ducked down beside her to see if she was injured.

She wasn't. Machiko Kurobashi had set her heart on revenge, and I had thwarted her, stayed her hand. She crouched there, weeping brokenheartedly. As soon as I understood that, I jumped back up and looked around for Christopher Davenport.

He was gone. Disappeared completely, taking his metallic smile with him.

"Stay here," I ordered Machiko. "You stay here. I'll go get him and bring him back."

Like most things, it was a hell of a lot easier said than done.

CHAPTER 21

I CHARGED OUT OF WATERFALL PARK JUST IN TIME TO see Davenport struggling with the lock on his car. A Nissan Pulsar with diagonal taillights. Barber pole striped taillights.

By then I had drawn my gun. "Stop or I'll shoot," I yelled across the lot. It was an empty threat. The park behind the parking lot was full of people and the school band had launched into a spirited version of "Louie Louie."

I didn't dare risk a shot, but Davenport didn't know that. He turned and looked at me, and then sprinted away down the aisle of cars with me running after him. He turned left up Washington and then ducked into the alley halfway between Occidental and First. I can run pretty damn fast in a pinch, and I was gaining on him as we came tearing down the alley toward Yesler and James.

I wasn't far behind him, but again there was a crowd of people in front of us, and I couldn't risk firing the .38.

Falling in with a large group of pedestrians, Davenport crossed Yesler while I dodged through to a chorus of honking horns. I was still in the middle of James, when he, along with a crowd of fifty or so people, filed down a steep iron-railed stairway beside the Pioneer Building.

That was when I realized that the group of pedestrians was actually part of a tour, a walking guided tour that makes hourly visits through what's known as the Seattle Underground, an area of town that was cemented over shortly after the great fire of 1889. Third floors were arbitrarily declared ground floors and the streets and sidewalks were raised to that level. Bottle-bottom glass in iron grids was built into the sidewalks to provide light to the businesses that continued to prosper down below there for the next ten to twelve years.

In the mid-sixties, fueled by post–World's Fair euphoria, an enterprising Seattle entrepreneur had mucked out and shored up parts of the underground and had begun offering guided tours in the city's dusty, rubble-filled basement.

I had gone on the tour once myself, with my son's Cub Scout den, and I knew from that visit that the stairs beneath the Pioneer Building formed the entrance to the last portion of the tour. It ended there with a locked door leading into the Underground's museum and gift shop.

So Christopher Davenport had made a big mistake. He had allowed himself to be trapped in a box canyon, a dead end.

The tour's guide had gone on ahead into another dimly lighted room while the last straggler held open the metal screened gate to let me in. "I got stuck in traffic," I said apologetically.

"No problem," he replied, and hurried off after his wife and kiddies.

I expected the place to be cool and quiet, but instead, just inside the door, a barred wooden gate led off to the left where three huge air-conditioning units threw off a tremendous amount of heat and noise.

"Come on in here so you can hear," the guide called from the next room. I did as I was told, edging into the room where a group of fifty or so people stood clumped around an old tin bathtub while the guide did a five-minute memorized talk. I worked my way through the crowd, looking for my quarry, but Davenport wasn't there.

When the guide wasn't looking, I sidled into the next room, where lighted displays showed various old-time store windows. My feet sounded hollow on the heavy wooden planks. This room was cool and damp and lined with cobwebs. Chris Davenport was nowhere in sight, and there were no side passages where he could have hidden. I tried the door to the museum, but it was securely locked.

I knew that once the guide had finished her talk, the audience would be free to wander around on their own for a few minutes before the door leading into the museum and gift shop was unlocked and the people were herded back upstairs.

There was no way for Davenport to get out ahead of time, and he was not mingling with the group. So he must have slipped away in that first room somewhere. Chances were, he was still there.

The guide was just finishing her talk as I came back through the middle room. She gave me a reproving glare, but I ignored her and went back to the entrance with its heat and noise, where muted sunlight filtered down the stairs and sifted in through the metal grating.

I could see now that there was a crawl space that led back up past the air-conditioning units. Davenport had to be there. It was the only place left where he could be hiding. Stepping quietly, I moved to one side of the wall just inside the door and waited.

A good five minutes passed. Soon I heard the guide's voice. "Everybody out?" she called.

I didn't answer. I stood pressed against the wall with the sweat running down my face, dripping into my eyes, blinding me. I didn't wipe it away. The waiting seemed to go on forever; then, suddenly, I heard a noise, a muffled scraping noise that was different from the steady thrum of motors.

He was back there, in with the mechanical equipment. I had him trapped. He moved forward cautiously, fumbling with the metal bar used to shut the wooden gate and discourage tourists from taking a wrong turn and straying off the guided path. Still I didn't move. I stood, holding my breath, wanting to have him clearly out in front of me before I made a move and showed myself.

Davenport backed into the light. He was carrying something in his hand, something heavy-looking.

"Stop right there," I commanded. "Drop it."

Instead, he swung around toward me. He was holding a hunk of iron grid studded with thick, purple glass. He moved so quickly that the piece of metal whacked into the barrel of my .38, knocking it loose from my hand and sending it skittering across the wooden walkway.

In a split second I had to choose between going for him and going for the gun. The Smith and Wesson was too far away. I dove for Davenport's knees and knocked him away from me. He grunted in surprise as the piece of metal dropped from his hand and fell harmlessly away.

We were even now. No, that's not true. We weren't even, I was better off. I could tell from the way he fell that he didn't know how, that he had never played a day's worth of tackle football in his life. Chris Davenport was a goddamned wimp.

He tried to squirm away from me, scrabbling toward the gun, but I caught him by the legs and hauled him back. I flipped him over on his back and held him one-handed by the neck of his shirt, while his bulgy little eyes almost popped out of his head.

"Let me go. You've got nothing on me," he screeched in panic. "You're choking me."

My knee was right there beside his crotch, itching to turn him into a tenor. Maybe even a soprano.

"I've got more on you than you know, you worthless little shit! After what you did to Kimi . . ."

"I didn't do that, I swear. It was Tabone. It was all Tabone's idea."

"Don't bother to confess," I told him. "I don't want to hear it, slimebag. I haven't read you your goddamned rights."

I pulled him to his feet. He stood there swaying, pulling at his throat as though I really had been choking him. I pushed him toward the wall and started to

retrieve my gun when he whirled on me, aiming a vicious kick at my head. Even though I dodged to one
side, the toe of his foot still caught my cheekbone. I
lost my balance and fell. On my hand. My right hand.
My broken fingers screamed with newfound pain.

Up until then I hadn't been mad. Not really mad.
Not with the black-blooded rage that filled me now.
He had scrambled up the steps toward the gate and
was tugging at it, but the gate was locked with a
lock that required a key on either side. It wouldn't
budge.

With my left hand, I grabbed his leg and twisted
it. I'm not often surprised by my own strength, but
adrenaline does wonders. Davenport went down
hard, yelping with pain. I fell on top of him, pin-
ning him to the dusty wooden plank floor.

Our faces were only inches apart as he struggled
to get loose, bucking and pitching in a futile attempt
to throw me off while I hung on desperately, with my
one good hand knotted in a handful of shirt directly
under his Adam's apple.

"Listen, creep. Tell me one thing. Who used the
bottle?"

"Tabone," he squeaked. "I swear to God, it was
Tabone. I only watched."

And that was when I hit him. Right in the braces.
With my splints. The braces popped apart, twang-
ing like so many broken guitar strings, turning the
inside of his mouth to hamburger. He screamed in
pain and grabbed for his mouth as blood spurted
from between his lips. He wasn't fighting anymore.
Gingerly, I got off him and stood up. He rolled over
on his side, coughing and spitting blood.

"Too bad, creep," I said, backing away. "Looks like you'll have to be rewired."

I left him lying there. He wasn't going anywhere. Retrieving my gun, I went into the third room, where I pounded loudly on the gift shop door. When the guide opened it, she looked me up and down in stunned surprise. Covered with muck and dust and blood, I could have stepped right out of *Nightmare on Elm Street*.

"What?" she demanded irritably. "You again?"

I nodded. "I think maybe you'd better call 911. There's a guy out here who's hurt. He'll need an ambulance."

"What about you?" she asked.

"You're right," I answered. "Have 'em send two."

CHAPTER 22

IT TOOK A LONG TIME TO GET THINGS SORTED OUT THAT afternoon. After all, I wasn't even on duty. As they hauled Davenport away in an ambulance, he was screaming police brutality and I was claiming self-defense. Without witnesses, no one was going to prove it one way or the other.

I never did get back to Waterfall Park. I had a long cut on my jaw where Davenport's toe had connected with my face, and I had to go up to Harborview and have it stitched shut. We were in adjoining emergency-room cubicles. Evidently they were still trying to stop Davenport's bleeding. Somebody finally shoved a fistful of gauze into his mouth and shut him up.

Ralph Ames came to the hospital to take me home. As we pulled into Belltown Terrace's garage he said, "By the way, we're having a little din-din."

I had stitches in my face, my clothes were still caked with blood and dirt. "We're not having company tonight," I groaned.

"Just a few people," Ames answered. "Archie's cooking."

How many is a few? I wondered, grumpily figuring I was in for another dose of Italian food, but when we got upstairs, there was no telltale odor of garlic lingering in the hallway.

As soon as we came into the apartment, a tiny ball of brown-haired braids and knobby knees flung itself at my legs.

"Unca Beau, Unca Beau," Heather Peters squealed. "Are your fingers all right? Are they? Daddy said they're broken. I'm sorry. I didn't mean to. I just wanted to put one more balloon in the car."

And that's how, a whole week later, I finally discovered what had happened to my hand. The fingers were still broken, but how they got that way was no longer a mystery, and consequently, they weren't quite such a mental problem for me either.

"It's all right, Heather," I said. "They're going to be fine."

Heather grabbed my hand, studied it, and then looked up at me with a serious frown on her face. "The bandage is kinda dirty, isn't it?"

"It certainly is," I told her, "and so am I. You wait right here while I go shower."

When I came back from the bathroom a few minutes later, Tracie Peters, who has made it her business to know where everything goes in my house, was busily helping her new stepmother set the table.

"It's nice of you to have us up like this," Amy said, "especially considering what you've been through this afternoon."

"No problem," I told her. "Anybody want a drink?"

Ralph Ames was doing the bartending honors. He handed me a MacNaughton's, and I retreated to the living room, where Clay Woodruff and Machiko Kurobashi, sitting together on the window seat, were deeply involved in a quiet conversation with Ron Peters, who was ensconced in his wheelchair.

As soon as she saw me, Machiko pulled herself up and limped over to me on her cane. She was still wearing the silk kimono, which emphasized her severely bruised and battered face.

I put down my drink. She grasped my good hand and held it, pumping it gratefully.

"Thank you," she said. "For what you do for me. For what you do for Kimiko. So I not go to jail."

"You're welcome," I said. I was tempted to add that it had been a pleasure to punch Chris Davenport's lights out, but I knew better than to admit that aloud to anybody, not even Kimiko Kurobashi's mother. As of that moment, the department was considering my actions in apprehending Davenport as use of reasonable force, and I didn't want anyone to think otherwise.

Clay Woodruff was standing directly behind Machiko with his hand extended as well. "Hope I didn't damage the lock on your car," he said. "If I did, let me know. It's just that once I knew Tad was dead, I had to go to his daughter, and I wasn't about to let you or anybody else stop me."

"But why did he come to you?" I asked.

"Once Tad realized the reason I hadn't testified

was that I hadn't been called, he began to put things together. He told me on Friday that he had begun to suspect that Davenport was cheating him. He said he was going back to Seattle to find out for sure.

"On Sunday morning, he showed up in Port Angeles again. This time he brought along a whole set of floppies, one of which he said would disable the virus. The rest were copies of his company records as well as his research on the new product. He gave them to me for safekeeping and made me promise that if anything ever happened to him, that I would go to Kimi immediately and help her develop and market that product."

"Which is?"

"A spread spectrum multiplexer."

"Pardon me?"

"It's brand-new technology that will make local area networks far more affordable by allowing more than one network on the same set of cables."

"I see," I said, although I didn't understand more than a word or two of what he said. Observing Ralph Ames' enthusiastic nod of approval, I figured whatever it was must be pretty good.

"What about that other thing we were talking about earlier?" Peters asked. "The device Mr. Kurobashi made for the man in the chair."

"I'm sure Tad never intended to market it, but I'll bet that kind of medical assistance computer program is a commercially viable product."

Ron Peters was nodding in agreement. "It sounds like a godsend to me, something that could make life easier for lots of folks."

"It's totally separate from Blakeslee's product

line. You could go ahead with that without having to wait to finish settling the RFLink problem in court," Ralph Ames commented. "And it has the potential to grow into being a good, solid business in its own right."

Woodruff had passed his glass to Ralph for a refill, and now he sat staring thoughtfully at the newly replenished drink. "Tad was the most creative guy I ever knew," he said quietly. "Believe me, if it can be done, I'll make it work. I owe him that much."

The determination in Woodruff's voice made it sound not only possible, but likely. However, Ralph Ames had brought up a touchy subject.

"What about Blakeslee?" I asked.

Ames grinned. "I was talking about that with Clay here a few minutes before I went to pick you up. We'll handle Mr. Blakeslee. No problem."

About that time the front door crashed open and Heather led Archie Winter into the apartment. Holding the platter high over his head, Archie carried a fragrant load of still smoldering barbecued ribs. So much for Italian food.

It was a quiet dinner. Tracie and Heather's unabashed interest in everything Machiko said and did made the meal less difficult for her and for everybody than it would have been otherwise. There's something life-giving about children, even in a time of mourning, something that helps people see beyond their immediate losses. Looking at them I was reminded once more of the final words on Tadeo Kurobashi's computer, and I had to agree with them. A child is indeed "one more hope."

Late that evening, long after everyone but Ames

had gone home, I had a call from the department. Just as I suspected, DataDump's handcart had been found near the railroad track a few blocks south of Industry Square. With the cart, officers discovered five bags of confetti—the paper stuff, not the shredded floppies.

Sunday afternoon Ralph Ames and Archibald Winter III left for Sea-Tac at the same time. Before leaving town, the two of them had come up with a program to provide interim financing to hold Micro-Bridge together and keep Kimi and Machiko above water until such time as the Kusumi family sword could be released for final sale. Ames' preliminary negotiations with Blakeslee had made things look a lot more manageable.

We put Archie on a United flight bound for New York and then walked to another terminal where Ralph would catch his Alaska flight to return to Phoenix.

"By the way," Ames said, as we waited in line in the departure lounge for him to hand over his ticket and board the plane. "I almost forgot. Dr. Wang's office called yesterday. You have an appointment scheduled for ten tomorrow morning."

With that, he handed his ticket to the flight attendant and disappeared down the jetway without giving me a chance to argue. I spent the afternoon alternating between being pissed and being appreciative, but Monday morning at ten, I dutifully presented myself in Dr. Lee Wang's reception room. He prodded and poked, asked me a bunch of pointed questions and took an almost equal number of blood samples. I answered the questions honestly, because there didn't seem to be much point in doing anything else. When he was through with me, Dr. Wang told me to come back on Friday.

That was the beginning of a long, busy week. In a search of Chris Davenport's car, crime lab investigators discovered a few stray pieces of floppy disk confetti although it was impossible to prove conclusively that the debris was actually material from MicroBridge. Why he took the computer disk bag and left the shredded paper, no one has ever been able to figure out.

The most damning evidence was found in his basement. One part consisted of a pair of blood-stained shoes. The blood turned out to be O negative, the same blood type as Tadeo Kurobashi's.

The other was a computer, a new computer still in its original container. The serial number matched the one still on file at the computer store where Tadeo Kurobashi had purchased his daughter's graduation present. We had that smarmy lawyer dead to rights.

In Illinois Alvin Grant was busily working his part of the problem. He called me Wednesday morning.

"What are you finding out?" I asked.

He laughed. "Aldo Pappinzino must be going soft in the head. From what I've been able to piece together so far, his youngest daughter fell in love with somebody outside the mob, a young guy who just graduated from college with a degree in electronics. They want to live in Seattle, and Chris Davenport was delegated to find a company the old man could buy for them as a wedding present. Bargain basement prices, of course, and Davenport targeted MicroBridge.

"It almost worked, except for one thing—Kurobashi wouldn't give up. He held on way longer than anybody expected. The wedding is two weeks from now. Pappinzino was getting antsy, so he sent Tabone out to apply a little pressure either to Kurobashi or Davenport, whoever needed it most.

"By the way, Tabone's been up on several suspected rape charges, same kind of MO as the one out there, but he's always been able to weasel out of it before. His extradition hearing is scheduled for two weeks from now. I want to see him try to duck this one."

The whole story was finally coming clear in my mind. "So when Tadeo figured it out, he enabled the virus and destroyed all his own company's records in order to keep them from falling into the new owner's hands?"

"That's the way I see it," Grant agreed. "Probably with both Tabone and Davenport right there in the room and helpless to stop it."

Grant's theory made sense to me. It must have driven those two bastards up the wall to be so close to getting what they wanted and then to watch the object of all their cheating and scheming disappear before their very eyes. In the intervening days I had talked to a couple of computer experts who had told me that any misguided attempt by Davenport or someone else to retrieve the information would only have made the virus work that much faster.

"And the verse on the computer made them think that Kimi might know the answer?"

"No, I don't think either one of them could have read it. It's more likely that they knew she had been there that night, maybe even saw Kimi leaving her father's office earlier in the evening and erroneously assumed that Tadeo had entrusted her with backup copies of the material he was destroying."

There was a pause. The case was at the point now where we had to turn loose of it and hand it over to the prosecutors. We were both worrying about the outcome.

"Are we going to nail all those crooks?" I asked, "or are they somehow going to slip through the cracks?"

"Not if I can help it," Grant answered. "We may not get 'em all on everything, but we've put a big chink in Aldo Pappinzino's armor. Somebody somewhere is going to be willing to make a deal in order to save his own skin, you wait and see."

I'm doing just that. And so is Alvin Grant. It takes time. We're keeping our fingers crossed.

On Thursday I had a call from Andy Halvorsen. He was phoning from his ex-wife's apartment in Spokane to tell me that Kimi had been released from Sacred Heart and was on her way to Honeydale Farm with Rita Brice.

"How're you doing?" I asked him.

"Better," he said. "Much better." He didn't elaborate on what that meant, but considering where he was calling from, I drew my own conclusions.

Late Friday afternoon I went to see Dr. Wang. He's

a slight man with gray hair, steel-rimmed glasses, and a heart to match.

"You have liver damage, Mr. Beaumont," Dr. Wang said bluntly. "Either you quit drinking or you die, it's just that simple."

Maybe that's why Drs. Wang and Blair get along so well. They have matching bedside manners. Brutal bedside manners.

"That doesn't give me much choice, does it?"

"No," Wang said. "It doesn't. Let me caution you, though, whatever you do, don't try to quit on your own. For a man who has been drinking the quantities you have for as long as you have, you must be under a doctor's care when you stop ingesting alcohol. Medically unsupervised withdrawal from alcohol can be very dangerous, even worse than from heroin. Do I make myself clear?"

"Perfectly," I said.

"You go home and think it over. I'll call you on Monday to see what arrangements should be made."

Big deal! Dr. Wang was giving me the whole damn weekend to think it over. That was mighty generous of him.

I went home. I poured myself a MacNaughton's and sat down in the recliner. After all, this was doctor's orders. He had told me very clearly not to try quitting on my own.

I was sitting there with the drink in one hand and looking at the bandages on the other when the phone rang. I suspected it would be Ralph Ames calling to check up on me, and I almost didn't answer.

"What's happening?" he asked.

"I feel like shit."

"What did the doctor say?"

"That I've got liver damage. That I have to quit drinking or die."

"Where?"

"Where what? My liver's right where it's supposed to be. Where the hell do you think it is?"

"I mean where are you going to go for treatment?"

"How should I know? Wang must have some ideas. He told me to call him on Monday."

And that's when Ames took over. "Look, Beau," he said kindly. "You shouldn't go for treatment up there in Washington. That would be a bad idea. You're too likely to run into people you know, people off the street. I know of a place down here, near Wicken-burg. It's called Ironwood Ranch."

"That sounds like a dude ranch."

"It used to be. Not anymore. It's tops. I know several people who've been through their program. Let me go to work on it and find out how soon they can fit you in."

"Okay," I said. "You do that."

And somehow, as I said the words, the anger I had felt about Ames and his interference in my life changed into something a little closer to gratitude.

Aimless Ames is a real friend, no question about it, and I'm damned lucky to have him.

Don't miss a single one of *New York Times* bestselling author J. A. Jance's novels featuring Seattle private investigator J. P. Beaumont, whom *Booklist* calls "a star attraction."

UNTIL PROVEN GUILTY

"J. A. Jance is among the best—if not the best!"
Chattanooga Times

The little girl was a treasure who should have been
cherished, not murdered. She was only five—too
young to die—and Homicide Detective J. P. Beaumont of the Seattle Police Department isn't going
to rest until her killer pays dearly. But Beaumont's
own obsessions and demons could prove dangerous
companions in a murky world of blind faith and religious fanaticism. And he is about to find out that
he himself is the target of a twisted passion . . . and
a love that can kill.

INJUSTICE FOR ALL

"J. A. Jance does not disappoint her fans."
Washington Times

It was a scene right out of a Hollywood "slasher" movie—a beautiful woman's terrified screams piercing the air, a dead body sprawled at her feet, blood staining the pristine sands of a Washington beach. But the blood is real, and the victim won't be rising when a director yells, "Cut!" In one horrific instant, a homicide detective's well-earned holiday has become a waking nightmare. Suddenly, a lethal brew of passion, madness, and politics threatens to do more than poison J. P. Beaumont's sleep—it's dragging the dedicated Seattle cop into the path of a killer whose dark hunger is rapidly becoming an obsession.

TRIAL BY FURY

"Jance delivers a devilish page-turner."
People

The dead body discovered in a Seattle Dumpster was shocking enough but equally disturbing was the manner of death. The victim, a high-school coach, had been lynched, leaving behind a very pregnant wife to grieve over his passing, and to wonder what dark secrets he took to his grave. A Homicide detective with twenty years on the job, J. P. Beaumont knows this case is a powder keg and he fears where this investigation will lead him. Because the answers lie on the extreme lethal edge of passion and hate, where the wrong kind of love can breed the most terrible brand of justice.

TAKING THE FIFTH

"Jance's [novels] show up on bestseller lists. . . .
one can see why."
Milwaukee Journal-Sentinel

There are many bizarre and terrible ways to die.
Seattle Homicide Detective J.P. Beaumont thought
he had seen them all—until he saw this body, its
wounds, and the murder weapon: an elegant woman's
shoe, its stiletto heel gruesomely caked with blood.
The evidence is shocking and unsettling, even for
a man who prowls the shadows for a living, for it
suggests that savagery is not the exclusive domain of
the predatory male. And the scent of a stylish killer is
pulling Beaumont into a world of drugs, corruption,
and murder to view close-up a cinematic dream at
its most nightmarish . . . and lethal.

IMPROBABLE CAUSE

"Jance brings the reader along with suspense,
wit, surprise, and intense feeling."
Huntsville Times

Perhaps it was fitting justice: a dentist who enjoyed inflicting pain was murdered in his own chair. The question is not who wanted Dr. Frederick Nielsen dead, but rather who of the many finally reached the breaking point. The sordid details of this case, with its shocking revelations of violence, cruelty, and horrific sexual abuse, would be tough for any investigator to stomach. But for Seattle Homicide Detective J. P. Beaumont, the most damning piece of the murderous puzzle will shake him to his very core—because what will be revealed to him is nothing less than the true meaning of unrepentant evil.

A MORE PERFECT UNION

A shocking photo screamed from the front pages of the tabloids—the last moments of a life captured for all the world to see. The look of sheer terror eternally frozen on the face of the doomed woman indicated that her fatal fall from an upper story of an unfinished Seattle skyscraper was no desperate suicide—and that look will forever haunt Homicide Detective J. P. Beaumont. But his hunt for answers and justice is leading to more death, and to dark and terrible secrets scrupulously guarded by men of steel behind the locked doors of a powerful union that extracts its dues payments in blood.

DISMISSED WITH PREJUDICE

"She can move from an exciting,
dangerous scene on one page
to a sensitive, personal,
touching moment on the next."
Chicago Tribune

The blood at the scene belies any suggestion of an "honorable death." Yet, to the eyes of the Seattle police, a successful Japanese software magnate died exactly as he wished—and by his own hand, according to the ancient rite of *seppuku*. Homicide Detective J. P. Beaumont can't dismiss what he sees as an elaborate suicide, however, not when something about it makes his flesh crawl. Because small errors in the ritual suggest something darker: a killer who will go to extraordinary lengths to escape detection—a fiend with a less traditional passion . . . for cold-blooded murder.

MINOR IN POSSESSION

"One of the country's
most popular mystery writers."
Portland Oregonian

All manner of sinners and sufferers come to the re-
hab ranch in Arizona when they hit rock bottom.
For Seattle Detective J. P. Beaumont, there is a
deeper level of Hell here: being forced to room with
teenage drug dealer Joey Rothman. An all-around
punk, Joey deserves neither pity nor tears—until he
is murdered by a bullet fired from Beaumont's gun.
Someone has set Beau up brilliantly for a long and
terrifying fall, dragging the alcoholic ex-cop into a
conspiracy of blood and lies that could cost him his
freedom . . . and his life.

PAYMENT IN KIND

It looks like a classic crime of passion to Detective J. P. Beaumont: two corpses found lovingly entwined in a broom closet of the Seattle School District building. The prime suspect, Pete Kelsey, admits his slain spouse was no novice at adultery, yet he swears he had nothing to do with the brutal deaths of the errant school official and her clergyman-turned-security guard companion. Beau believes him, but there's something the much sinned-upon widower's not telling—and that spells serious trouble still to come. Because the secret that Pete's protecting is even hotter than extramarital sex . . . and it could prove more lethal than murder.

WITHOUT DUE PROCESS

"Jance paints a vibrant picture,
creating characters so real you want to
reach out and hug—or strangle—them.
Her dialogue always rings true, and the cases
unravel in an interesting, yet never contrived way."
Cleveland Plain Dealer

What kind of monster would break into a man's
home at night, then slaughter him and his family?
The fact that the dead man was a model cop who
was loved and respected by all only intensifies the
horror. But the killer missed someone: a five-year-
old boy who was hiding in the closet. Now word is
being leaked out that the victim was "dirty." But
Seattle P. D. Homicide Detective J. P. Beaumont isn't
about to let anyone drag a murdered friend's reputa-
tion through the muck. And he'll put his own life
on the firing line on the gang-ruled streets to save a
terrified child who knows too much to live.

FAILURE TO APPEAR

"Jance's artistry keeps the reader
guessing—and caring."
Publishers Weekly

A desperate father's search for his runaway daughter
has led him to the last place he ever expected to find
her: backstage at the Oregon Shakespeare Festival.
But the murders in this dazzling world of make-
believe are no longer mere stagecraft, and the blood
is all too real. The hunt for his child has plunged
former Seattle Homicide Detective J. P. Beaumont
into a bone-chilling drama of revenge, greed, and
butchery, where innocents are made to suffer in
perverse and terrible ways. And many more young
lives are at stake, unless he can uncover the villain
of the piece before the final, deadly curtain falls.

LYING IN WAIT

"[Jance] will keep the reader up nights."
Pittsburgh Post-Gazette

Else Didriksen is no longer the beautiful, troubled teenager who disappeared from Detective J. P. Beaumont's life thirty years earlier. Now she is a homicide victim's widow—frightened, desperate, and trapped in a web of murderous greed that reaches out from a time of unrelenting terror. And the dark, deadly secrets that hold Else prisoner threaten to ensnare Beau and new partner, Sue Danielson, as well—and to rock their world in ways they never dreamed possible.

NAME WITHHELD

There are those who don't deserve to live—and the
corpse floating in Elliot Bay may have been one of
those people. Not surprisingly, many individuals—
too many, in fact—are eager to take responsibility
for the brutal slaying of the hated biotech execu-
tive whose alleged crimes ranged from the illegal
trading of industrial secrets to rape. For Seattle Detective J. P. Beaumont—who's drowning in his own
life-shattering problems—a case of seemingly jus-
tifiable homicide has sinister undertones, drawing
the haunted policeman into a corporate nightmare
of double deals, savage jealousies, and real blood
spilled far too easily, as it leads him closer to a killer
he's not sure he wants to find.

BREACH OF DUTY

"A thrill . . . One of Jance's best."
Milwaukee Journal-Sentinel

The Seattle that Beau knew as a young policeman is disappearing. The city is awash in the aromas emanating from a glut of coffee bars, the neighborhood outside his condo building has sprouted gallery upon gallery, and even his long cherished diner has evolved into a trendy eatery for local hipsters. But the glam is strictly surface, for the grit under the city's fingernails is caked with blood. Beau and his new partner, Sue Danielson, a struggling single parent, are assigned the murder of an elderly woman torched to death in her bed. As their investigation proceeds, Beau and Sue become embroiled in a perilous series of events that will leave them and their case shattered—and for Beau nothing will ever be the same again.

BIRDS OF PREY

"[A] fast-paced thriller . . . Vivid and well-drawn."
Tampa Tribune

The Starfire Breeze steams its way north toward the Gulf of Alaska, buffeted by crisp sea winds blowing down from the Arctic. Those on board are seeking peace, relaxation, adventure, escape. But there is no escape here in this place of unspoiled natural majesty. Because terror strolls the decks even in the brilliant light of day . . . and death is a conspicuous, unwelcome passenger. And a former Seattle policeman—a damaged Homicide detective who has come to heal from fresh, stinging wounds—will find that the grim ghosts pursuing him were not left behind . . . as a pleasure cruise gone horribly wrong carries him inexorably into lethal, ever-darkening waters.

PARTNER IN CRIME

> "*Partner in Crime* will have fans of J. A. Jance
> hopping in anticipation with just three little words:
> Beau meets Brady."
> *Seattle Times*

The dead woman on a cold slab in the Arizona morgue was a talented artist recently arrived from the West Coast. The Washington State Attorney General's office thinks this investigation is too big for a small-town *female* law officer to handle, so they're sending Sheriff Joanna Brady some unwanted help—a seasoned detective named Beaumont. Sheriff Brady resents his intrusion, and Bisbee, Arizona, with its ghosts and memories, is the last place J. P. Beaumont wants to be. But the twisting desert road they must reluctantly travel together is leading them into a very deadly nest of rattlers. And if they hope to survive, suddenly trust is the only option they have left. . . .

LONG TIME GONE

"Brims with richly drawn characters,
atmospheric locales, and more twists and turns
than a bucket of snakes. . . . *Long Time Gone* is
crisply written and filled with suspense."
Tucson Citizen

A former Seattle policeman now working for the
Washington State Attorney's Special Homicide
Investigation Team, J. P. Beaumont has been hand-
picked to lead the investigation into a half-century-
old murder. An eyewitness to the crime, a middle-aged
nun, has now recalled grisly, forgotten details while
undergoing hypnotherapy. It's a case as cold as the
grave, and it's running headlong into another that's
tearing at Beau's heart: the vicious slaying of his
former partner's ex-wife. What's worse, his rapidly
unraveling friend is the prime suspect.

Caught in the middle of a lethal conspiracy that
spans two generations and a killing that hits too
close to home—targeted by a vengeful adversary
and tempted by a potential romance that threatens
to reawaken his personal demons—Beaumont may
suddenly have more on his plate than he can handle,
and far too much to survive.

JUSTICE DENIED

"Jance's success . . . lies in the strength of
her characters and the craftiness of her stories.
[*Justice Denied*] has plenty of twists and more than
enough hard-boiled banter to keep fans reading."
Booklist

The murder of an ex-drug dealer ex-con—gunned
down on his mother's doorstep—seems like just another turf war fatality. Why then has Seattle Homicide Investigator J. P. Beaumont been instructed to
keep this assignment hush-hush? Meanwhile, Beau's
lover and fellow cop, Mel Soames, is involved in
her own confidential investigation. Registered sex
offenders from all over Washington State are dying
at an alarming rate—and not all due to natural causes.

A metropolis the size of Seattle holds its fair share
of brutal crime, corruption, and dirty little secrets.
But when the separate trails they're following begin
to shockingly intertwine, Beau and Mel realize that
they have stumbled onto something bigger and
more frightening than they anticipated—a deadly
conspiracy that's leading them to lofty places they
should not enter . . . and may not be allowed to leave
alive.

FIRE AND ICE

"A gripping tale that's easily one of her best."
Publishers Weekly (✱Starred Review✱)

In Seattle, six women have died terrible deaths—wrapped in tarps, doused with gasoline, and set on fire—their charred remains unceremoniously scattered in various dump sites around the city. Investigator J. P. Beaumont is working overtime to unravel a killer's grisly pattern. In the Arizona desert, Sheriff Joanna Brady of Cochise County investigates the cold-blooded slaying of the elderly caretaker of an ATV park, heartlessly run over and left to die—the innocent victim in a brutal turf war . . . or possibly something far more sinister.

Two cases separated by thousands of miles are drawing closer together by the hour—and drawing Beau once more into Brady country. Sparks flew the last time they joined forces. This time, it'll be murder. . . .

BETRAYAL OF TRUST

"San Francisco has Dashiell Hammett,
Boston has Robert B. Parker,
Fort Lauderdale boasts John D. MacDonald . . .
Seattle has J. A. Jance!"
Seattle Times

When her teenage grandson is discovered with a snuff film on his phone, the governor of the state of Washington turns to an old friend, J. P. Beaumont, for help. The Seattle private investigator has witnessed many horrific acts over the years, but this one ranks near the top: a girl strangled to death while an unseen camera looks on. Even more shocking is that the crime's multiple perpetrators could all be minors.

Along with Mel Soames, his partner in life as well as on the job, Beaumont soon discovers that what initially appears to a childish prank gone wrong has much deeper implications, reaching into the halls of state government itself. But Mel and Beau must follow this path of corruption to its very end, before more innocent young lives are lost.